Broken Kei

by

Jen Wylie

∞ Untold Press ∞

Broken Kei

Book Four of The Broken Ones

First Untold Press Publication / August 2018
ISBN: 978-1-945893-02-5

Published by Untold Press LLC
114 NE Estia Lane
Port St Lucie, FL 34983
Untoldpress.com

RODUCED IN THE UNITED STATES OF AMERICA

10 9 8 7 6 5 4 3 2 1

Dedication

This book is dedicated to the newest member of the family, my nephew Evan! May your life be an amazing adventure! (Or you stay home and read lots of books while surrounded by bubble wrap, your mother and I would be fine with that, too!)

Acknowledgements

Thank you to everyone for waiting so long for this book! I know it's taken me forever to finish and I greatly appreciate your patience and support!

Of course, I'd probably still be writing this if my sweetheart and my boys hadn't continued to harass me to get writing and encouraged me to not give up. Lots of love and hugs to you guys! Thank you!

I'd also like to send out some huge thank you's to the wonderful ladies who helped proofread! Thank you so very much to: Kris Lynch Arnett, Tambra White, Kendra Gaither, Lynn Vroman, and lastly to my awesome cousin Theresa and my amazing mom! You all rock! Flings rainbows!

Chapter 1

Broken Fey

Aro wrapped her arms tighter around Kei as the horse stumbled on the uneven ground. A gust of frigid wind whipped around them and she turned her face, setting her cheek against his head where it rested on her shoulder. He sat in front of her, legs hanging over one side, hands limp in his lap. Her thighs burned and her back ached from the effort of holding him for so long. Even thin as he was, she struggled to keep him in the saddle as the horse plodded along. She didn't care. He was back and that was all that mattered.

He wasn't conscious. Damon had broken his mind, but he was back.

Closing her eyes, she sucked in a slow breath as a tremble ran through her. Somehow, she would figure out a way to fix him. Kei believed in her, Damon said she could, so…she would find a way.

"Do you need to stop?"

Looking over the horse's head, she saw Baelan walking backward, watching for her response. The Elf moved slowly and smudges of black sat below his eyes showing his growing exhaustion, but he continued plodding along the frozen fields and leading the horse. She noted the tightness around his mouth. The Dragos paid a visit to his mind as well, causing enough pain to drop the Elf to his knees. Perhaps the pain still lingered, it wasn't something they could heal.

"I'm fine," she lied. "I just want to get home."

Looking beyond him, she narrowed her eyes. The faint glow of the pre-dawn sky gave enough light for her to see the familiar road ahead. They were nearly back in Westport.

Nodding once, he turned and continued his careful and slow pace.

He would never argue with her. He would, in fact, do absolutely anything she asked.

She hated it. She hated him.

He'd killed her. Pretending to help her, he overdosed her on riath and left her to bleed out on the floor after her fight against rogue Elves intent on killing her.

The Elven pirate, Roan, saved her life. When he promised to keep her safe, she agreed to stay with him in the city. He didn't, despite his best efforts. Yet, he sent Baelan and the bodies of the other Elves back to Rivenward and then took care of her once more. She died, but somehow, he brought her back.

Everything had been over...or so she thought, until her killer arrived on her doorstep, beaten and scarred and begging for her to give him a chance to redeem his honor. She'd almost killed him, but Bo reminded her she wasn't that kind of person. She didn't kill unarmed men on their knees before her. So, she let the Elf use his Elven rune magic and bind himself to serve her. She had no idea what to do with him, how to be someone's...master. She hated suddenly being one.

He did anything she asked. He followed her everywhere, had in fact, followed her outside the city when she left to retrieve Kei from Damon, the Dragos who'd stolen him.

Baelan got quite the shock to find she went to meet a dragon. The terror on his face would have been amusing, except she'd been too furious to pay much attention. He kept her from attacking Damon though, and possibly that saved her life. Once the dragon left, Kei once again lost consciousness and the Elf helped bundle him in a cloak and hat and get him up on the horse.

She still didn't trust him and doubted she ever would. Sometimes just looking at him brought forth such a sense of loathing she–

"I can hear you," he suddenly muttered, just loud enough for her to hear. He glanced over his shoulder. "Or is that your intention?"

"I..." She didn't know what to say. Embarrassment heated her face, which only made her angrier as she concentrated on protecting her thoughts. Though considering he was supposed to serve and obey her, she found his sudden comment almost amusing. Perhaps the Elf still possessed a bit of backbone.

"Even though your mind is closely guarded," he continued, "you tend to let your guard down and yell your surface thoughts, especially when you're angry. In case you didn't know," he added.

No, she hadn't, but it didn't surprise her. There were so many things she didn't know. Roan told her to learn from the Elf, but trusting him enough…. She shook her head. Even knowing Roan was right, she shouldn't waste such an opportunity, she just couldn't do it. She wanted him gone, out of her sight so she didn't need to be constantly reminded of the past. Hopefully he wouldn't be around for very long.

Baelan stopped walking, yet didn't turn to face her.

"What?"

His shoulders curved in, but still he kept his back to her. "Most likely I will be bound to you for quite some time. Possibly even until you're old and gray and pass of old age. I wanted you to understand this."

The words hit her, hard. Her mouth worked, but words just wouldn't form. Were her thoughts still leaking out? Never mind that, what did he mean? She'd be stuck with him forever?

"I *killed* you," he said firmly, as if that explained everything.

It didn't, not at all. She had no idea how the spell he cast worked.

"I'm not going to die of old age," she finally said.

He turned then, his head tipping to one side. "The Fey fury you take in may slow it down, give you additional decades, or even centuries, but you will age, and you will die."

Eyes wide, she could only stare at him, her breath caught in her throat. No one had ever told her that. She knew the fury she took from the Fey would change her, had changed her already, but for it to extend her life....

Clearing her throat, she finally answered, "I meant I would be killed before then. Die fighting."

Turning, he began to walk again. "That is what I am here to prevent."

She cursed and wasn't quiet about it. Trying not to mull over everything he'd just said was harder than it should have been.

Tucking the cloak around Kei a bit tighter, she tried to stretch the cramp from her neck. The sun began to peek over the mountains as they reached the road.

She sent a quiet thought to her boys. *We'll be home soon.*

Bo and Garen didn't ask too many questions. They already did when she first contacted them after they set back out to the city.

Through the Fey bonds she shared with Kei, she could feel almost nothing. His constant sleeping worried her. It shouldn't, it being barely morning, but a nagging fear he'd never wake up wouldn't go away. Holding him snug against her with one hand, she raised the other to rub at her gritty eyes.

Soon, they'd be home. She would sleep and eat and then…then she'd try to figure out how to fix the damage Damon caused while tearing the centuries old prophecy from Kei's mind. Her breath hitched at the thought and she closed her eyes again. For months, the Dragos tortured him, ripping his mind apart piece by piece to get at the prophecy Kei's parents had bound, and hidden, within him.

It wasn't going to be easy, but then again, nothing ever was.

∞ ∞ ∞

Bo met them at the gate to the fortified little part of the city they now called home. The two-story stone house, stables, paddock, and little bit of land had been walled when they bought it. However, having Elves wanting to kill her because they thought her to be their prince's weakness forced them to increase their security. The walls were now higher, with watch areas. The gate now fortified and barred. Though the Elves after her were dead, or in Baelan's case, magically bound to serve her, it didn't mean they wouldn't still take precautions. There could always be more.

Closing the gate behind them, Bo then moved to her side and raised his hands. "I'll take him in."

Nodding, she awkwardly shifted Kei's unmoving body down into Bo's arms. Tall, broad shouldered, and with arms like small tree trunks, he easily cradled Kei's slight form against his chest.

Slipping down off the horse, she winced and groaned as sore muscles protested the sudden movement.

"You need to get some rest, pup," Bo commented, his scarred face grimacing as he looked her over. "Did you eat?"

Food. Yes, Bo packed them some and she'd forgotten about it. "I will later." She jerked her head toward the back of the house. "I need to go. Can you get him to bed?"

"Of course."

Garen, still glamored to look like a dog, bumped his head against her thigh. *We'll take care of him. You take care of yourself right now.*

She gave his head a scratch. *I will.* She didn't speak out loud. Baelan still didn't know their pet dog was really a Were hidden by an Elven glamour. Not completely trusting the Elf, they still hadn't told him.

Garen trotted away to catch up with Bo and she slowly moved to the front of the horse, giving it a pat on the neck. Baelan stood silently, still holding the reins. He'd dropped the glamor he wore out in the city. Human ears once more were pointed, brown hair and eyes returned to silver.

"Can you take care of the horse?"

"Of course."

"You know how?"

For a moment, a look of disbelief momentarily crossed his beautiful face, followed by an irritated frown. "Yes," he answered through gritted teeth.

Not caring if her comment upset him or not, she headed for the privies. For a moment she missed living with Roan. His house had them *inside*. She couldn't deny that for some reason she missed the cold-hearted man. Occasionally, she'd seen a different side of him. After spending the winter with him, she allowed herself to admit she thought of him as a friend.

When finished, she entered the house by the side door and stepped into the kitchen. Stripping off hat, gloves, and her cloak, she tossed them on the counter before heading for the bath room.

Bracing her hands on the small table holding the pitcher and wash basin, she stared into the mirror for a long moment. She looked worn and tired, much older than seventeen. Part of that may have been all the scars. Dark brown, messy hair framed her face, falling halfway down her back. Dark circles smudged around eyes now the same golden hue as a Fey's. Shaking off her weariness, she washed her hands and face.

Her feet dragged as she made her way upstairs. Worry for Kei gnawed at her insides. Perhaps some of that was hunger, too. The need to check on Kei overwhelmed any desire to eat.

At the top of the stairs she paused, looking into Kei's room and finding it empty.

Garen stepped into the hall from her room. *Down here. Bo could use some help.*

Her breath caught in her throat as she raced down the hall and through the door on the right. A slightly crazed laugh erupted out of her.

Bo sat with Kei on the bed, trying to hold the unconscious Fey up in a sitting position as he struggled to remove his shirt.

"I'll help," she said quietly. Her foot caught and she stumbled as she tripped over one of Kei's boots.

Bo cursed under his breath. "Sorry, pup."

"No worries." Sitting beside Kei, she helped get his filthy shirt off as Bo held him.

"I'd like to get him out of these pants, but I couldn't find anything else to put him in."

Guilt swarmed through her. "I gave them to Baelan."

"He'll be fine for now. I'll run out and get something once the market opens. Once he wakes up we'll get him into the bath."

Pulling the blankets back, they maneuvered Kei into a comfortable position and tucked him in.

"Did you get some sleep?"

Bo shook his head, crossing his arms and staring down at Kei. "I will." He glanced over at her. "Get ready for bed. You look like you're going to fall over. Or do you want to eat first?"

She shrugged a shoulder. "I'm not hungry." Hearing movement behind her, she turned.

"Elaina is here," Baelan said quietly.

Bo raised his eyebrows and immediately headed for the door. "I'll be right back."

Baelan frowned, his eyes on the sleeping Fey.

"What?" She barely kept the panic from her voice.

He hesitated and then just shook his head.

She'd caught him doing that quite often during the last few days and she stared at him sharply. Why would.... She sighed and rubbed her forehead. Of course. "You may speak freely."

Gray eyes snapped to her in surprise.

The shock in them made a small smile curve her lips, and at the same time an uncomfortable knot formed in her stomach. "Don't worry. If I don't want to hear it, I'll let you know."

He nodded once, sharply, and then turned his gaze to the floor. "Why is he here?"

She snorted. His comment shouldn't have surprised her. "Bo put him here. He knew I'd not leave his side, and this way I can at least get some sleep."

"I see."

He probably didn't, but she didn't feel like explaining herself, or her relationship with Kei. He'd figure it out eventually. Or not. He likely still thought she and Roan had really been lovers.

Bo walked in, a steaming bowl in one hand. "Elaina brought some soup." He glanced at Kei. "Do you think he'd eat?"

She shook her head. Through her link with Kei, she could feel he wasn't even close to being awake.

He held the bowl out to her. "Then you eat, and get changed, and get some rest. Elaina and I will head to the market."

"And afterward you get some sleep, too," she insisted, taking the bowl.

"Of course." He grinned and winked. "There's a whole pot downstairs. Eat up."

"Thanks, Bo," she said softly.

He ruffled her hair. "Everything will be fine." His eyes turned to Kei. "He's home now."

He left and she sat on the end of the bed, forcing herself to eat. At least Elaina and her sisters were wonderful cooks. Baelan shifted by the door and she groaned inwardly. Holding the bowl on her lap, she turned to face him. "Go and eat. And get cleaned up, and go to bed. I don't care what order you do the last two," she added, taking in his weary appearance.

He shook his head slightly. "I would prefer to stay close to you."

Her eyebrows rose. The couch downstairs was too far away? "Sleep in Kei's bed then. It's just down the hall." She finished her soup while he continued to just stand there. The Elf was going to drive her insane. Standing, she walked over and handed the bowl to him. "Go. I need to get changed." She waved her hands at him when he still didn't move. "Eat, sleep. Consider that an order."

Lowering his head, he turned for the door. "As you wish, master."

Narrowing her eyes, she resisted the urge to swat him over the head and just slammed the door closed behind him.

∞ ∞ ∞

She woke shortly after noon. Kei did not.

He remained a silent, still body beside her, his face pale, eyes sunken and dark. If it weren't for the gentle rise and fall of his chest, she would have thought she'd lost him.

The day passed slowly as she remained by his side. Garen joined her often, sprawled at the end of the bed, either with his head across Kei's legs or curled up against him. Bo and Elaina came and went, sitting in the chair to hold Kei's hand.

Baelan hovered, a silent gray shadow along the edges of the room. Sometimes he brought food or water. Except for then, she ignored him.

17

Another day went by. Kei didn't move. She spoke to him; out loud, with mind-speech. They all tried. He didn't answer. They tried to get him to eat and drink. Though they could part his lips, his jaw seemed locked shut. Even pinching his nose closed didn't work. They kept trying.

Another day brought the same. She refused to leave his side. Every day she struggled, trying not to panic, not to let the growing fear and hopelessness overcome her. Why hadn't he woken up? She needed to remain strong and believe in him, just in case he could feel her. Holding their bond tightly, she constantly sent him her love and support. It was exhausting, but she didn't give up.

She would never give up. Not on Kei.

Never.

Chapter 2

Just Another Scar

Aro placed her hand on Kei's forehead and then gently smoothed a lock of hair to the side. He felt cooler to the touch, not his usual overly warm self.

Clenching her teeth, she locked down her worry and fear and kept her expression calm as she pulled her hand away and slipped it into Kei's hand once more.

Elaina shifted forward from her seat beside the bed and gently wiped a wet cloth against his cracking lips. Bo sat in another chair beside her, elbows on his knees and head in his hands.

She glanced down at Garen where his head rested across the Fey's lower legs. He'd been trying to read Kei's surface thoughts for days, but always found nothing. She stopped asking but knew he continued to try.

Do you think Hale could help? About such things, she used mind-speech with the boys, even if Baelan wasn't in the room. The Elf had good hearing and was so silent she often didn't even notice if he was near.

No, Garen replied softly. *He's too young.*

She'd asked if Garen could go into Kei's mind and gotten a long drawn out explanation of why he wouldn't. Or couldn't.

He'd never been in Kei's mind before. He didn't even know for certain if the Fey had such a place. Were did, Elves did. Most humans didn't. Since Fey weren't telepathic, it was quite possible they didn't either. Like the odd human, it was possible for them to create a mental barrier, but Garen wasn't certain what he would find, or not. It would be too easy for him to become lost. Even if Kei did have a special place in his mind, the Were wasn't sure what state it would be in. A broken mind could be a dangerous place.

When she'd pressed and sensed Garen's panic, she dropped the matter. It had been inconsiderate of her to even ask, considering he'd already lost a part of himself. When young, the Were lost his connection to his human form and spent more than a century as a wolf.

What about Silas or Raythe? She wasn't sure how old the Were twins who worked for Roan were.

I don't know. He paused. *Dealing with their alpha, should something happen, would be an issue.*

She nodded absently. The last thing they needed was further reason to have the Were angry with them. They were lucky enough the Were king hadn't come for them over the winter after learning she made them a pack. Suppressing a shudder, she pushed those thoughts away. Her nightmares of the Were king chasing her down and killing her were bad enough. Reality could be so much worse and was something she just didn't have the strength to deal with now.

They sat in silence for a while before Garen raised his head and looked to the hall.

Baelan walked in, carrying a fresh pitcher of water.

Have you considered the Elf?

Her lip curled in contempt as she watched him walk across the room to put the pitcher on the side table. *I don't trust him.*

The Elf stopped abruptly, head lowering as his shoulders curved in. Long, slender fingers clasped the pitcher tightly but still she saw them tremble. He didn't look at her, just remained frozen as she glared at him.

Calm your anger. It does no good now, Garen muttered.

Her emotions tumbled about. Turning her attention back to Kei, she took a deep breath. Garen was right. Now wasn't the time to get angry again about having the Elf here. It didn't matter how she felt about him. There wasn't a thing she could do about it.

No matter what she did, he constantly hovered around her. Even sending him out on errands didn't give her a lot of alone time. He always returned quickly whenever she sent him off to the market. She'd even sent him with Bo to get furniture for his own room, the empty one next to hers. They hadn't been gone long. He never used the room either. Stupid Elf.

Elaina turned and rested a hand on Bo's shoulder. "I need to get to the tavern."

Aro glanced at the window, noting it was close to noon.

"Can you…" Elaina paused. "Could you help today, for a while? Father wasn't feeling well last night."

Bo looked over to her and Aro nodded. *Go. I'll be here. Spend some time with her. You need a break.*

So do you, pup. He turned back to Elaina. "Of course."

Garen jumped off the bed as they rose. *I need to go outside. I'll be back soon.*

Bo paused at the door. "Do you need anything?"

She shook her head. All she needed was for Kei to wake up, but he couldn't give her that.

"I'll bring over something for dinner later."

She forced a smile as they all left. The silence of the room weighed down on her. Strong. She must stay strong. *I'm here, Kei. Please, wake up.*

Closing her eyes, she squeezed his hand and once again tried to reach him through their Fey bond. She pushed and pulled, held him tightly, begged. Like every other time, only the numbness met her actions. How long did he have left?

A rising sense of desperation washed over her. Her options had run out. Kei wouldn't live much longer like this.

"Come here," she said softly. Soft, quick steps crossed the room and opening her eyes, she looked up at Baelan.

"How may I serve you?"

Did he say such things on purpose? She scowled in response. His head tipped slightly to the side and he frowned.

The gesture reminded her so much of Prince. A sudden pain clenched her chest and she quickly looked away. Rot, she still missed him so much.

Clearing her throat, she ignored the Elf and brought her thoughts back to where they should be. Prince was gone. Kei was here, and he needed her.

It took a moment before she could speak. She didn't want to ask Baelan for his help. Trust wasn't the only issue. She worried something could go wrong. She'd never forgive herself if something happened to Kei.

Shifting, she sat up to kneel beside her Fey, keeping her eyes on his face. Baelan waited patiently at the end of the bed.

"He's not waking up," she finally said, still not looking at the Elf. She pulled Kei's hand into her lap and held on tightly. "I can't...I don't know...." She shook her head and pressed her lips together tightly for a moment, fighting to stay calm.

"What would you like me to do?" When she didn't answer right away, he continued softly, "I don't know how to heal others. Or a broken mind."

"Can you see if he's in there?" She turned her head to look up at him. "If there's anything of him at all?"

His gray gaze regarded her for a moment before he nodded and walked around the bed to sit in one of the empty chairs. Placing his hand over Kei's, he closed his eyes.

Aro held her breath.

"There are no surface thoughts," he said after a moment.

She knew that, though wasn't going to share that information. "Can you try looking further?"

A faint frown crossed his face. "He has a mental shield up, though it is weak."

She caught the surprise in his tone and unconsciously leaned forward as hope rose within her. "Is that good?"

"Most humans and Fey don't have them. If he was lost to you, I would not expect it to be there. I will try to—"

Kei's eyes snapped open.

She briefly saw them glowing a violent red before he screamed and shot upright.

"No!"

The hand she held jerked up, catching her hard under the chin. As she began to tip to the side the hand swung about with unnatural speed, striking her so hard across the face the force sent her right off the bed. Something crashed, and she heard Baelan's shocked curse.

"Kei!" Scrambling to her feet, she sprang back to the bed. Only moments had passed, yet already he'd fallen back down. As she quickly crawled toward him she watched claws recede from his twitching hands. He stared up at the ceiling, eyes wide and the fury already fading. Before she could say a word, the light was gone and his lids slowly closed.

"Kei!" Once again kneeling beside him, she took his face in her hands. He was there. She hadn't lost him yet. A slightly hysterical laugh escaped her until she choked. Blood filled her mouth. Perhaps she bit her tongue? She didn't care.

"Arowyn."

The strangled whisper caused her to turn. Baelan sprawled up against the wall, legs tangled over the fallen chair. His wide eyes locked on the Fey. He'd never seen a Fey in a fury before.

"You must have startled him." She paused. "Perhaps he thought you were Damon."

He blinked twice and then looked at her. All color drained from his suddenly stricken face. With the grace only an Elf could have, he untangled himself from the fallen chair and sprang to his feet. Before she could say a word, he grabbed a handful of cloths from the side of the bed and flung himself across Kei to slap them to the side of her face.

It wasn't until then the burning pain registered.

Panicked gray eyes searched her face as she just stared at him in surprise. It took her a moment to figure out Kei must have struck her with his claws. Lowering her eyes, she blanched seeing blood spattered across her arms and the bed sheets. From the amount of it, she had more than a little scratch.

"You're fine, my lovely. You're fine," Baelan said quickly, pressing harder against the cloth.

A disbelieving smile twisted her lips at his concern and she winced as the movement brought a sharp sting of pain to her cheek. She swallowed blood and tried not to gag.

Baelan inhaled a sharp breath, his brows drawing together. He leaned closer, his forehead close to hers as he pulled the cloth back. Jerking back, he pushed the cloth back swiftly.

"It's not healing. Why isn't it healing?" His eyes found hers and she almost laughed at the rising panic within them.

"Is it that bad?" She didn't want to waste the very little bit of fury she had remaining. Once it was gone….

His eyes widened. "It looks like he tore half your face off," he snapped brusquely. A frown crossed his lips. "Doesn't it hurt?"

She snorted. The pain was there, but it was nothing compared to the pain of being beaten by Elves and the healing that followed, or being nearly gutted by one of the Vor.

The Elf caught her thoughts, his gaze dropped, and he shook his head slightly. "You need to heal," he said softly. "You're losing a lot of blood."

"Fine." Closing her eyes, she easily slipped within herself and then deeper. Losing all sense of self didn't leave her as disorientated as it once did. It only took a moment to find the two wounds across her face.

One cut followed along her jawline. It wasn't too deep, but she quickly gathered her power and stopped the bleeding before looking to the one above it. It slashed from cheekbone to lips, parallel to the other. It took longer to stop this deeper gash from bleeding. In one spot it cut right through her cheek, which explained the blood in her mouth.

With the bleeding stopped, she concentrated on slowly mending her flesh. Working slowly used less power and caused less pain.

She felt the cloth pull away and heard a deep relieved sigh. Keeping her eyes closed, she continued to heal. As her power waned, she hesitated on using it all.

Fingers gently grasped her chin as Baelan moved her head to the side to get a better look. "Almost done," he whispered.

Deciding there was no point in saving the little that remained, she completed the healing on the top wound, pushing a little more in so not even a scar remained. She focused on the cut on her jaw. The skin mended and her brows drew together in concentration as she tried to find and pull forth every bit of power within her to complete the healing.

A trickle of soft light burned within for a moment and the healing completed. Shock filled her as she jerked her head out of Baelan's grasp. What was…

She swiftly locked down all her thoughts and emotions. Opening her eyes, she relaxed to see the Elf only studying her face.

"Well done."

Lowering her gaze, she struggled not to panic. She'd pulled power from Baelan. From an Elf.

She wasn't supposed to be able to do that.

If the Elves found out she could… A shiver ran through her body and she closed her eyes, trying to remain calm and keep breathing.

Cloth moved across her face and she started, her eyes opening quickly.

Baelan gave her a faint, beautiful smile. "Let's get you cleaned up."

Nothing in his expression led her to believe he noticed her little bit of thievery. Pushing her thoughts far into her mind, she just nodded. Nothing happened. Nothing happened. Act normal.

Turning her attention to Kei as she slipped off the bed, a sudden smile formed on her lips. "He's still there," she said faintly. Hope blossomed within her.

"Yes, he is." Baelan grabbed a few more cloths and wiped his hands. "If you'd like to go down and bathe," he said, his voice suddenly quieter, "I'll change the sheets." He shifted from one foot to the other and dropped his head.

She didn't know what bothered him now. Understanding the Elf seemed an impossible task. Glancing down, she grimaced at the blood covering her. She didn't want to leave Kei, but she was overdue for a wash. Heading downstairs, she quickly gave up trying to figure the Elf out and closed herself into the bath room. Setting the water running into the tub, she stripped off her clothes, almost giddy as she thought about Kei. She hadn't lost him yet. Somehow, she'd figure out how to bring him back.

As the tub filled she contacted Bo and Garen, giving them a shortened version of what happened. They were just as excited. Garen didn't resist throwing in an "I told you so" either.

Once settled into the warm water, her thoughts turned again to the power she'd unintentionally stolen. A small spark remained within her and she marveled at the difference between it and the power she took from the Fey.

When she pulled fury from them, she somehow was able to separate raw power from the actual fury. It was a rough, bright light within her. The fury itself was a wild seething mass of black and red. It gave the Fey the power to grow claws and fangs, as well as giving them extra speed and strength. For a long time, she let it seep away until Roan informed her power was power. The fury had a specific purpose for the Fey, but she could still use it for whatever purpose she required, such as healing. She didn't understand how it worked, only that it did.

The power she'd taken from Baelan intrigued her. It reminded her more of raw power than fury, but with a softer feel. If there'd been more within her she would have attempted to see if she could pull it apart as well.

Shaking her head, she quickly discarded any other thoughts. If the Elves discovered she could take their power, she wouldn't live long. She had to make sure she never did it again. Grimacing, she finished washing her hair and cursed herself for having too much curiosity. Wondering if she could take power from the Were, or even the Dragos, would certainly get her killed. She had enough enemies as it was.

After getting out of the tub and pulling the stopper, she frowned. She forgot to bring clean clothes down. After drying off, she jumped as a knock came at the door.

"I have clothes."

Her brows rose in surprise as she quickly tucked the towel around herself. "Just set them inside." The door creaked open a bit, a pile was shoved through the crack, and then the door closed again. Perhaps Baelan could be useful after all.

"Thank you," she called, though wasn't sure if he remained outside or not. He'd likely frown at her for being polite to him, but she didn't care. Her family raised her to have good manners. She wasn't about to stop because the stupid Elf thought treating a servant with respect was wrong.

∞ ∞ ∞

Aro paced her bedroom, every few moments her eyes going to Kei. Baelan had cleaned up her blood and changed the sheets while she bathed. He was gone now, though whether he was cleaning or burning the sheets she didn't know or care. She had time to herself without his hovering.

Her thoughts spun once again, going over what happened with Kei, trying to decide if she should have Baelan attempt it again.

Chewing her lower lip, she worried over her lack of power. If he went into a fury again she didn't know what would happen. She'd seen him in his fury multiple times before, but he had some semblance of control then. Deep in her soul she always knew he'd never hurt her. He didn't seem to have that now. She understood why; his fear and pain overtook everything else. Eventually she'd get through to him, but....

Grimacing, she shook her head. Learning to heal was something new. She'd gone most of her life not having the gift. How had she come to depend on it so quickly? It didn't matter, she would be extra careful. Getting Kei back was the most important thing.

"Arowyn?"

Her feet stopped moving and a weary sigh escaped her before she could stop it. Turning, she saw Baelan behind her, holding her brush.

"I can brush my own hair," she snapped. His mouth opened, but before he could speak she continued, "I don't care if my hair is in knots. Kei is more important than that."

"Of course," he answered quietly, his gaze dropping to the floor. Turning swiftly, he returned the brush to her dresser. "Is there anything else I–"

"No." Sometimes she just wanted to strangle him. She hated, *hated,* being waited on.

Pacing once more, she tried to re-gather her thoughts. Should she try to tie Kei down? That would likely make things worse. Not knowing everything Damon had done to him didn't help. She didn't know what might trigger his fury.

Finally, she stopped and turned, her eyes seeking the Elf. She found him standing against the wall by the door, head bowed, his silvery hair once again hiding his face. Her brows drew together in confusion. For some reason his hands clenched and unclenched over and over at his sides. She cleared her throat.

His head shot up, pale eyes immediately latching onto her face.

"I'd like to try that again with Kei. I want to try to keep him with us longer, so I can let him know he's here and not still with Damon."

His head tipped to the side as he frowned. "He was conscious when we retrieved him."

"I know, but I can't otherwise explain why he reacted like he did. He's…lost. Perhaps he doesn't remember. Maybe he thought it was a dream? I don't know."

"May I suggest we don't stand as close this time?"

A slight smile quirked her lips. "Sounds good to me. Do you have to touch him?"

He shook his head. "I'm not going into his mind, just pushing beyond his shields. Do you plan to subdue him? Or would you like me to?"

Hesitating, she turned to Kei. If the Elf knew she could no longer heal, he'd probably try to send her out of the house. "I'll–" Her answer died abruptly, Roan's words suddenly echoing in her head. *You need to think, Arowyn.* "Rot," she muttered.

Baelan remained silent as she stared at Kei for a long time. Being impulsive wasn't going to help her. She needed to think about others, even Baelan. Not telling him could have disastrous consequences. It still galled her to share with him though.

"I have no power left," she finally said abruptly. "I used the last to heal my face."

When he remained silent, she turned back to face him. He regarded her with a curious look on his face, which she didn't understand at all. She needed a rotting book on how to understand the stupid Elf.

"How do you…get more?"

A shoulder rose and fell. "Next time I take a Fey's fury, I keep some of it."

"I see." His brows drew together as he looked over at Kei. He didn't say anything else.

"So, I'll hold him whie you do your mind thing."

His head snapped back around to stare at her and the pained look on his face almost made her laugh. Then his entire body began to tremble and she huffed out a sigh, setting her hands on her hips. Putting herself in possible danger apparently gave the Elf fits. "Fine. What do you suggest, then?"

∞ ∞ ∞

Baelan eventually stopped panicking. He then took her question literally and thought for quite some time. Now he stood in her bedroom doorway, in front of her, ready to slam the door closed if needed. At least she was still in the house.

Behind her, Bo shifted restlessly. Garen rubbed his head against her hip, trying to give her comfort. The Elf insisted Bo be here and Garen took it upon himself to join them. She couldn't really complain about that. They were family.

Peering around him, she waited for Baelan to make contact again…and waited. Glancing up, she could only see part of his face in profile. Pale, jaw clenched.

Catching her look, he gently pushed her back. "Ready?"

At her nod, all their attention returned to Kei.

A moment later the Fey's eyes once again snapped open. She briefly saw their red glow before he sprang up in a flurry of sheets and claws, a scream tearing from his fanged mouth.

Stumbling from the bed, Kei whirled around, claws slashing at nothing and still screaming. Screaming and screaming.

Her heart lodged in her throat, tears springing to her eyes. She pushed forward but Baelan blocked her way.

"Not yet," he whispered sharply. "Wait for the fury to fade."

The need to help Kei nearly made her frantic. She tried to force the Elf to the side, but his thin form held like a stone wall.

"Let me by," she snarled, wishing she still had fury within her to lend her more strength.

Beyond him, Kei suddenly stopped his frenzied fight against the air, a last scream dying on his lips. He sank to his knees, curling in on himself and clutching his head.

"Stop. Please stop. I can't. Please." His pleas came out hoarse and strangled.

Baelan finally relaxed and stepped to the side. She sprang past him, falling to her knees next to Kei and throwing her arms around him.

"Shh. I'm here. You're safe now. He doesn't have you anymore. You're safe, Kei."

"Stop! I can't..."

The pleading in his voice broke her heart. Bending over him, she held him tighter. "I'm here. I'm here. No one will hurt you. Come back to me, Kei." She moved her hands to his wrists, leaning over his trembling, frail body. "I'm here," she said over and over, both with words and in her mind, hoping he'd hear her.

His claws receded, and she pulled, leaning back and shifting him against her. Adjusting him in her arms, she then brushed stray locks of hair away from his startling pale face.

"Look at me. Look at me. I'm here."

Wide eyes, now orange, lifted to her face. Through heaving breaths, he whispered her name.

"Yes, Kei. I'm here. You're safe. Stay with me."

"It hurts." A shudder ran through him and he winced. "Can't."

His lids began to close, and she gave him a hard shake. "Stay with me, Kei." *I need you. I love you!* "Tell me what to do. What's wrong?"

He struggled to keep his eyes open and finally succeeded. A hand grasped hers as she went to stroke his cheek. "Broke it. Broke it all. Can't hold on, Aro. Can't–" Another shudder ran through him and tears welled in his eyes. "Falling apart. The pieces. I can't..."

She held him tighter, rocking him. "We'll fix it. Just stay with me." His eyelids began to flutter again. "Kei!" She shook him again. "You have to stay with me."

"Aro, it hurts." Heart-wrenching sorrow filled his eyes as tears slipped down his face and his hand tightened on hers. "Can't hold on," he whispered.

"You can," she insisted. *I'm with you, always.* "Kei!" Her shout roused him once more. "Forever beside you I shall stand," she whispered, locking her gaze with his. "Together or apart, always I will be with you."

Forever, he finished, a whisper in her mind.

A faint smile pulled at her lips and she sniffed, blinking back tears. There he was.

"Help me," he stuttered out. "I can't…"

"I will. I will," she promised.

"Aro."

Raising her head, she found Bo crouched before them. He quickly held out a cup of warm broth. Taking it from him, she put it to Kei's dry lips.

His eyes fluttered and he turned his head away. Frustration made her clutch him to her more tightly and give him another shake. "You have to drink." *Please, Kei. I can't lose you.*

His lips parted and she tipped the cup, carefully watching to make sure he swallowed and it didn't all end up running down his face.

Between one sip and another, he stopped drinking. When she looked back to his eyes she found him once again staring at nothing.

"Kei!"

Bo quickly took the cup from her before she could throw it. Holding Kei to her chest, she bent her head over him, not wanting the others to see her tears.

A hand touched her shoulder and she jerked away.

"You should–" Baelan began softly.

"Leave us alone!"

She'd fix him. Somehow.

Jen Wylie

Chapter 3

Baelan

Something woke her in the night. Staring into the dark, she squeezed Kei's hand and then tried to go back to sleep.

After getting him back into bed, they all stayed up late talking about what happened, trying to figure out what was wrong with him, what to do. They didn't have any answers and she had to force herself not to break down in tears. Tears didn't help. They didn't do anything at all.

The boys hadn't been too impressed she'd forgotten to pull some fury from Kei. Stupid, stupid.

She'd fallen asleep imagining the hurt she'd do to Damon if she ever saw the rotting Dragos again. Returning to those thoughts, her eyes began to drift closed once more.

A rhythmic thumping invaded her senses and her eyes snapped open as she listened. The sound quietly met her straining ears again. What was it? She sat up in bed, trying to figure out what could be causing it. Not the old house. It stopped, and then began again.

Shifting to her better Fey sight, she got out of bed and made her way to the bedroom doorway, her bare feet making no sound. Sticking her head into the hall she paused, listening again.

Across from her room, Bo's door hung partially open. A loud snore startled her, and she shook her head with a small smile. She loved Elaina and felt so happy she and Bo were soon to be married, but hoped the woman already knew about the snoring. On second thought, she didn't want to think about if the woman knew first hand or not.

The door creaked open a little more. *You hear it?*

She could barely see Garen in the dark, but nodded. "What is it?"

Your Elf is having another bad night.

What does that mean?

He's not...adapting well. He paused and then continued, *I smell blood.*

The Were's comments left more questions than answers, but the mention of blood sent her moving out of her room. What was wrong with the stupid Elf now? *Why didn't you wake me?*

I was about to.

Did you check on him?

A wolfish snort answered her. *He is your responsibility, not mine.*

An angry retort died suddenly on her lips and she just stared into the dark. Garen was right. No matter how much she tried to deny it, accepting Baelan put him in her care. That was how she was raised. Had he been anyone else, it wouldn't have given her a second thought. She cursed under her breath. Consequences of her actions kept coming back to haunt her.

I hate that you're right, she muttered. His answering mental chuckle didn't improve her mood.

Frowning in irritation, she started down the hall a few steps and then paused, trying to locate where the faint sound came from.

Her eyebrows rose. He was in his room for once.

I'm here if you need me.

Turning slightly, she gave the Were a stiff smile. "Thank you," she answered quietly. "I'll be fine. Keep an eye on Kei?"

Of course.

She stepped quietly into Baelan's dark room. Almost no light came in through the window and even with her sharper Fey sight she could barely make out the sparse furnishings. The bed against the wall separating their rooms sat empty and she frowned.

The thumping began again, and she squinted, finding a dark shape in the corner to her right. Walking slowly, she tipped her head to the side, trying to figure out what the Elf was doing. She should have brought a light with her.

A swift movement in the shadows startled her, but not as much as the sudden small golden ball of light that formed above Baelan's raised hand. It rose slowly to her height and then just hung there above the Elf. Had she spoken her thought out loud?

Her gaze snapped back to him. The Elf sat in the corner, facing her but with his eyes closed. His legs curled to the side, shoulders hunched, both hands now resting limp in his lap. Slowly, his head banged against the wall, over and over.

"Baelan..." she whispered. The sudden rush of concern shocked her, and for a moment she tried to push it away. Closing her eyes, she shook her head and let out a sigh. She couldn't hate him forever and seeing him like this... It brought out a part of her she couldn't deny. She wasn't a monster.

"What's wrong?" When he didn't answer, she said his name again.

"So many shadows," he eventually whispered. "Dark. It's so much darker now. Lost. Lost...in the dark. But I can hear it. Crunch. Crunch."

Had the Elf lost his mind? Moving forward, she crouched down in front of him. Her breath caught in her throat when she noticed the blood on his wrists and hands. Her eyes shot up to his face and then she noted the dark smear on the wall. He'd banged his head bloody.

Shifting to her knees, she leaned forward, cupping his cheek and holding his face in place. "Stop."

He did, immediately. Beneath her fingers, she felt him tremble.

"What's wrong?" He didn't answer. "Baelan, tell me what's wrong."

"I can't do this," he whispered so quietly she had to lean forward to hear him.

His words made her grimace. "You chose this." She paused. "Is it really so bad? I know I've maybe not been nice to you...but you did kill me, and I didn't want this. But I didn't think I was being–"

"No. No," he said softly, cutting off her words. A faint bitter laugh came with a soft shake of his head as tortured gray eyes met hers. "You don't understand."

She was so very tired of hearing those words. "Tell me. Explain to me why things are so bad you're hurting yourself. Why are your runes bleeding? Why–"

Raising a hand, he cut her off again, though she didn't mind. She wanted answers. He rested his bloody head against the wall and closed his eyes.

Why did the stupid Elf have to be so heart-stoppingly beautiful? She shouldn't want to comfort him.

Long lashes fluttered a moment before he opened his eyes again and spoke. "A number of years ago, I used this same spell."

Her mouth dropped open in surprise. "On yourself?"

His disdainful look made her mouth snap closed again. Stupid question.

"Yes. I offended a lord. He was quite taken with the old ways, and I suggested this to make amends. He agreed and I spent two years serving him." Frowning, he looked away. "He was not kind, but I survived and did what..." He shook his head. "I did what I had to do."

His vague story left her with so many questions she didn't even know where to start. "The spell only lasted two years? How do you know how long you'll be with me? You said for as long as I lived."

Tipping his head back, a slightly crazed grin crossed his face. "I have no idea. Time is decided by the spell. I don't know how it works. Considering I took your life, it wouldn't surprise me if I would serve you for quite some time."

"But not until I die?"

He shrugged a shoulder. "You did survive, so probably not. Perhaps a decade or less."

"You lied to me," she said angrily.

"No." A shoulder lifted and fell in a shrug. "It is possible."

She wanted to strangle him again. He'd reminded her though, not to trust him. Another thought occurred to her. "But you don't have an amulet. How can you even stay outside of Rivenward for any length of time?"

He regarded her quietly for a moment before his fingers went to his chest. "You saw my runes." She nodded. "One will ensure I remain connected to my home."

Her brows drew together. "Why didn't Prince have one?"

"It was created within the last few decades. Before he left. He has one now, as well."

A smile spread across her face before she could stop it.

A look of pity filled his eyes. "He'll not be coming any time soon. Another reason he sent me."

So quickly, her happiness faded. "Why?"

He hesitated before speaking. "She bound him," he said quietly. "When he first arrived home. He said she deceived him and bound him. He can't leave Rivenward until he is free."

Her mouth opened on a gasp. She...the queen. His own mother. No. No. "Bound like you are to me?"

He shook his head. "Not this spell, but I don't know which, or what else it does."

Nodding, she looked away. There wasn't anything she could do for her prince, but she could try to make the most of the gift he'd sent her. First, she needed to try to fix some of his crazy, if she even could. "So back to what is wrong?"

He closed his eyes again. "The spell requires I serve. I feel your needs and must meet them. With you...I feel needs, but you either refuse to let me serve you, or for some reason I can't even figure out what it is you are needing. When I fail to remove the need, the spell itself punishes me, first bringing pain and then the runes will bleed." He held up his wrists.

They were bound with strips of cloth, and looking up, she saw the runes around his neck were, too. Thinking about it, she thought they had been for a while but hadn't thought anything of it. Now she knew it was because of the blood and she winced.

"You said they'd do that if you thought of harming me."

He opened his eyes again. "Yes, that as well."

Silently she watched him, thinking on everything he'd said.

With a roll of his eyes, he pointed out the obvious. "I have been in constant pain. Every day it grows. It doesn't go away. I can't even sleep through it anymore."

She winced as a wave of nausea washed over her. "I didn't know."

He looked away and shrugged a shoulder again. "I know, Arowyn. You are not a cruel person, even if you have a temper at times."

She ignored that comment. "So... I need to let you do things?" She grimaced. Him waiting on her hand and foot would drive her mad. A thought crossed her mind. "Can I give you specific things to do? Or would you still feel the need to brush my hair?"

"Verbal commands take precedence," he answered.

"Then problem solved," she said with a grin. At his incredulous look, she explained. "Roan said I should make use of you, so I will. You can help me train. Teach me about the Elves…or whatever else. Certainly, I can keep you busy with things like that, so you don't drive me crazy."

His solemn gaze turned to the wall, yet he nodded.

She frowned. He didn't seem overly happy. "Is there something else?"

Dropping his eyes and tipping his head down so his hair shielded his face, he whispered a quiet, "No."

"Tell me," she commanded.

His shoulders slumped. "It is nothing you can do anything about. I am simply…lost. Everything has been taken; everyone, everything I own, my country. I've lost everything. It is…difficult, coming to terms with this."

"I understand," she said quietly, a knot forming in her throat. "I lost everything, too," she reminded him. "It hurts, and it will for a long time. But you'll find a new place and new friends. Maybe even a new family like I did." She paused. "You have your life. You even have your power. Things could be worse."

Raising his head slightly, his sad gray eyes stared at her for a long moment. "Even with the pain, most of the time I do regret killing you," he finally said.

Most of the time? Leaning back, she held out her hands. "Come on, let's go get you cleaned up."

He looked incredulously at her hands, but eventually slipped his into them and she pulled them both to their feet.

Letting his hands fall from hers, she turned and headed into the hall. Silently, they made their way downstairs and to the bath room. Pulling a stool out, she gestured for him to sit and filled the bowl on the small table with water.

"I can clean myself."

"I know." She found a cloth, wet it, and then started to clean the blood from the side of his head. His eyes locked on his hands, clenched in his lap. "So," she said after a few moments, "who are you really?"

His eyes flicked up to hers, clearly once again startled. At least she kept him on his toes.

"I've seen you shy and afraid, and how you are now, and those are both different from the Elf I first met. Which one is you?" When he didn't immediately respond, she added, "Remember you are free to speak, any time."

He looked away, a frown crossing his beautiful face. "Do you remember the Dragos saying I was...unstable?"

Her eyebrows rose. "You heard that?"

With a grimace, he nodded, still not looking at her. "He wasn't far from the truth, Arowyn. Being what I am..." The Elf took a deep breath and started over. "I didn't want to kill. I wasn't given a choice. I did as I was told, or I would die. That was made quite clear to me."

Again, too many questions flooded her mind. "Someone forced you to be an assassin?" She couldn't even imagine what it would be like to be *forced* to kill.

"If I wouldn't take my place in court, then I would be made use of," he said flatly.

The fact he'd become an assassin instead of going to court made her wonder just how bad court was. Some of Prince's comments suggested it was a dangerous place. Again, her mind filled with questions and she remained silent a moment as she sorted through them. She dismissed her questions about court. However, clearly someone in power had done this. Who? Why? "Then why were you punished? What the court did, it seems so...harsh."

He laughed, and the bitterness in it shocked her more than his amusement. "They did not punish me for killing you. It was because I got caught."

She could only stare at him.

He shook his head. "I became a liability, and those are always quickly disposed of. If not for the prince, quite likely I'd have been killed."

"I see." She worked on rinsing blood from his hair. "Who did this to you?"

Angry eyes met hers. "The queen. She is not one to cross, Arowyn. The prince made the right decision in not bringing you home with him. You'd not be alive now if he had."

His words sent a chill down her spine and worry gripped her stomach. Prince could take care of himself. She needed to remember that.

Baelan once told her he'd killed her because she was hurting Prince, she knew that much. But his words made her think further. "Were you to kill me?"

"Your death had not yet been ordered."

The tone of his voice drew her attention and she went over his words again. "You believe it would have been though?"

"Yes. I have no doubt. I was not her only assassin, but I was the best," he continued. "You being...human, others would have been sent before me. Had they failed, I would have been sent eventually." His voice softened as her eyes grew wide. "I am here for a reason. Prince Shael sent me to protect you."

"From his mother," she whispered, still shocked.

"Those she would send. Will send, yes. Vesrin and the others acted on their own. It is quite likely others will as well, trying to gain favor or to hurt him, though I imagine they'll now be more...discreet in breaking our laws. But should the prince continue to behave as he has, others will come."

"Surely he knows this?"

Baelan snorted. "Of course he does. So, they bait him. They push and push, and he cares for you too much not to react. You are his weakness," he said softly.

Yes, she'd heard that before, and didn't want to get into that argument again. "I see." Clearing her throat, she brought the topic back to her question he'd tried to evade. "So, who are you then?"

"I am who I need to be."

He looked away again and she paused in her cleaning.

What a strange thing to say.

∞ ∞ ∞

Baelan brought her bread and burnt fried eggs for breakfast. Still in bed, she eyed the eggs warily, trying not to wrinkle her nose. "Not much of a cook?"

"I have trouble with eggs." A faint, unsure smile curved his lips and disappeared.

With a snort, she took the tray, shaking her head. Had he just attempted a joke? Hopefully, he didn't think their talk last night suddenly made them friends. Yet, something between them had changed. She didn't quite hate him as much as before. Pausing a moment, she forced a smile. "Thank you."

"Bo's gone off to the tavern already."

Her eyebrows rose. Was it later than she thought? She hadn't slept well. Just dozed on and off between spinning thoughts and a few nightmares she thankfully couldn't remember.

Picking at the food, she tried not to look at Kei too often. He remained a motionless body beside her, breathing, but nothing else.

Baelan cleared his throat, yet when she looked at him his eyes rested on the Fey. "He doesn't have much longer," the Elf informed her gently.

Her gaze darted back to Kei. Being with him all the time, she didn't notice the changes. His breaths came soft and shallow, his golden skin had a sickly pallor to it. He'd lost so much weight his cheekbones stood out sharply against the hollows of his cheeks.

He wouldn't die. He couldn't. They had to save the Fey. She couldn't do it without him. Besides, he'd promised he'd never leave her. Her throat closed up, her appetite disappearing.

Holding her barely touched food out, she took a deep breath after he quickly took it from her hands. "I want you to teach me how to go into someone's mind."

Baelan dropped the tray.

∞ ∞ ∞

He didn't speak as he cleaned up the mess on the floor and she left the flustered Elf to his thoughts until he stood, tray in hand, and gave her a helpless look.

"I need to go in and help him." She looked over at Kei. "I've run out of time. I can't wait for him to wake up on his own. I don't think he's going to," she admitted softly.

The Elf heaved out a sigh. Turning, he walked over to set the tray on her dresser. "You're human, Arowyn. This is something I can't teach you."

She could have told him then, of the fortress she built in her mind, of how she even created a Were pack with her boys, but she didn't. She had no idea how much he already knew, but didn't trust him enough to give him more if he didn't already know. "I want to try."

He shook his head, but then nodded, not able to deny her need.

Did he hate her for that? She didn't ask. She didn't care.

"Now?"

"Yes."

A resigned sigh left his lips, but he came around the side of the bed. "You understand I must go into your mind?"

Her stomach churned and she swallowed back bile at the thought. She didn't want him there, not ever.

She had no choice. She would do anything for Kei. "I do."

He knelt beside the bed. "Lie down. Close your eyes."

A breath shuddered out of her as she did as he asked. Fingers slipped tentatively into hers. Though she knew he needed to touch her, she couldn't stop the flinch. "Give me a moment, and then come in."

Diving into her mind, she opened her eyes and looked around. Was there anything she didn't want him to see? Her gaze settled on the small tree growing alone in the barren dirt. Striding over to it, she couldn't help the small smile that came to her lips. She still didn't know what it represented, but certainly it signified something good. The little tree had grown, almost reaching to her chin now. Stroking the leaves gently, she then stepped back and spread her hands.

"Hide," she whispered.

A misty fog rose around her. Walking backward, she watched until the tree disappeared from her sight. Hopefully Baelan would appear by her and not see it. She'd done her best.

"Arowyn?" As if she'd called him, his voice echoed in the now foggy landscape. "Master?"

"Here. And don't call me that," she added.

He came out of the fog, thankfully from the opposite direction. The mist clung to him, swirled around him, and her breath caught at the sight. It suited him, accentuating his strange gray beauty. Head tipped up, his eyes focused on the fortress behind her, she couldn't help but stare. How could such a sweet and seemingly innocent face belong to an assassin? Gritting her teeth, she called his name, bringing his attention to her.

"How did you do this?" His voice held noticeable awe.

"In case you hadn't noticed, I'm not a normal human," she answered wryly.

"Apparently," he murmured, his eyes once again drawn to the towering walls behind her. After another long moment, they flicked up to her cloud-filled skies, then down and around as he surveyed the rest of the barren landscape. "So…" he paused and cleared his throat. "I've not done this before."

"Just do your best."

He ran a hand nervously over his hair. Neither of them mentioned the dangers she now faced. "You know how to heal, so you've moved yourself out of your mind and into your body." She nodded, even though she didn't have to. "Going into another's mind is similar, yet opposite. You will push your consciousness outward. You've felt the connection, when you mind-speak with others. Going into a mind is an extension of that. We touch," he held out a hand, "as a conduit in finding where we will go."

"Do you have to touch," she interrupted, remembering how Garen hadn't touched her the first time they met, and he briefly went into her mind to see an image of the missing Bo.

His brows drew down as he frowned. "That is how it is done. Perhaps some needn't, but becoming lost along the way would become much more likely."

"Understood."

"We will practice with my mind, going back and forth. I will guide you, which will make it much easier." His gaze flicked up to her fortress again before he held out a hand. "Think of me, of entering my mind."

Gingerly, she slipped her hand into his, surprised to find it shook slightly. "I can do this," she assured him.

Lips pressed tightly together, he held her gaze for a long moment. "Don't let go of my hand."

"I won't."

He paused and did the thing where he went to say something and then changed his mind. For a moment he stared down at their joined hands and then rolled his shoulders and straightened, turning his gaze back to her. "Ready?"

With a nod, she closed her eyes and concentrated on Baelan. She felt a pull...a shift, and for a moment, disorientated.

"Open your eyes."

Chapter 4

Within Minds

Baelan's mind was…unexpected. Opening her eyes, she found herself standing within a dark forest, the Elf beside her and still holding her hand.

The black trees drew her attention. Tall, spindly things with reaching empty branches, they looked…burnt. Despite the lack of leaves, the shadows they cast appeared larger than they should be. She couldn't see the sky above her, yet a faint light came from somewhere. As she stared, trying to figure it out, a breath whooshed out of him.

"Don't look too closely." His fingers squeezed hers briefly before he let go, drawing her attention back to him. His eyes darted about and he frowned, pushing hair from his face with trembling hands. "Come, this isn't a good place."

He took off through the strange trees surrounding them. After a step, she paused at the crunching sound beneath her feet and looked down. The ground was covered with bones. "Baelan?"

Stopping a few steps ahead of her, he turned, but didn't meet her gaze. It occurred to her then, he didn't want her in his mind any more than she wanted him in hers.

"Is it…safe here?"

Jen Wylie

A twisted laugh escaped him. "Of course, my lovely. Everyone here is already dead." He gave her a dark smile. "Almost." With that he turned and stalked off through the twisted, black trees. Stopped. Turned abruptly and went in the opposite direction.

Her mouth opened and closed a few times before she quickly followed. Almost? What did he mean almost? Almost dead or almost everyone? A shiver ran down her spine.

"Baelan, wait!"

She walked gingerly, the crunching of the bones beneath her feet unnerving. Pausing, she looked around and shuddered. This dark forest, the bones, they reminded her too much of some of her own nightmares.

Silence surrounded her, and she jerked her head around. "Baelan?" Moving forward, searching the dark shadows, the crunch of bones beneath her feet echoed too loudly.

"Come, come with me…"

She rushed forward at the sound of his singing voice. Why was he singing?

My darling one,
My everything,
To the sea, to the sea.

Of course, he had a beautiful tenor and the lilting tune of the simple song was almost comforting as she hunted for him within the shadows.

"Baelan," she half-whispered.

Come, come with me,
Side by side,
On the cliffs,
By the sea, by the sea.

She followed his voice, pausing once more when wisps of a faint glowing fog began to swirl around the bases of the trees. It gave her more light though, so she continued to follow his voice.

Watch, watch with me,
My darling one,
The sun set,
On the sea, on the sea.

She sped up, worry setting in as no matter how far she walked he never seemed to get any closer. Jerking, she almost tripped as something snagged her pants.

Horror choked her scream away. A boney hand clutched her pants. The fingers moving, trying to grab her leg.

"Baelan!" She kicked the hand away and bolted toward his voice, raising her hands to protect her face from slapping black branches. Brighter light ahead urged her on and she broke into a small clearing, only to stop abruptly.

Glowing fog swirled around the Elf as he sang and danced. She couldn't look away from the morbid sight as he swung his partner around. A skeleton. He danced with a skeleton.

"Die, die with me," he sang softly now, his spinning dance slowing.

My forever,
My sorrow,
In the sea, in the sea.

He stopped, staring down at the grinning skull with such sadness her breath caught. Then he stepped back abruptly, spreading his arms. The bones crashed into a pile by his feet...and he laughed.

Looking up, his wild eyes met hers and he tipped his head to the side. Smiling brightly, he danced off into the trees.

Words evaded her. The Elf truly was insane.

Bones crunched next to her and she jumped, turning quickly to find...Baelan.

"Did you get lost?"

"No...I..." Whipping her head around she searched the shadows and swore she did briefly catch sight of silver hair before it disappeared. Was there more than one of him? Could it be a trick?

A small smile curved his lips and she narrowed her eyes at him. "Come along then," he said lightly, like she hadn't just seen the most terrifyingly bizarre scene ever.

"Wither me," she muttered, dashing after him quickly.

∞ ∞ ∞

"Where *are* you?" Somehow, she'd lost the rotting Elf again. Tramping over the crunching bones, she glared into the shadows. They weren't supposed to be playing games. She was supposed to be learning so she could save Kei.

"Here," he whispered in her ear.

She jerked and turned, but he wasn't there.

"You understand, don't you," he continued softly. "I saw it in those lovely eyes. Bones, bones, bones..."

Clenching her fists, she spun around again. "Stop it."

"Bones are death. You know death, don't you, Arowyn?"

His words slammed into her and she froze, closing her eyes. "Yes."

"We are more alike than I thought." His fingers slid gently across her cheek, but when her eyes snapped open he wasn't there.

She shook her head at his words. She wasn't an assassin, a killer. She wasn't crazy. Searching the shadows again, she still couldn't see him. With an irritated huff and a touch of fear, she set out again. "This isn't funny. We're supposed to–"

Arms wrapped around her from behind, pulling her to the side. "Don't step there."

She froze again. He didn't let go of her. The heat of his body pressed against her back, his breath once again by her ear. The soft warmth of it, of him, disarmed her. It shouldn't have. What was he doing to her? "Why?"

"Trap."

She scowled. "I think your whole mind is a crazy trap," she muttered.

"Yes, actually. It is. Very good, my lovely." His cheek pressed against hers. "You pass the test."

"Test?" She turned in his arms, glaring up at him and not caring he didn't step back at all. No, she wasn't going to play *that* game. Not with him. "You're supposed to be teaching me."

A childish grin crossed his lips and he laughed as he tipped his head to the side. "The lesson is the test. Or the test is the lesson. You understand now, minds are dangerous places. You never know what you'll see. You must always be on your guard and," he leaned in closer, his nose almost touching hers, "fear can kill you. Some traps manifest your fear. Understand?"

Nodding, she fought not to let him intimidate her and make her step away. His gaze dropped to her lips and her eyes narrowed. Rotting Elf. Raising a hand between them, she slapped it against his chest and pushed him a step away.

"Good." Moving past her, he grabbed a hand and pulled her along behind him. "On we go." Still walking swiftly, it wasn't long before he spoke again. "Are you really afraid of skeleton hands grabbing your feet?"

How much had he seen? A stupid question. This was his mind, he probably saw everything.

"Wrong question perhaps? Are you afraid of me kissing you?" He turned his head to see her response. "Or just feeling anything at all for me?"

Glaring at him, she didn't answer. Crazy Elf. She didn't feel anything at all for him but anger and some lingering hatred. And pity, she decided.

He chuckled and turned forward again, singing under his breath. "Walk, walk with me..."

"I hate the sea," she whispered.

His singing stopped abruptly, but he kept walking.

Finally, he pulled her into another clearing. Eyes wide, she stumbled behind him as he walked into the center and then stopped. With a soft sigh, he closed his eyes and tipped his head back.

Sunshine lit his face, the light accentuating his strange ghostly beauty. Long dark lashes fanning out against his flawless skin. His striking features highlighted by his beautiful silver hair. Even the scar he hated so much seemed to fit him. He was so brokenly stunning she wanted to reach out and slide her fingers down his cheeks. Across his perfect Elven lips...

Quickly turning her gaze to the flowers surrounding them, she smashed down such thoughts. It wasn't him. His mind was playing tricks on her. He was doing it on purpose.

Turning her head away, a tower in the distance caught her attention. An overwhelming rush of sorrow crashed into her and she quickly looked away, blinking back tears. *Wither me, his mind is insane!*

The flowers were an easy distraction. She'd never seen so many different kinds. So beautiful and bursting with many colors.

A place of such beauty and light existed in his twisted mind? "What is this place?"

His hand squeezed hers and it disturbed her she hadn't even noticed he still held it. "Everyone has good moments in their life. I treasure the few I have and keep them safe." His lips quirked into another smile. "It is also the only place in here that won't try to drive you insane."

Her eyes found his again, and the calm, sane look on his face confused her even more. "Can I make a place like this?"

"In your mind, you can do as you wish. You know that."

She supposed she did, but had never done much more than build her fortress.

"Now that I've found it again, we will practice coming here. Only here." His fingers tightened on hers as she tried to figure out what he meant by that. "Always come here if you enter my mind, Arowyn. It is the only safe place for you." Once she nodded her understanding, he took one more look around, a quiet sated sigh escaping before he pulled her closer. "Now, back to your mind."

Back and forth they went, over and over again until Baelan finally allowed her to enter his mind on her own. When she managed to do so, and even ended up in the flowered clearing, she couldn't help jumping up and down among the flowers at her success.

"Well done, my lovely," he said with a soft smile.

"Now we try Kei?"

He shook his head in amusement. "Not yet. Now we practice this." He made a shooing motion at her. "Back you go. Find your way home again."

So she did, over and over again, until Baelan finally called a stop.

Opening her eyes, she blinked a few times, staring up at the ceiling. A pulsing pain burned behind her eyes. The stiffness of her muscles made themselves clear as she sat up with a wince.

Baelan rose slowly beside her, catching himself on the bed before straightening. Looking up at him quickly, his pale face alarmed her.

Rot, he'd been kneeling next to the bed all this time. Glancing around the darkening room, she realized they'd been practicing most of the day. Looking quickly at Kei, she saw what she expected. He hadn't moved at all. She returned her attention to the Elf standing beside the bed.

"Baelan…" She couldn't think of what to say.

"You did well today," he said into the silence, not looking at her. He shifted slightly, trying to be inconspicuous about stretching strained muscles. "Now rest, we will do more tomorrow."

"But…"

He turned his gray gaze on her for a brief moment before quickly dropping it again. "It takes more out of you than you realize. You need to rest."

Looking away, she nodded. She hadn't been about to argue with him. Clearing her throat, she ran her fingers through her messy hair. "Thank you."

"There is no need to thank me," he reminded her stiffly. "Can I make you something to eat?"

She shook her head. She did need to use the privy, though. "Bo should be home soon. I imagine he'll bring something."

"Is there anything else—"

"No," she interrupted. "I would just like you to rest." Looking up at him again, it struck her then how different he acted within his mind. More like the first times she'd met him, not like a cowed servant. He moved toward the door as she debated mentioning it. As he reached it, she did. "You didn't act like this…in your mind."

He froze and then immediately bowed his head. "I… I…"

"I like you that way better," she said softly.

Silver hair parted as he looked up at her in surprise.

"You're all sorts of crazy," she continued with a small smile. "But that is you, not," she waved at hand him, "this." He continued to stare at her, and she had no idea what he was thinking. "Get some rest. I'll need you tomorrow," she finally said.

With a slight bow, he slipped from the room.

Elves drove her crazy, they really did.

∞ ∞ ∞

Bo brought home food and the smell of it pulled her away from Kei and down to the kitchen. She grinned when she saw Elaina with him and pulled the young woman into a quick hug.

"I can't stay long," Elaina said. "How are you doing today?"

The worried look on her face made Aro grimace, but she quickly forced a smile. "Much better. Made some progress today."

Bo raised his eyebrows.

Later.

His eyes narrowed, but he didn't press. Bo was just wonderful like that. Elaina was a lucky girl.

Garen stood off to the side, scarfing down something that didn't look appetizing. *Do I want to know what that is?*

Lifting his head, he gave her a wolfish grin. *Nope.*

Making a face, she ignored his mental laughter.

Working side by side, Bo and his soon-to-be wife unloaded a basket on the counter and began filling plates with food. Elaina's eyes flickered over her shoulder toward the hall, and she reached to take another plate down from the cupboard.

Aro turned, though she didn't know why she bothered. Of course, it was Baelan hovering by the kitchen doorway. Pushing away the flare of irritation rising within her, she jerked her head, inviting him in.

He shuffled in, head slightly bowed, though his eyes kept darting up and toward the food. She wondered when he last ate, then got angry she worried. A breath huffed out of her and she snapped her mouth closed.

"Nice to see you, Baelan," Elaina said softly, with her usual sweet smile. Aro didn't miss how she nudged Bo's arm and gave him a questioning look.

"A pleasure as always, Miss Elaina," the Elf replied quietly.

Bo frowned and then shrugged his massive shoulders. "Go sit," he said, handing her a full plate.

"Thank you." She settled into a chair at their small table and dug into her meal. Her eyes closed in bliss as she chewed. Elaina and her sisters were the best cooks ever. Looking over at Bo, she leaned sideways to see if he'd started to get a gut yet. He hadn't, but then the barmaid kept him busy, and they'd all been under a lot of stress with Kei. And Elves. And Were. Thinking about it all almost made her lose her appetite. Almost. She shoved another forkful of food into her mouth.

"Do sit, Baelan," Elaina instructed, as Bo pulled out the chair to the right of Aro for her, before sitting himself across from her.

The Elf sat to her left, bowed his head, and began to slowly eat. She shouldn't have been surprised he took his time, cutting small bits and eating neatly. Just like Prince always had.

Frowning, she shoved more food into her mouth and chewed quickly to vent her annoyance. *Don't think about it. Or him.* Now wasn't the time. With some effort, she stuffed her feelings for Prince back into her fortress.

For a while, they ate in silence, which she would have found odd if she hadn't been starving and had a thousand other thoughts running crazy through her mind.

Elaina elbowed Bo. He frowned, they shared another look, and then he cleared his throat. Aro watched in amusement, wondering what it could be they wanted to say. Her eyebrows rose. Maybe Elaina was pregnant? She didn't know what else could have them acting like they did.

"Just say it already," she finally said.

Bo gave a loud laugh, startling Baelan enough he choked on his food. She shouldn't have been amused, but couldn't help it. Smacking him harder on the back than he needed, she grinned when he looked over at her.

"I'm not sure..." Elaina began when everyone was settled once more.

Bo placed one of his large hands over hers. "Always speak, love. It may be nothing, but then again, perhaps it is."

Nodding once, she gave him a small smile. The look in her eyes as she met Bo's gaze, so full of love, made Aro's heart twist. She wanted *that*. Why couldn't she have it? Would she ever?

"A man came to the tavern this afternoon. He asked about someone, and I have to say, his description fit you fairly well."

Baelan didn't notice right away that the barmaid looked at him. When he did, he sat back and sucked his lower lip between his teeth. "Was he human?"

Elaina sighed and looked down. "He seemed to be...but, he was one good looking man, almost pretty." She paused a moment. "Like you. He reminded me of you."

Aro leaned forward. "What did you tell him?"

"Nothing, of course!"

Baelan frowned. "Did he ask about Arowyn?"

Elanina shook her head, and he relaxed, nodding slightly. At Bo's hard look, Baelan continued. "I am outcast. Others will hunt me. It has always been so." At Elaina's stricken look he leaned forward. "You needn't worry. I will deal with it." Pausing, he looked over at Aro.

Did he want her permission? Giving him a confused look, he let out a sigh.

Garen suddenly stuck his head on Baelan's lap and stared at his unfinished plate.

You did not just do that, Aro thought at the Were.

He didn't move his head, but his eyes turned in her direction. *I'm still hungry.*

They finished eating in silence. Aro pretended to ignore Baelan sneaking bites of food to Garen.

"We need to get back to the tavern," Bo finally said.

"I will clean up," Baelan offered.

They left him to it. Aro ran outside to the privy, surprised to find the weather certainly had started to warm up, before heading back up to sit with Kei.

She dozed off at some point and woke with her head on Kei's unmoving shoulder, her arm laced through his. With a quiet sigh she got up, moving slowly from the room to avoid stubbing her toes in the darkness. The quiet of the house proved Bo and Garen hadn't returned from the tavern yet, so it wasn't nearing morning.

A faint light in Baelan's room caught her attention as she neared the stairs, and she paused, glancing in through the partially open door. A golden globe hung in the air, making the scars crossing his leanly muscled back shine as he pulled a dark shirt over his head.

Looking away quickly, she hurried down the stairs, glad lanterns left in the lower hallway and kitchen for Bo gave her light to see by.

Returning from the privy, she rubbed at her arms as she entered the kitchen. Though the days were warming up, the nights certainly had a chill to them.

A sudden unease stopped her abruptly as she stepped into the hall. She'd learned quickly enough not to ignore her instincts. A shiver ran down her spine as she looked toward the main door, eyes searching the shadows, ears straining for any sound. Turning toward the stairs, her breath lodged in her throat and she froze.

Baelan stood directly in front of her, dressed completely in black, his sword at his hip. The shadows and lamp light played tricks with his hair, turning the silver to dark gold. His face however, caused her body to tense, fingers moving to the dagger at her belt she always carried with her.

"I will return shortly." Though he kept his voice low, there was no trace of his usual soft and meek tone.

The assassin stood before her now, and she had to admit he certainly looked the part well. Forcing herself to relax, she simply watched him.

He regarded her with dark stormy eyes for a moment, before walking past her. Their hardness, lack of emotion, nearly made her reach for her dagger again.

Turning to watch him, she shook her head. He didn't even walk the same. The words "be careful" sat at the edge of her tongue, but she swallowed them back. Instead, she called out, "Help yourself to anything in the training room."

He stopped, turning his head just slightly in her direction before he gave a sharp nod.

Ensuring her thoughts were still firmly locked away, she kept herself relaxed as she turned her back on this deadly killer and walked back up to her room. Never, ever, did she want him to think she was afraid of him. She wasn't, just more…shocked. He was so *different*. Why did his personality change so much? He acted like completely different people sometimes. He was moodier than she was.

The Baelan who killed her hadn't been this one. If it had been, she most certainly would have stayed dead, of that she was certain. She found it a bit disturbing to realize he had no trouble killing, no matter what state his mind was in.

Taking her spot next to Kei again, she didn't wonder if the Elf would come back. He would. What trouble he might cause did make her worry. Hopefully Baelan knew how to clean up after himself in a human city.

She kept a lantern burning on the side table.

Jen Wylie

Chapter 5

Assassins

For once Baelan wasn't hovering by her door when she woke in the morning. If it was morning. The faint light in the room wasn't the sun, but the lantern.

Rising on one elbow, she kissed Kei on the forehead and got up. She'd check the house and see if Baelan was back. Maybe his return had woken her.

Bo's snores echoed in the hallway and when Garen didn't peek out to check on her, she assumed he slept as well. Baelan's room remained empty, so she quietly made her way downstairs. The lights in the hall guided her steps and she paused at the bottom, sensing...something. Listening carefully, she heard only the pop and crackle of the fireplace in the living room. It hadn't been lit, had it? She scanned the hall, grimacing as she moved forward, stopping before the first of many dark stains trailing from the main door.

She followed them into the living room, pausing a few steps inside.

Baelan sat on the floor by the fireplace, leaning up against the side of a chair, legs stretched out as he stared into the flames.

She walked up to him, dropping to crouch beside his dark-clad form. The clothes hindered her view of how injured he was. Considering the amount of blood he'd trailed into the house, she assumed badly. Especially since he should have been able to heal most wounds.

After a moment, his gaze left the flames and found hers. The assassin stared at her, his face void of emotion.

"How did it go?"

He blinked once, before turning his gaze back to the fire. After a long moment he finally answered her, his voice low and brittle. "I tracked him to the west side of the city. He was waiting for me."

"A trap."

"Yes. He knew I'd come." His gaze returned to her. "There were four of them. I recognized two. Assassins."

Her brows rose at that. "That's...not good."

"No," he agreed. Silence stretched on for a long moment as they stared at each other.

"Did any get away?"

He of course frowned, which brought a faint smile to her lips. "No."

She forced herself to not look away from his penetrating gaze first. "So, we're good then?"

His eyes narrowed and then he grimaced and shifted before looking away. "No. We are not good. They were after you, Arowyn. They know of your connection to the inn. They knew I was protecting you. They needed to kill me first, to be able to get to you."

His words shocked her. "How could they know?"

"Most likely they discovered it while watching the house. Seeing me here," he elaborated.

"Did they tell anyone else is the question."

"Yes," he agreed. "It certainly is." His jaw clenched as his eyes narrowed.

Looking him over again, she saw the firelight shining on wetness on his clothing. Blood. In more than one place. Had he just recently returned or was he still bleeding? Rotting Elf, getting hurt protecting her. How was she supposed keep hating him when he did things like that? "How bad is it? Do you need anything?"

"I am fine," he said stiffly.

Stupid Elves. Leaning forward, she shocked him by cupping his cheek and turning his face toward her. "You may serve me, but I am responsible for you. I take care of *you*, too. You are not alone, Baelan," she finished softly.

With her words, the assassin disappeared. She wasn't sure who remained, the meek servant or the carefree Elf, since his face suddenly contorted in pain. Sucking in a gasp, he tried to turn his face away.

She held it firmly, her eyes searching his face and trying to meet his gaze again. "Baelan." Finally, he looked at her, completely at a loss. She smiled faintly. "Come, we'll get you cleaned up and tended to, then into bed."

His gaze dropped again, but he nodded. She managed to get him up and they headed for the bath room. As she settled him on a chair, she cupped his face again, forcing him to look at her. "You did well tonight. Thank you." More words came tumbling out, and it surprised her how much she meant them. "I'm sorry you got hurt. Because of me."

His brows drew together as he stared into her eyes, searching to see if she spoke the truth. His confusion didn't surprise her. She'd been back and forth between hating him and being almost nice since he came. For some reason, it made her chest hurt though.

She cleaned him up and tended the wounds he'd not yet healed, even changing the wrappings he now always wore on his wrists and neck. He assured her he would be well as soon as he got some rest.

She followed him up to his room and settled him on his bed. "You did get rid of the bodies?"

When he just blinked up at her, she cursed. She'd be up for a while more then, contacting Silas or Raythe to let them know. Random dead Elves on the street was not a good thing.

He tried to sit up, but she gently pushed him down and forced a smile. "I'll take care of it." The worried and lost look on his beautiful face pulled at her insides. For some reason her fingers stroked the hair back from his face, and though his brows once again drew together in confusion, he settled back in bed. Rotting Elf.

"Sleep now," she said gently.

Leaving the room quietly, she rubbed at her temples. What was wrong with her? She hated him, didn't she? Why did she feel the need to be nice to the man who killed her? It didn't make any sense.

"Wither me," she muttered, heading for her own room. Getting back in bed, she closed her eyes and sent her thoughts to Roan's Were.

∞ ∞ ∞

Aro peeked into Baelan's room and watched him silently for a moment. Once she saw the faint rise and fall of his chest she walked as quietly as possible back to her room.

Taking a moment to stroke her fingers gently down the side of Kei's face, she forced a sudden wave of panic away.

"Soon, Kei."

Once Baelan woke up, she fully intended to convince him it was time for her to go into the Fey's mind and somehow find a way to fix him. Time was running out, slipping through her fingers like sand. She would not lose Kei. She wouldn't.

Stepping to the window, she leaned against the wall and looked up at the blue sky, watching a few wispy clouds float by. A bit past noon, the house was quiet. Bo and Garen had gone to the tavern, with strict instructions for her to contact them if she planned to do anything with Kei. She'd updated them on everything before they left, including Baelan's evening out as an assassin.

She frowned and shook her head slightly. When he confided in her that he didn't know who he was, she'd not considered what he meant. The killer last night hadn't been him, but seemed to be a totally different person. She didn't know how that was possible, or what it meant. Clearly, he was crazy, but she didn't know how, or if, she could help him.

It sent her mind spinning that she wanted to. Part of her still wanted to hate him, needed to hate him. But she couldn't. Bo was right, it wasn't who she was. She needed to remember that, not lose herself to everything that had happened.

Sometimes it was hard to let go.

Sometimes it was hard to hold on.

Closing her eyes, she let out a slow breath. Her talk with Raythe late in the night went well enough, until he started talking about Roan...

Have you spoken with him at all?

Um...no. Things have been—

Miss Arowyn, he cut her off. Silence. *He asks about you. Every day.*

I don't think it's a good idea.

I understand, you love someone else. That's a whole other matter. I thought you two were friends, though. I apologize if I was wrong. He did a lot for you, and...I think you helped him, too. Helped him see beyond the walls he's built.

It's complicated.

It always is.

With everything going on, it was easier to try to forget about the pirate. She didn't want to remember how he'd found her after escaping the Elves who'd taken her. Didn't want to remember the pain of withdrawing from the riath, or their arguments...or their parting.

Jen Wylie

She didn't want to think of *him*. If she did her mind went places she didn't want it to go. How if circumstances had been different, if she hadn't already given her heart to Prince...

But things were as they were. She couldn't change the past and didn't want to.

"He's my friend. That's all," she muttered to herself. "Stop being stupid."

Roan? Are you there?

She waited, wondering if he was maybe too busy, or too far away, or too—

Arowyn!

The surprise, happiness, and pleasure in his voice made her smile even as guilt stabbed at her heart.

To what do I owe this pleasure?

His formality made her smile again. *I just...*she floundered suddenly. She hadn't thought about what they'd talk about. *I don't...*

He chuckled. *No reason is ever needed. I enjoy hearing your voice.* When she didn't respond, he asked, *How have you been?*

The simple question put her at ease, and she quickly found herself telling him of what happened since she'd gotten Kei back. When she mentioned finally asking Baelan to teach her to go into someone else's mind, Roan had remained quiet long enough for her to begin to chew her bottom lip in worry.

I would have thought it would be obvious, Arowyn. I will admit to being disappointed in you. I hope your lack of sense has not ruined your chance to heal the Fey.

Her stomach churned and she bit down on her lip, hard. She should have been angry at his words...but he was right. She hated that he was. *I don't trust him,* she answered, knowing how weak the statement sounded.

He let out an irritated sigh. *We've discussed this. Trust is not an issue you need to have while the Elf is bound. It is impossible for him to harm you. I told you to use him, yet it seems you haven't at all.*

Because he's confusing! This whole thing with him being my servant... I don't... I hate him. Part of me hates him, she amended. *And that is the problem. He's annoying and frustrating and I can't stop thinking how he killed me, but...*

*But...*he prodded when she finally stopped her rant.

But I've found myself wanting to take care of him. Pitying him. He is seriously all sorts of crazy, did you know that? ...and I want to fix him. He's too rotting pretty, she finally mumbled.

Roan chuckled. *This is what makes you you. Though you can kill without batting an eye, you also have one of the most loving and compassionate hearts I've ever seen.*

Maybe I'm as crazy as he is.

Or...you are who you need to be to deal with the future set before you. To heal the Fey you will need to fight, but they will also need that heart of yours to heal centuries of madness. Perhaps you underestimate the power of kindness.

Perhaps, she said, mostly to stop his lecture. A headache was forming between her eyes.

Promise me you will think on what I've said. That you will think, Arowyn. He waited, until she finally muttered she would. *Good. I must leave for a meeting now. I hope you will call on me again. Know you are welcome to, day or night, at any time.*

I wouldn't want to bother you if you're trying to fall asleep. If he was sleeping, he'd not hear her at all.

He chuckled. *I find I do not sleep as well lately. My bed is disturbingly empty.*

His words shocked her silent for a long moment. *G-goodbye, Roan,* she finally stammered, deciding to ignore the comment. *And yes, I promise to talk again soon.*

After he said goodbye, she thumped her head against the wall next to the window. His words brought an uncomfortable heat to her face. A sudden thought made her pause and look out the window. Perhaps he hadn't kept her in his bed just to make sure she didn't die, like he'd told her. Maybe, like her, he just needed someone near at night to keep the nightmares away.

Despite her annoyance at Roan for making her feel awkward, she took a moment to go over the rest of their conversation again. His disapproval at her hesitance to use Baelan struck her hard.

Sitting in a chair next to the bed, she took Kei's limp hand in hers and watched him breathe. "I'm sorry, Kei. I'll fix it. I'll fix you." Leaning forward, she pressed a quick kiss to his forehead before hopping up and walking purposely from the room.

She headed for the kitchen. Baelan would need food before she put him to work.

∞ ∞ ∞

Setting the tray down on a small table beside his bed, Aro frowned down at the still sleeping Elf. Last night she hadn't thought his injuries to be very bad, yet still he slept, not even stirring at her entrance. Perhaps she'd been wrong. She'd become too complacent and used to people being able to heal so quickly. Of course, that he remained wounded meant he didn't have the power to heal them. If some of the wounds were deep, an arrow or knife wound, he could be out for a while as he slowly healed internal injuries.

Rot.

She needed him up…but didn't want him to fall over dead. Which, in itself, was surprising.

Her teeth ground together in frustration. If she had power, she could have given him some. The shocked look on his face would have been quite amusing, too.

She pulled the blanket down, eyeing the bandaging on his side. No blood seeping through. Good. Most, but not all, of the smaller cuts were gone now. Also good.

Her attention turned to another wound on his shoulder. It quite reminded her of her own. That the Elves he fought shot him up with arrows rather irritated her. Blood showed on this one. Leaning over him, she reached forward to see if perhaps the bleeding happened in the night and it was healing now.

She didn't even see his arm snap up, his hand just suddenly grasped her wrist so tightly she clamped her teeth down on a painful gasp.

For a moment she struggled for balance, then her eyes flicked over to his. She held back a grimace at the hard face and unwavering eyes meeting her. Wonderful. Assassin Baelan. The scar curving around his eye and then slicing across his cheek made this Baelan even more terrifying.

Holding his gaze, she remained still. "Good afternoon, Baelan." Pleased her voice didn't waver, she continued, "I brought lunch, and was checking your wounds." Her gaze moved to the bloody bandage on his shoulder. "You were, or are, still bleeding."

"I am fine."

The deeper quietness of his voice still surprised her. Still, she nodded once, then turned her gaze to where he still tightly grasped her wrist. He was certainly going to leave a bruise. "If you break it, I won't be able to heal it." When he didn't release her, she reluctantly turned her attention back to his face.

"Why are you here?"

Making up excuses likely wouldn't work with him, so she stuck with the truth. "I need you well so we can continue with Kei. He doesn't—"

"I understand," he interrupted. He released her wrist.

When she moved to check his bandage again though, his hand came up again. Raising both her hands in surrender, she straightened and took a step back. "Fine, I won't touch it."

"I don't require your care."

"Understood," she muttered. "Are you up? Do you want to eat?" She picked up his tray.

He sat up stiffly. "I don't need you to–"

"Sure, sure." She huffed in exasperation, set the tray back down, and then turned toward him, hands on her hips. Impossible Elf.

He glared up at her. She frowned down at him. It was like he could be totally different people. The thought sent her mind spinning as they continued to stare at each other. She remembered her time in his mind. Could it be more than just insanity and mood swings?

Eventually, she broke the silence. "Is there…" How to say it? "A few of you inside?" She tapped her head.

His head tipped a bit to the side. "Yes."

Having him actually confirm it sent her reeling. "Why…How…" His gaze turned icy and she took in a long breath. "What brings…this you forth?"

His face returned to the hard mask of indifference, and also now slightly condescending. "I kill."

"Yes, but you're not an assassin now."

"Danger," he answered. "I am to protect you."

"The…" she fumbled for the right words. "The other you seems capable enough."

"I am better."

She didn't doubt that.

"I am at your disposal. Should you require someone eliminated."

The thought turned her stomach. "I won't ever ask that of you," she said quietly.

"Last night–"

"I did not ask you to kill them."

His brows drew together slightly, then his head tipped a bit to the side as he regarded her. Rot, but he was beautiful. Frightening, but still beautiful. Such a strange combination.

When he didn't speak, she gestured to the tray. "Eat. If you're feeling well enough, come find me." She headed for the door, pausing at the threshold. "I don't mind you protecting me.

Any other killing, possible or imagined threats…speak with me first. And I meant what I said before."

"As you wish," he said, inclining his head. She turned to leave but looked back as he spoke again. "And, Arowyn," his fingers moved to his chest, "I am Bay."

Silence filled the room for a long moment as she processed that, and tried to figure out how, exactly, she should respond. Finally, she tipped her head in greeting. "It's nice to meet you."

She felt like an idiot, but he gave her a slight nod in return.

As she left she felt his eyes on her and clenched her teeth, holding back a shiver.

∞ ∞ ∞

He glided quietly into her room a while later, stopping inside the door to watch her pace.

"Feeling better?"

"Yes, very much so, my lovely."

Crossing her arms, she tapped her fingers as she kept walking, keeping him in sight. "Different you."

Baelan chuckled and gave a slight nod of confirmation. However, his stiff shoulders told her he wasn't entirely happy about her knowing. After a quiet moment, while she just stared at him, he looked away.

"He shouldn't have told you," he muttered, fingers fiddling with the ends of the wrappings on one wrist.

"Huh." What a strange thing to say. She walked some more. The whole thing just didn't want to make sense. "And your name is…?"

"Baelan."

Of course. She cleared her throat. "So…are you all there, all the time?"

He forced a smile, apparently resigned to the situation. "No. I suppose you could say we take turns coming forth, except it is who is needed, or expected, at the time." His face screwed up slightly. "Except him. I think he's always at the edges, watching."

"Bay."

"Yes."

"This is… I don't even know…" She shook her head.

He took a step forward, then stopped, his face suddenly pained. "You are the only one who knows. Who understands."

"What? How can that be?"

"I haven't had anyone close. Not for a long time," he answered. "Others see who they need to see. This me," he gestured to himself, "is the one most often out."

She shook her head. "I don't see how others wouldn't notice."

"*Everyone* has different aspects of themselves." A mocking smile lit his face. "Look at you. You bounce from angry to kind to sad so quickly it makes my head hurt."

She nearly argued, but then realized he was right. Rot, she wasn't going to break up into pieces like him, was she?

He either heard her thought or guessed from her frozen state and wide eyes. "It is unlikely. Your…situations have not required you to protect your very self. You haven't broken," he said softly.

"But–" She began, suddenly worried.

"Arowyn, I have suffered longer than you've been alive. Much longer," he added, looking away. She had no response to that and after a moment of silence he cleared his throat and then straightened. "So, my lovely, are you ready?"

Her brows drew down as she frowned. He still looked terrible. "Are you?"

A shoulder lifted in a shrug. "I am well enough. It should not take much power. We will go in and I will analyze the situation. If it is unsafe, we will return and plan."

She wanted to argue but didn't. Dying wouldn't bring Kei back.

After letting Bo and Garen know they were going to start, she and Baelan set up the chairs next to the bed so they could each reach Kei's hand.

Taking a seat, she looked over at the Elf as she slipped her trembling hand into his. She glanced down as he twined their fingers together.

"I won't let anything happen to you," he murmured.

Breathe. In. Out. She could do this. She'd survived Baelan's crazy mind.

"Ready?"

When she nodded, they both reached out to Kei. She took his hand as Baelan grasped his thin wrist.

"Remember, I'll come to you, then we'll go together into Kei. Do not let go of me. For any reason. When we are done, or if I think we need to leave, I will pull us out. Understand?" When she didn't answer quickly enough, his fingers tightened around hers. "Do you understand?"

"Yes. Yes, I do," she said quickly, heart pounding in her chest.

"Relax. Start when you're ready."

She tore her eyes from Kei's prone form to look at Baelan. His gaze met hers, serious, unwavering. Yes, she could trust him. Closing her eyes, she went inside herself.

Baelan stood beside her when she opened her eyes, his fingers squeezed hers briefly and then she twirled and twisted and was gone again.

"We're here."

Jen Wylie

Chapter 6

Broken Mind

She hadn't thought much about what Kei's mind would be like; a forest had come to mind, perhaps a fortress like she'd made.

Absolute darkness.

Silence.

For a moment she panicked, her breath lodging in her throat as her heart beat frantically. Had something gone wrong? Had she died again?

A hand squeezed hers, allowing her to breathe again. "I am here."

She looked to Baelan in relief, blinking as he created one of his golden lights above them. His hard, cold features made her stiffen. Not Baelan. Bay. How dangerous could Kei's mind be for the assassin to come out?

Looking around again, her brows rose. "I see lights, in the distance." Glancing at him, she saw a slight frown cross his face as his eyes narrowed. The lights grew, and she squeezed his hand, unsure what to do. "Are they coming closer?"

"Yes." He glanced up, his head tipping to the side. "Perhaps not a danger though."

Jen Wylie

Looking up, she saw more faint twinkling lights, like a sea of stars. They kept spinning around, circling something. She didn't know what exactly. Hopefully Kei.

"Quite unusual."

Tense muscles relaxed at his flippant tone. A smile twitched on her lips as they looked at each other and she saw Baelan had returned.

"What now?"

"Now we–" His gaze flicked over her shoulder, eyes widening suddenly. "Move!" Releasing her hand, elbow shoving her to the side, his hand flew up, the sudden bright blue rune blinding her.

She looked down as she stumbled, trying to clear the spots dancing in her eyes. Between one footfall and the next she noticed the nothing below her. No ground, water, nothing but blackness. With that realization, she dropped, an audible gasp filling her lungs as she uselessly kicked and swung her arms, trying to catch hold of something, anything.

She spun wildly, her hair whipping across and around her face. Wind buzzed in her ears, drowning out her panicked breaths and pounding heart. Even knowing she needed to calm down, she couldn't. Especially when she somehow turned herself to see the sphere of lights above quickly moving away.

Frantic noises escaped her mouth, combinations of gasps, whines, and whimpers. Her thoughts became a chaotic mess. Would she fall forever? Did Kei's mind have a bottom, or did it not matter, because she'd fallen into a trap and her sudden fear would never let her go.

Tears streaked her face, blurring her vision.

She still fell.

Forever, she fell.

I'm so sorry, Kei...

Stop moving, silly girl.

Not Kei, Bay. Blinking rapidly, she did as told and held her arms and legs still. Above, she noticed a small gold light quickly coming closer.

Hair still whipping around her, she clenched her fists, trying to calm the hysteria that wouldn't go away, her fluttering heart and constant quick short breaths. He'd never be able to reach her. She'd just keep falling and falling...

But he did draw closer. Soon she saw him, toes tipped down, body stiff and strait and arms pressed close to his sides, his silver hair a flowing cape above him. A beautiful figure in the dark.

As he neared, she couldn't help but scramble to try to reach him, arms flailing in her panic.

Stay still.

He passed her and she twisted, a cry escaping her lips. She'd lost him. He'd gone too far...

The jarring motion of landing in his arms made her bite her lip, drawing blood. She couldn't get close enough, hooking her legs around his as she wrapped her arms around his neck and tried not to cry.

"Shhh. I've got you." Stiff, he hesitated, patting her back awkwardly as she plastered her shaking body against him. After a moment, he finally wrapped his arms around her and held her tightly. "I will always catch you," he said softly. A hand stroked her hair as she stuck her face into his neck and tried to remember how to breathe.

Her brows drew together as she looked up at him, not understanding. She understood the words, just not which Baelan had said them. The tone didn't match any of the ones she'd grown to recognize. Hard features, dark gray eyes. But...the assassin never spoke with such a soft, almost gentle voice.

"You shouldn't have let go," he said stonily.

Ah, there he was. Maybe she'd lost her mind. An annoyed smile crossed her lips as she pulled back from the assassin. "I didn't. *You* let go of *me*."

He turned his head to the side, a nearly invisible frown on his face. After staring off into the distance for a moment he finally returned his attention back to her. "You are correct. He…we…" He frowned again. "I apologize."

Loosening her arms a little, she rested her head on one and closed her eyes, still trying to get herself back in control.

"The lights are shards, of glass or mirror perhaps. It would be unwise to get in the way of one."

"Understood." Pushing back, she locked one hand firmly into his and refused to look down. Resting one foot on top of his helped. *I'm on solid ground. All is well.* He didn't comment. "Back up we go, then? I think the lights are likely circling him."

"Agreed. I will try to maneuver us to avoid as many shards as possible."

Nodding, she held him tightly as they moved upward. Should she apologize for well…literally falling apart? A wave of nausea washed over her and she cleared her throat. "This isn't going as planned," she muttered.

"Things rarely do," the assassin answered softly.

She looked up at his face quickly. He never spoke softly, yet he'd just done it twice. He kept his face tipped upward, apparently intent on their destination.

"We are coming closer to the outer shards. It was a stray one which distracted me last time. Link your arm with mine. I can cast a rune if needed."

She did as he suggested, then her own gaze turned upward as they moved below the lights. "What do you think they are? Protection? A trap?"

He remained silent for a while before answering. "It is likely they are fragments of his shattered mind. Perhaps remnants of what was here previously. Maybe memories."

The thought made her chest hurt and she clenched her jaw against the tears suddenly burning her eyes.

"I don't see him."

Using her bond, she searched for Kei. "Keep going."

As they drew closer the number of stray shards increased. After Bay threw out his third rune he stopped and she looked up at him in surprise.

"This isn't working." As a hovering rune glowed beside her, Bay suddenly grasped her arms and pulled her around to his other side. Where she would be more protected, she realized. Like she was a doll, he adjusted her, tucking her body against his, moving her one arm behind him and the other to his chest. He then settled his arm around her and held her close.

"Hold on to me."

She did and then waited. When nothing happened, she looked up at him, and was surprised to find the assassin gone.

"Well, this is delightful, isn't it, my lovely?" He looked down at her with an amused smile.

"Uh…yes? Why are you here?"

A shoulder rose and fell. "I am better at such things." He gave her a curious glance. "He didn't want to leave you, which is…" His voice trailed off and he shook his head, not completing his thought. The smile appeared again. "Apologies for letting go before. The shard moved quicker than expected." His head tipped to the side. "I rather didn't think you'd fall either. Perhaps we should have done a bit more training."

"Apparently," she muttered.

They began to move forward. At first, she thought they just moved slowly, but then realized with no reference points, she'd simply misjudged the size of the spinning lights before them.

"Are you certain he is inside?"

Once again, she used her bond with Kei to search for him. He'd grown closer and the direction remained the same. "Yes."

His grip around her waist tightened. "I have to ask how you know." When she didn't answer, he continued, "It won't be easy moving through that. Assuming there is a hollow center, I may not have enough power to make it through to there. If so, I'll take us out. If we make it inside, and he's not there, I won't be strong enough to go through again. We'll have to try another day."

She didn't want to tell him, even knowing him finding out soon was inevitable. Trusting him remained difficult, an obstacle in her mind she had trouble crossing.

Closing her eyes for a moment, she finally just spit the words out. "We are bound." Her words were met with silence. "You know, Fey bindings–"

"Yes," he interrupted. "I understood."

He didn't say anything else and she turned to look up at him. "That's all you're going to say?"

His head tipped to the side slightly as he gave her a condescending smile. "I'm quite certain you've been asked often how that was even possible. Obviously, it just was. You don't seem to follow many of the magical rules. I also imagine Kei has been told on numerous occasions how foolish it was."

Pressing her lips together in annoyance, she just nodded.

"Therefore, no need to repeat myself."

"You just did."

He bumped her with his hip and scowled. They'd drawn even closer to the condensed area of shards and he stopped, his free hand outstretched to the side as he somehow deflected the increasing number of shards coming at them.

"I'm going to shield us. Do I have to tell you again not to let go of me?"

"No," she snapped.

"Good. It would help, if you could imagine us protected also."

"I don't have any power."

"In your mind, not all is about power. Obviously, since you are here."

Rot. She hated when she appeared stupid. "Understood."

"Strength of will. Do what you can. We've been here quite some time as it is. You'll be tired, and likely have a headache when we return anyway. Ready?"

Swallowing nerves, she nodded.

After a few moments, she felt him relax against her. "Shield is up," he murmured. "Now you try."

She had absolutely no idea what to do. Grimacing, she closed her eyes. Nothing really felt different. With a frown, she attempted to push her senses outward. There...something surrounding them both. A solid circle of light, Baelan's power, mixed with something else. The only thing she could think to do was concentrate and try to imagine it stronger, adding her own strength and will, weaving it through what the Elf had already made.

He sucked in a deep, shocked breath. "Yes. How...?"

Slumping against him, she opened her eyes. His remained closed, his brow furrowed and face tight. "Good?"

"How you can manage to do that, yet not stand, is beyond me."

She snorted.

"I must concentrate, my lovely. Guide me through, but do try to not distract me otherwise."

Turning her head toward the shards, she took a steadying breath. Soon she'd see Kei. Find out what was wrong. Fix him. "I'm ready. Forward."

The sudden onslaught startled them both, but Baelan managed to hold the shield. Every now and then she told him to keep going.

His grip on her waist tightened. Slight tremors wracked his body. She gritted her teeth, hoping they'd get to the middle soon. Finally, they broke through the worst of it.

Craning her neck, she looked around. Her fingers tightened on his shirt. "Up! Forward and up!"

The remnants of a stone slab drew closer. The floating stone looked strangely out of place, but the figure crouched on it broke her heart.

Baelan stopped on his own when they cleared even random shards. She nudged him. "Just a little closer and I can stand."

"Arowyn," he said sadly, doing as she asked.

Once close enough, she hopped onto the stone. For a moment, she kept one hand on the Elf to make sure nothing happened. Steady, a deep sigh lodged in her throat as she looked to her Fey.

Her sweet, wild, dying Fey.

Tears threatened, and she blinked rapidly before taking a few steps.

"Aro," Baelan said quietly. "Remember we are intruders here. Do not startle him."

No, she certainly didn't want to do that. Deep breath. A few more steps.

Kei crouched before her, hair a wild mess, arms around a large ball of swirling blue light in his lap. Rocking back and forth, he would touch his forehead to the ball now and then, lips moving but no words reaching her ears.

Even though he looked horrid, for some reason he wasn't in as bad a state as his real body.

Soon she stood only a few steps away, yet he hadn't seemed to have noticed her.

"Kei," she whispered tenderly. "Can you hear me? It's me, Aro."

The rocking paused, then started again. "Aro," he repeated. Over and over and over.

Looking over her shoulder, she cast a dismayed look at Baelan. He gestured her forward.

Carefully, she moved closer until she stood next to him, and then crouched down. "Kei," she said more firmly. "I'm here. I'm here with you."

He continued to rock and repeat her name.

"Rot," she muttered, blinking back more stupid tears. She tentatively rested a hand on his shoulder and called his name.

"You're not real." He squeezed his eyes closed. "Not real. Not real."

"Yes, I am, and you need to wake up. Look at me!" She squeezed his shoulder as she leaned forward. "I'm here! Look at me!" Swallowing thickly, she calmed herself and pressed a hand to her heart. "Feel me, Kei. I'm right here."

He stopped rocking and slowly turned to face her. His eyes widened and then brimmed with tears. "Aro…" Blinking, he shook his head. "You can't be here."

Not quite sure what he meant by that, she shrugged. "I learned how, so I could save you. You're dying!" Her voice rose as her agitation grew. She wasn't sure how much time she had here with him. "Tonight. Tomorrow. Your body is going to die. You need to wake up. Now."

His gaze returned to the ball of light. "But I need to protect Aro. I tried. I tried to keep her."

Looking at the ball, she frowned. Did it contain memories? Memories of her? Her heart ached, that he'd fought to keep those. "Kei," she tried again. "I'm here. And I'm alive and out in the world waiting for you. I need you. Out there, not in here."

His brow furrowed and then he looked at her again, his beautiful golden eyes meeting, searching hers. "Aro? I'm not… I don't understand. You're here?"

Relaxing slightly, she smiled. "I'm here. I'm always with you. I'll always need you. Right now, I need you to wake up."

"My Aro…" Kei's gaze shifted to look behind her. His eyes narrowed. "Who is he?" Before she could answer, his teeth clenched and furious eyes snapped back to her. "He is bound to you!"

"It's...It's only one way," she stuttered out, shocked at the sudden anger in his voice and wondering how he knew.

"Why is an Elf bound to you?"

"Prince sent him to protect me," she said gently, trying to calm him down. It was mostly truth. Telling him now how Baelan had betrayed and killed her wasn't a good idea.

Her words didn't help. "I protect you!"

"From Elves?"

"I'll kill anything for you, Aro."

A smile came to her lips. Perhaps she was strange for feeling touched by such a comment. "Not stuck in here you can't. You need to wake up."

His brows drew down and his shoulders slumped as he looked around. "I don't know how. Everything is broken."

"We'll fix it. Together."

He nodded but turned his attention back to his ball and began to rock again.

Aro turned to Baelan, who still hovered near the edge of the stone. "I don't..." She shook her head, forcing herself to remain composed. "What happened to him? What can I do?"

The Elf regarded the Fey for a long moment then gestured to the blue ball of light. "He holds remnants of memories. As you know, the Dragos broke him. It seems likely he had a conscious mind space prior. Though, it is also possible what the Dragos did resulted in him having one now." He turned his gaze to the black surrounding them, and the flashing shards whirling around them. "I would assume those are the memories Damon tore away. He will need to somehow retrieve them to get them back." His gray gaze returned to her. "First, he will need to have a place to put them. He needs to create...something in this space."

"Like my fortress, or your forest."

"Yes."

"And I am supposed to help him."

"So, it would seem."

She closed her eyes for a moment. Why, why, was nothing ever easy? She had no knowledge on how to do this. Sure, she'd built her fortress, but at the time didn't know what she was doing.

"Rot," she muttered. "Kei. Kei, I need you to pay attention and to listen. I don't have a lot of time." Giving his shoulder a shake, he focused on her again. "You need to make a safe place for the memories you have. That's all for now. Everything else you can fix later. Those," she gestured to the swirling shards, "won't be going anywhere."

"I don't know how. I don't…remember? Did I know?"

He looked so lost it broke her heart. "I don't know, Kei. But you can do it. In your mind, you can do anything. Make anything. This is your world."

He frowned at her, but nodded.

"I have a fortress in mine. Baelan has a forest."

Kei looked over her shoulder toward the Elf, then tipped his head to the side in confusion. "What is he doing?"

Turning, she saw the Elf sitting on the edge of the stone, legs hanging over. He swayed slightly as he hummed and swung his legs back and forth. She stared for a long moment, not quite sure what to say.

"He's strange," Kei said softly.

"You've no idea." Shaking her head, she turned back to Kei. "So, you understand what to do?" She leaned forward earnestly. "You have to wake up soon. I'll be there, waiting for you."

"I will, Aro. I promise."

Leaning forward, she kissed his forehead and then stood. "Baelan, I'm ready. Kei…" She struggled to get the words out as Baelan came to her side. "I love you. I'll see you soon."

"I love y–"

She wasn't quite prepared for the pain when she opened her eyes. Groaning, her body fell forward, only to be caught in strong arms.

"I swear, pup, you'll be the death of me."

Blinking up at Bo, she winced and closed her eyes again. Pain pounded her entire head. Every muscle ached. "How long?"

"At least half the day. Did you find him?"

A smile crossed her lips. "We did. He should wake up soon." Her smile faded. "He's so broken, Bo. Ugh, I need to use the privy."

"And then to bed with you." He easily gathered her up in his arms.

As he turned her and headed for the door, she saw Elaina helping Baelan stand. "Do I need to tell you to go to bed?"

He shook his head, face pale. "Not today."

Thank you, for everything.

Despite the pain evident on his face, he managed a small smile. *You are welcome, my lovely.*

Chapter 7

Sometimes an Idiot

She dreamt of her brothers. For once not nightmares, though perhaps those had come first. Muddled memories faded as she woke with a groan. Her head still hurt, and her body felt like she'd fallen off a cliff. Thinking of falling caused a shudder to run through her. Another thing to add to her list of fears. Hopefully she wouldn't start having nightmares of it, too.

Habit moved her hand out from her side, searching for Kei...and met nothing. Jerking up, she rolled over, eyes wide as she stared at the empty spot beside her. Her hands frantically, uselessly, patted at the sheets.

Her keening wail echoed in the empty room. She'd been too late. He was gone. Dead. Just like when Avery died, and they'd taken his body away when she wasn't looking. How could they? How could they not have woken her?

Keeeiii!

Shaking, blinded by tears, her stomach heaved and she lurched forward to vomit over the side of the bed.

Aro.

Kei? Kei!

He was alive. His surprise and worry hit her in the gut through their bond. Why hadn't she looked for it first before panicking? Perhaps she was losing her mind.

Gasping, her fingers curled into the sheets as Bo's voice roared into her mind.

Whatever you're doing, stop! Kei is losing control here and is going to drown in the rotting tub.

To Kei, *I'm sorry, I panicked when you weren't here. Everything is fine.*

To Bo, *Sorry! He wasn't here and I thought... I'm sorry.*

He sighed. *He wanted you to sleep,* he said more softly. *Get some more rest. You need it. We'll be a while. I'm trying to get him cleaned up. Elaina's gone to the tavern to cook. I sent Baelan and Garen to the market.*

She cleared her throat, wincing at the burn. *I will. Sorry.*

No worries, pup. Go back to sleep.

Falling back on the bed, she pushed her fingers against her eyes. Sweat beaded her forehead and she took a slow breath. The smell of her vomit made her nauseous and she sat up, blinking rapidly as the room swayed and she suddenly shivered.

Managing to stand, she grabbed a handful of cloths from the bedside table and threw them on the floor, swirling her bare foot around to somewhat clean up her mess. She noticed the empty bucket beside the table just in time to drop to her knees and be sick again.

Sides aching and eyes watering, she cursed when she finally finished and realized what was happening. "Rotting riath." After so long why was it back to haunt her?

She should have noticed the signs the last few days, her pacing and jitters, the occasional nausea. With her borrowed Fey power gone, it'd snuck up on her again. Maybe she would never be rid of it. It eventually killed humans, merely gave the other races dreams, and she was...something in between. Roan had never been certain what would work when he tried to break her addiction.

Bo, can you bring Kei to me as soon as you're done?

Of course.

She wanted to tell him. She knew she should, but hated the idea of being weak. Of them seeing it. She didn't want to see Kei again like this. Maybe it would go away. "I'm an idiot," she muttered. "At least I know I'm an idiot."

Another wave of heat washed over her. With a groan, she used one of the chairs pushed against the wall to help herself stand and then lurched for the bed. She missed, managing to grab some sheets to mostly slow her slide to the floor.

"I hate my life."

Aro, what's wrong?

Baelan's worried voice stabbed her between the eyes. She winced, pressing her lips together tightly. Him she would lie to. He was the last person she wanted to see right now. *I'm fine. Just woke up and Kei wasn't here. Panicked a little.*

I'll head back.

No, she snapped. *I am fine.*

Do you need anything from the market?

Closing her eyes, she pictured a few choice ways she might kill him. *No, I don't!*

The Elf looks like he just got kicked, Garen said with some amusement.

Thunking her head back on the floor, she closed her eyes against the growing pain tearing through her insides. She knew pain. She could deal with it for a while. Hopefully Bo would bring Kei up soon. Such a wonderful reunion it would be. "Hey, I need your fury or I might die."

Time always moves so slowly when you actually want it to go by fast.

She curled herself into a ball. The pain grew, her insides trying to become her outsides. Her body shook. Sweat leaked from every pore one moment and the next wracking shivers took hold. Every moment, the growing need for riath pushed at her. Sleep. Dreams. Everything would be perfect if she just...

"I don't want it. I don't need it!" She would have screamed the words if she could. She didn't need it. Just Kei. *Kei* would make the pain go away.

The last thing she wanted was for Baelan to feel her need and start running around the city to find her the drug. But then maybe he'd give her too much again. Maybe she'd see her prince one more time. She missed him so much. So so much. If only he were here. Why wasn't he here? She loved him so much. But he...but he...

A sob escaped, and then another. She pounded the sides of her head with her fists, trying to get her thoughts to just...stop. Another round of pain ripped through her, turning her sobs to gasping whimpers. Maybe she should...

Clutching her head, gritting her teeth, she squirmed on the floor. No no no no. Don't want it. Don't want it.

Her door flew open, slamming against the wall. The pain wouldn't let her move, wouldn't let her look. She hoped it was Kei.

Fur tickled her face, a cold nose touched her check. *Can you hear me now, Aro?*

Somehow, she managed a nod to answer Garen's question. Had he been trying to speak with her before and she hadn't heard him? Considering how distracting the pain was, it didn't honestly surprise her.

Is it the riath?

Gritting her teeth, she nodded again.

Bo and Kei are on their way up. Just hold on. I'm here. He pressed his head against her. She moved an arm clutching her stomach to wrap around his neck and pressed her face into the comforting warmth of his fur.

Breathe, she just needed to breathe. Another tremble shook her entire body and she gasped against the pain.

"Aro? Aro! Will you just...move dog!"

Her furry haven disappeared. *Rotting Elf.*

Hands gripped her cheeks, forcing her to look up into frantic gray eyes. "Who did this to you?"

She blinked at him and then started to laugh hysterically. "You did."

Baelan stared at her, brows drawn together.

His hands dropped from her face and he fell back, finally understanding. As she shivered and twisted and clutched at the floor, trying to escape the never-ending tearing, ripping pain, he just stared at her.

Garen nudged her face and gave her cheek a small lick.

"Ah, pup." Strong arms scooped her up, holding her close to a massive chest. Bo tucked her head under his chin for a moment, holding her tightly. "What am I going to do with you? When will you learn?"

"Maybe," she gasped out, "tomorrow."

He shook his head, his grip loosening somewhat as he shifted her. "Look, Kei is here."

Tears welled in her eyes, but she still saw him sitting on the floor next to Bo. Face pale, dark circles under his eyes, but alive and smelling strongly of soap. From his frown and furrowed brow, she knew he was confused and worried, and she wished for time to explain. As she reached a hand for him, he grasped it tightly and pulled it to his chest. His glistening eyes began to change. He knew what she needed.

"Take."

She did, but not too much. She knew he'd been using his power to stay alive and didn't want to weaken him. Even when she stopped pulling it from him, she didn't let go of his hand, as Bo held her while she fought the riath inside her.

Other than the sounds of her struggles, the room remained silent as she fought to rid herself of the pain. Eventually she succeeded and wilted against Bo, her breath coming in short pants. He stroked her sweat dampened hair. Kei didn't let go of her hand.

"All good now, pup?"

"Yes," she managed to croak out. "Just need...sleep."

She rocked as Bo rose and carried her to bed, settling her in gently. Kei somehow still didn't let go of her. She blinked at him, suddenly noticing they'd cut his hair.

His frail hand smoothed hair from her face. Fingers stroked her cheek. "Rest."

Her eyes drifted closed. The pain was gone. The constant love drifting from their bond accompanied her to sleep.

∞ ∞ ∞

The kettle began to whistle, and she hurried to move it off the stove. She'd woken early, before anyone else, and taken the time to bathe and wash her hair and then prepare a simple breakfast.

She didn't know how long she slept. Her memories of the riath episode were a bit foggy. Had she just slept through the night or had she lost another day?

It didn't matter really, so she didn't dwell on it. Kei was back. He was alive. The fear of losing him had finally disappeared and she could breathe again. Her face felt strange from smiling so much.

She felt Kei stirring. *Good morning!*

Aro. A rush of his relief filled her.

Yes, I'm up and well. I'll be up with breakfast shortly.

She managed to take a tray upstairs without spilling anything. Nudging Kei's door open with her foot, she peeked inside and smiled to see him sitting up in bed. Seeing him with such short hair still startled her a bit, even more than how horribly thin he was. "Good morning."

His smile was small, and tired, but there. "Morning, Aro," he said softly.

Setting the tray on the bedside table, she pulled up a chair, sat, and handed him a plate. "Eat up. Did you sleep well?"

He nodded, shoveling eggs into his mouth. Good, he had an appetite.

Eating more slowly, she continued to fire questions at him. "Things are going well?" She tapped the side of her head, and he nodded. "Good. Do you need any help?"

He stopped chewing to stare at her, his face growing pale. Forcing himself to swallow, he shook his head. "No. No."

Sensing his rising panic, she raised her hands and leaned forward. "Kei. Kei. I won't. Only if you ask."

Squeezing his eyes closed, he calmed himself by taking a few long, slow breaths. "I'm sorry," he finally whispered. "I just... I remember the pain. So much..."

"I understand. I do." After what Damon did to him, she didn't blame him for not wanting anyone in his mind. It would be impossible for her to ever forget feeling Kei's pain for months with their bond, and it had been a muted thing. She couldn't imagine what he felt. She pushed those thoughts away. He was back now. He was safe.

They ate in silence for a while, until Kei finished. She took his plate, handed him a mug of tea, and then returned to her meal.

"I don't..."

She looked up from her food when he didn't finish, meeting his intense golden gaze.

"I don't remember very much," he finished slowly, handing her his mug with a slight crinkle of his nose.

"I know," she soothed, setting it down. Guess he didn't like that kind of tea. "The memories are still there. You'll get them back."

He frowned and then looked away. "I don't remember this room."

"You weren't here long. It's not—"

"I barely remembered Bo." His face scrunched up. "Or Garen. Or that he—"

Clearing her throat loudly, she shook her head.

With a loud sigh, he looked down at his hands. "Right. Bo told me."

She set her plate to the side and then leaned forward and took his hand. "We'll get through this, together. Like we always do."

He squeezed her hand, locking his gaze on it as he sat silently for a while and absently played with her fingers. "I remember this. I mean...when we bound to each other."

Her smile grew, her heart warming. "Good. That's good."

"I wasn't going to fight him," he finally said after another silence, speaking slow and quiet. "I knew it wouldn't matter." His eyes flicked up to meet hers. "I wanted it over. So I could return to you." She forced a small smile and his gaze returned to their hands. "But then he s-started." He spoke more quickly, stuttering over the words he tried to force out. "T-tearing through my mem-memories. Peeling them off, one b-by one. Then he...he..." His jaw tightened, and he swallowed. "Then he tossed them away. And I...I realized when he d-did...they were g-gone. I couldn't ...I couldn't remember them any-anymore."

"Oh, Kei." She clasped his hands tighter.

Tipping his head back, he closed his eyes. Tears slipped down his cheeks. He continued, but once again speaking quiet and slow. "I fought him. Holding on to what memories I could of you. Of us."

She shifted over to sit on the side of the bed and pulled him into her arms. "I'm so sorry."

Gripping her tightly, he hid his face against her neck. Hot tears wet her skin and she struggled not to cry...and failed. She held him for a long time, not speaking. Sometimes there were no right words that could be spoken. Nothing she could say would make things better.

Eventually, he pulled back to look at her. With a sad smile, he brushed the remnants of her tears from her cheeks and then cupped her face in his hands. "I love you."

"I love you, too," she answered hoarsely.

Lowering his hands to take hold of hers, he held her gaze.

It took her a moment to notice the question in his eyes. *Oh. Oh, rot.* She instinctively began to pull back.

He broke their gaze, looking to the side, a wry smile crossing his lips as his cheeks flushed. "I wasn't sure..." His voice trailed off. "But not remembering so much is–"

"Hard." Squeezing his hands, she forced a smile and tried to ignore the slight heat in her cheeks.

He released her hands and leaned back, clearing his throat. "So, is there someone?"

She blinked in surprise for a moment. "For you or me?"

His head tipped slightly to the side. "Both?"

"You, not that I know of. Me..." Her cheeks warmed again. "Do you remember Prince?" It didn't surprise her when he grimaced, and she smiled. "You two never did get along."

"Bo said we got him home?"

"We did."

"And he's still there?"

She knew where this was going and sighed. "Yes."

At least the confusion on his face didn't look feigned. "So... you're in love with a man who lives in a different county, behind a magical wall, is an Elf, and who you may or may not ever see again?" Before she could respond, he kept going, speaking each word painfully slow. "And even if you did, he is an immortal and a prince, so nothing would ever come of it."

"That sums it up nicely," she muttered.

Surprisingly, he smiled. "Good. Avoids me dealing with anyone courting you."

There was her Kei.

"You have failed to mention," said a low voice behind her, "the prince's enemies who would very much like to see you dead."

Kei frowned, his now orange gaze flipping back and forth between her and Bay.

She turned to glare at the Elf.

"He should know," was all he said.

Shaking her head, she turned back to Kei. "It's a long story, which I will tell you about soon. I'm safe right now."

His eyes returned to their normal gold. "Who is he?"

She paused. "Bay, um…Baelan. I met him while you were gone. He's just recently…come to join us."

"Prince Shael sent me to protect her. Among other things," he added, before leaving just as quietly as he'd come.

"We'll get to that," she said in response to Kei's questioning glance. "So, I guess it would be best to give you at least a brief account of everything."

"Bo started last night. How we met on the…the slave ship."

"Good. Well, you've told me some of your past. I should start there, and then we'll keep going. Do you remember anything?"

Kei nodded slightly. "He stopped where my parents bound the prophecy to me. I was around ten. I remember everything before then." He grimaced. "And everything since Damon took me. The prophecy. He'd ramble on about what everything meant." He stared off to the side, a muscle in his jaw ticking.

She took his hand again. "We can do this later."

A shiver ran through him, then he shook his head and turned his attention back to her. "No, I need to know. Are we still…" His eyes searched hers.

"Yes, Kei. As soon as you're strong enough, we're going to heal the Fey."

∞ ∞ ∞

A soft knock at her door woke her. By the time she sat up, the door had opened.

"Aro," Kei whispered, his voice wavering.

"What's wrong?" Sitting up, she turned up the lamp by her bed. Tangled emotions pulsed down their bond, but it was the fear that sent her own heart racing.

"I…I remembered…"

Lamplight flickered off his glistening eyes and she quickly raised her arms, fingers beckoning him in. He closed the door quietly and paused a moment before springing across the room to her bed.

She thought he'd sit at her side, but instead he flipped the blankets and crawled in next to her, his body laying as close to hers as he could get. He mashed his face into her neck, his arm going around her.

"What is it?" She wrapped her arms around him, holding his trembling body gently.

She didn't understand his mumble, but his breathing increased. The arm around her shifted. His hand slid under her shirt and she froze until his fingers began frantically moving up and down the long scar on her stomach and curling up her ribs.

Ah, he remembered the Vor attack when she almost died.

Resting her hand lightly over his, she kissed the top of his head. "See, it's healed. I'm fine. I'm fine."

He gasped for breath against her neck, shaking his head. His tears wet her skin. She stroked his hair with one hand, his arm with the other. "Shh. I'm fine," she murmured into his hair.

Her words didn't seem to matter. He broke into body wracking sobs, his grip tightening. Curling into him, she held him tighter.

Her door opened again, and she glanced up, her eyes meeting Baelan's. They shared a startled look before his gaze took everything in and he quickly stepped back and closed the door.

I apologize.

Wait! It's not–

It is none of my concern, he interrupted.

"Wither me," she muttered.

Kei tipped his head up, red eyes meeting hers, and his brow scrunching together. "Was someone just here?"

She smiled tenderly down at him and brushed tears from his cheeks. "It's fine."

He blinked, more tears falling, and sniffed. "I should go," he said softly, pushing away. "I'm sorry."

"Shush, you." She pulled him back, not surprised when he eagerly sank back against her. "That was a...bad memory."

They curled up together in silence for a while as his trembling settled. "I can't lose you," he suddenly whispered.

"You won't."

"You're all I have."

She placed a kiss on the top of his head. "Not true, you have Bo and Garen, too."

"Not the same," he mumbled.

She couldn't argue with him. She understood what he meant.

Chapter 8

Broken Home

Despite Baelan's brief appearance in Kei's room and hers, she didn't see much of him over the next four days. Even when she did, it was always the servant or assassin. She wondered if he avoided her because of the episode with the riath.

She didn't mind, appreciating the lack of constant hovering. Kei kept her busy a good portion of the time. With Garen often curled up on the bed with him, she told him of the past. Other than asking the occasional question, he didn't speak much, which didn't really worry her. Kei had never been very talkative.

Most of the memories weren't hard to speak of. Some that were, she glossed over, hoping Kei wouldn't be angry with her when he did remember. Some though, needed to be told in full. Avery's death had been the hardest. He still contained memories of his old friend. Even though these days she tried not to cry, she allowed herself to this time. Holding Kei, they shared their tears, and afterward she thought maybe it had helped her to overcome her grief.

Soon enough she got Kei up and moving around again. He still took frequent naps, sometimes just to sleep, often to try to repair his broken mind and retrieve more memories. During these times, she began taking care of herself. She'd been a mess the last few weeks over Kei and needed to get herself back in shape and form. Now and then Elaina would also draw her aside to speak of her upcoming marriage. Before bed each night, she'd speak to Roan, at least for a little while.

Being busy again put a spring in her step to add to her smile. Each day Kei grew stronger. Bo and Elaina finally decided to wed in only a few days' time. Aro didn't even have to worry for Kei. He'd easily be strong enough for the trip to the registry hall and back. Getting married in Westport didn't take long but the celebration afterward would go on long into the early morning hours. Since it would be held at the tavern, it would be easy to sneak Kei home to rest if he needed it.

Hale stopped by to visit, pleased to see her up and about, and even more thrilled when she asked him to train with her for a while.

He left before noon, to meet his brother for lunch at the tavern, and she smiled as she saw him out. She'd miss the young Were when they left.

Her smile faded as she walked down the hall, a knot forming in her stomach. Her storytelling with Kei had gotten to the fight in the warehouse. She'd stopped just before Baelan betrayed her. At least Kei wasn't aware of when, exactly, her death happened in the timeline. From his frown, he knew it was close though, and that she was intentionally avoiding it. Of course, he didn't know why.

A headache began to form, and she rubbed her temples. How was she supposed to tell him? Once she did, how did she keep him from killing Baelan? She knew he'd go into a fury, she didn't doubt that at all.

Stalling, she peeked into the kitchen and waved at Bo and Elaina, smiling as they pulled away from an embrace. "Late lunch today?"

Elaina blushed at her joke as Bo mock-scowled at her. "It will be if you interrupt us," he said with a laugh.

Shaking her head, she decided not to bother them. Hopefully they'd be done soon, and eating would distract Kei. His intake of food had slowed down a bit, but not much.

A loud thump upstairs startled her out of her thoughts. Another followed and then the slamming of a door. "Kei?"

Baelan appeared at the top of the stairs, eyes wide and hair disheveled as he plunged down them. "Sorry, sorry, sorry!"

She ran for the stairs. "What did you do?"

He stopped at the bottom but wouldn't meet her eyes. "I told him."

He didn't need to tell her what. She froze and stared at him for a moment before smacking him up the side of the head. "Idiot! Are you trying to get yourself killed?"

"What's going on?" Bo stepped out of the kitchen, all humor gone. Crashes and bangs continued above them.

"Baelan's provoked Kei. I can handle it, just stay out of the way. And protect Elaina," she added. Baelan hadn't left. "Go! Now!" The sound of the door breaking down upstairs stopped her rant.

"Aro, he's–"

"Get out of here!" Not waiting to see if he listened, she bolted up the stairs. "Rotting…stupid… Elf."

Kei barreled into her as she reached the top, all fangs and claws and blazing red eyes. A terrifying Fey in full fury.

Except she wasn't afraid of him. Crazy crazy…

Pushing her hands against his chest, she tried to gain his attention. "Stop! Stop it now, Kei!"

He bared his teeth and tried to move around her, but didn't hurt her in any way. "He. Killed. You."

"I know. And I know why. And he's paying for that now by serving me. Get control of yourself!"

His eyes blazed as he turned his attention to her. "He. Killed. You!"

She fought to keep him from passing her, but he'd grown stronger than her already. Knowing she was going to lose, she chose another tactic and began pulling his fury from him.

They sparred against each other as he tried to pass. Even lost to the fury, he still tried not to hurt her. Suddenly his eyes blazed and he roared. Pushing her to the side, he flung himself down the stairs.

She hit the wall hard and swore, looking up in time to see Baelan dart into the living room. He still hadn't left? "I'm going to kill him myself," she muttered, running down the stairs.

If Kei didn't first.

The worst part was she couldn't blame Kei. In his shoes, she'd have the same reaction.

Growls and crashes echoed through the house.

Get out of the house!

But you might–

Out! Now! Rotting stupid Elf.

Swinging around the banister, she hurled herself through the doorway to the living room. Kei stalked Baelan around the furniture. A chair flew through the air. Baelan blocked it with a rune and it crashed to the side.

Kei charged him and another rune sent the small table into the air between them. With a roar, the Fey tore at it with his claws before managing to push it aside.

She swore again. Their house would soon be destroyed at this rate. Glaring as the Elf pushed more furniture into Kei's path, she stepped farther into the room.

I told you to get out of the house!

Yes, well...

Now, run by me. And leave this time!

He did, nimbly slipping by the Fey with the grace only Elves possessed. She sprang forward, but Kei's strength and speed still overwhelmed her as he mindlessly tried to follow the Elf. Wrapping her arms around him, she twisted and turned, throwing her weight to unbalance him.

They crashed to the floor in the hallway. Before he could throw her off, she held on tighter and pulled at his fury with everything she had.

She had a lot.

He had a lot of fury.

The sudden silence hurt her ears as she slumped over him, heart pounding in her chest, breaths coming in quick gasps. How had he gotten so strong so fast? The fury roared and spun within her. Wild. Savage. Barely controlled.

Kei shifted under her, curling in on himself. Pushing back, her heart broke at the soft whimper coming from his lips. With a shaking hand, she traced her fingers down his cheek. "Shh. All is well."

He blinked up at her and she let out a deep breath in relief to see his golden eyes. "Aro." His voice cracked and he grimaced, closing his eyes again. "Sorry," he whispered.

Leaning down, she pressed a kiss to his forehead. "Nothing to be sorry for. Just rest. We'll talk. I'll…explain."

He nodded slightly but didn't open his eyes.

The fury within her howled, pulsing along every nerve. She gritted her teeth. Had it ever been this bad before? She needed to let it go. Pressing a hand to the floor, she tried…but nothing happened. Wood and stone and space… the basement. She needed ground. Dirt.

"Wither me." Her jaw hurt, she clenched her teeth so hard. It didn't stop the tremors running along every limb. Every small hair on her body stood on end.

"All good now, pup?"

She managed to raise her head and look to Bo. "Well enough. Can you take him up." She paused. "If his bed is gone, use mine."

"You look like you're going to fly into pieces."

She snorted at his blunt comment. "I'll be fine. Just need to get outside."

"Go on then."

Somehow, she managed to push herself to her feet. The fury swelled and shrieked within her. Black and red. Fight. Kill. She stood to the side as Bo scooped up Kei and headed upstairs. Still shaking, she walked into the kitchen, freezing when she saw Elaina staring at her with wide eyes.

"Aro?"

She winced. Had Elaina ever seen her with blazing red eyes? "I'm fine. No fangs or claws," she said through gritted teeth, forcing a fake smile. Elaina didn't move. Aro eyed how many steps it would take to get to the door to the side yard.

Fight. Destroy. Kill.

She closed her eyes and swore under her breath. "Excuse me." Her fist slammed into the table, shattering the top, and breaking her fingers. The power needed to heal them wasn't enough to make much of a difference. It just hurt. At least it did help change the course of her thoughts.

Elaina continued to stare at her, wide-eyed and hands now over her mouth.

"I'll replace that," she somehow managed to say before forcing her legs to move to the door. Once she reached it, she flung herself outside.

Remembering the stairs would have been good. She tumbled and fell, landing on her side. Rotting fury. Forcing herself to her hands and knees, she put both hands to the ground and let it go.

The explosion was new.

She hit the side of the house and then stared in surprise at the decent sized hole in the ground. Blinking, she looked down at the dirt covering her. "Wither me."

Exhausted, she just leaned her head back against the house and closed her eyes.

When Baelan sat down next to her, she didn't even move. It'd been too hard of a day already. She was too tired to yell at him.

Leaning back against the house, he set his forearms on his raised knees. "I am so very sorry, my lovely," he said cautiously.

Snorting, she shook her head.

"I thought it would be better if I told him. I know you didn't want to."

"I didn't want to because I knew how he'd react," she snapped.

"Ah."

She really did hate Elves sometimes. They sat in silence for a while. "Where have you been," she finally asked.

He shifted uncomfortably, fingers fiddling with the wrappings on his wrists. "After..." He cleared his throat. "I had to do some thinking. And I didn't think you wanted to see me. After being reminded..." His voice trailed off. "I tried to keep the others away," he said after she didn't respond.

"The not hovering was nice," she admitted.

He sighed and dropped his hands. "I can't help that, Aro."

"I know."

Turning to face her, he opened his mouth and closed it a few times before speaking. "I didn't mean for all of this," he finally whispered. "It was supposed to be painless. I didn't want you to suffer. I didn't know..." Groaning, he turned and sat back against the wall. "I'm sorry. I didn't know."

Closing her eyes against the emotions flooding her, both old and new, she tried to come up with some response that made sense. "I've told you, I understand why you did it. You didn't want him to suffer because of me. Killing me was...extreme. But I understand it. That I survived, and what I have endured since then, wasn't your fault."

"Yes, it was." When she frowned at him, he continued, "You are human, and I didn't see you as a person. I still didn't want you to suffer...but you weren't important."

"Am I a person now?"

He nodded.

"Bo? Elaina? All of us humans?"

"Yes," he answered softly.

"Good."

She was surprised he'd figured that out. Many of the other races saw humans as something less. Humans weren't immortal, had no magic or powers, so were thought to be lesser creatures. Especially by those who had little to no interaction with them.

"Baelan," she said in exasperation, "You need to stop torturing yourself. I think we both need to just...move on. I need to. There are too many other crazy things I need to deal with right now."

"Like being covered in dirt?"

"That is one of them." She grimaced. "I've never blown holes in the ground before, but then I don't think I've ever taken that much fury and released it."

He frowned. "This could be a problem in the future. With what you plan to do."

She shook her head. "I've taken from other Fey. Kei is so much stronger than them." He wanted to ask why, she could tell, but for some reason didn't. Perhaps he had his own ideas.

Wincing, she sat up. Her whole body ached. She held the full amount of fury she could handle still within her. The ache wasn't from an injury. Maybe dealing with the fury itself? She'd never understand how all of this worked. "I need to get cleaned up, and talk to Kei, and then we need to go to the market to replace everything we broke."

He grimaced.

She chuckled. "You'll be busy for a while."

Once inside, the broken table surprised Baelan. His, "I didn't do it!" rather amused her. She took a little time in the bath room to get the worst of the dirt off. When she came out, she found Bo waiting in the kitchen.

"How is Elaina?"

"She went back to the tavern. She'll be fine. Would have been better if she hadn't looked in the living room."

"I'm going to go see Kei and then I'll drag Baelan to the market." She turned to the Elf. "Actually, go see what we need to buy." With a slight bow, he left.

Wait. Where's Garen?

We were going to head right back, so he stayed at the tavern. I imagine he's trying to beg scraps in the kitchen.

She closed her eyes in relief for a moment. Suddenly noting the Were's absence had given her a bit of a panic.

"Kei's in your room. He rather destroyed his again. He's calm for now."

"I'll take care of it." She looked to the side. "I'm sorry Elaina had to see that and was in danger. I know–"

He rested a large hand on her shoulder. "I think she understands our life better now. And she was never in danger, pup. I know that."

Pressing her lips together, she nodded. "I'll go sort Kei out then." Walking by him, she grabbed and squeezed his hand. "Thank you."

"Always here."

∞ ∞ ∞

Spring had certainly come to Westport. The sun beat down on them, giving a comfortable warmth. Aro wrinkled her nose. The warmer weather also brought back the cloying city smells. She wouldn't miss that when they returned to the forest.

After finding Kei curled up asleep, she'd grabbed some clothes and quickly cleaned up. While discussing what needed to be replaced, she and Baelan ate with Bo, who would stay while they were gone to keep an eye on Kei.

The damage hadn't been too severe in Kei's room. He'd only overturned the bed and his dresser, though he broke the chair and door. Baelan thought they might be repairable. The kitchen table, couch, chairs, and tables in the living room were likely not. Apparently, some Elves were quite gifted in making and repairing such things, though Baelan admitted to never being interested in learning how. He would try, however, if they had no luck replacing them.

The carpenter they'd bought furniture from previously had very little in stock and lamented the lack of wood in the city. None had yet been harvested and no new shipments from the west had arrived either. She did at least purchase a new kitchen table, even though it was a bit smaller than she liked, and one chair. After arranging delivery, the owner grudgingly suggested another carpenter closer to the docks. After all the effort of finding the shop, they only bought one chair for the living room.

"It's not as though you use the room very often," Baelan commented as they headed back to the market.

Glancing over at him, she frowned. Not at his words, but how he chewed his lower lip and hunched away from her, worried what she might do. "Very true," she finally answered. For some reason, she wasn't particularly upset over the destruction in the house.

"I am sorry I—"

"It's fine," she interrupted, sending him a small smile.

He stared at her for a long moment before nodding. They walked in silence for a while. "What did you need from the market?" *We're being followed.*

Her brows rose, and she glanced over at him. He acted as if nothing were amiss. She hadn't even noticed how he constantly scanned the area around them. How he walked relaxed, but ready. "Bread. We're out of honey." *Humans or Elves?* "Perhaps some different tea."

One Elf, two humans.

"Kei didn't like the last kind." Looking up ahead, she saw they were still a good distance from the market.

"Do you have everything for Bo's marriage?" *What would you like me to do?*

She rubbed at the back of her head. "I have the dress Roan bought me." *Wait a little.*

He tilted his head as he looked at her. "You didn't get a new one?" At her frown, he continued, "It's not like you can't afford it."

"I don't like dresses. Or fittings. It will be fine. Do you have something?"

He actually stopped walking. Starting again, he couldn't hide his surprise. "You wish for me to go?"

"Well, they can only bring up two others each. But there is a standing area." She frowned. "I'm not sure how they do it here. Bo said something like that. Either way, I assumed you'd be coming with us to the tavern after. So, do feel free to find something appropriate." *Are they still there?*

"Very well." *Yes.*

We can lead them—

No. You will not be put in danger, he interrupted sharply.

Fine. She looked at the shops around them and then stopped. "Kei needs a hat. I might as well look now." *Can you slip off and—*

"I'll wait outside." *Yes.*

He followed as she crossed the street, trying not to look around and see who followed them. *Don't kill them if you don't have to.*

Of course.

She paused at the door to the hatter's shop. "I'm not sure how long I'll be." *If you do, then clean up.*

"Take your time." *I know.*

As the door began to close, she glanced back, rubbing her temple. That double conversation had given her a headache. *Be careful.*

It took her longer to find a hat.

When she walked out, box in hand, Baelan waited by the door. "That was quick," she murmured as he took the box from her. He shrugged a shoulder. She paused before they headed back into the crowded street, giving him a quick look over.

I'm fine.

She smiled, but licked her thumb and leaned forward, wiping some blood spatter off his cheek. "You had a little something…"

His cheeks flushed and he quickly ducked his head, silver hair falling over his face.

Rotting adorable Elf. More often than not, it was hard to hate him.

"Come, let's finish so we're back for dinner."

No one drew his attention in the market, thankfully, and they quickly set about gathering the few items she wanted. Soft music, barely loud enough to be heard over the crowd, caught his attention more than once.

"What is that?"

He smiled slightly. "Just a simple pipe."

"I like it," she decided. "Do you play?"

The smile faded as he looked out over the crowd, avoiding her gaze. "I used to."

She dropped the subject and sent him off in search of honey while she moved through the market toward home. The music grew louder as she moved closer to the booths, stopping in front of one with a variety of instruments. A thin man noticed her interest and pulled the pipe away from his mouth, smiling brightly at her.

"Is that your best one?"

Grinning wider, he shook his head and pulled out another pipe, this one with faint carvings of vines and leaves.

"It's gorgeous. Is it–"

"Elven, yes. But very expensive."

She glanced over her shoulder but didn't see Baelan. For a moment, she hesitated, then decided yes, she would get it for him. Then she could have him play for her. Surely not for any other reason. "I'll take it."

She barely haggled with him. "Is there a case?"

Nearly bouncing, the man whipped one out from behind the booth and told her the price. She narrowed her eyes and he cut it in half. "Good enough." She looked over her shoulder again. "Wrap them quickly, please. It's a gift and I don't want him to see."

"Yes, yes. Of course."

Baelan caught up with her by the bread stand and she watched him carefully, wondering if he'd seen. He didn't give her any strange looks, so she assumed not. On the way home, she tried not to second guess her impulsive decision. She could still change her mind.

She really did like the sounds it made though.

∞ ∞ ∞

After eating, she pulled Kei toward the front door.

Baelan, I'm going to talk to Kei about what happened. Out front.

You would like me to make myself scarce then?

Yes, please.

Kei cast her curious glances as she led him outside but didn't say anything. He'd not said a lot since he'd gone into a fury. She tried not to worry about that.

Sitting on the small bench under the apple trees, she stared up, smiling at the tiny buds forming. When would they bloom? She must remember to have Bo let her know.

"I want to talk to you about Baelan." He went to rise, and she grabbed his arm, pulling him back down. "Just sit and listen. Then you can yell at me."

He frowned, but finally nodded, sitting back against the bench and crossing his arms.

113

Taking a deep breath, she started. "He didn't just randomly do it, and he wasn't sent to do it. He killed me because he thought I was a threat to Prince, and Prince was his friend." Pausing, she shifted to face him. "Prince hasn't done well since he returned." This got a surprised look at least. "He was weak when he arrived, which didn't help, but…" her voice dropped to a whisper, "his mother bound him. It is similar to what Baelan has. I don't know what all it does. Though, I do know he can't leave Rivenward."

Kei's eyes widened. "Why would she do that?"

"I don't know. She's not a good queen and is getting worse. So, not only that, Prince has acted differently than he had before he left. Many people aren't happy. They found out he has…feelings for me. I became his weakness. It's why those Elves kidnapped me." He nodded, remembering her telling him before. "Baelan just wanted to protect him. To remove his weakness."

Kei scowled. "That almost makes sense," he grumbled.

"Well, Baelan isn't like other people," she said slowly. "He's honestly rather crazy, so it made perfect sense to him."

"He is…odd," Kei agreed.

"Well, he's stuck with us, so you'll see what I mean."

They sat quietly as she planned what to say next. "I hated him. For quite a while," she admitted. "When he showed up here, begging for me to accept him, I almost killed him. I was going to kill him as he knelt at my feet. Unarmed." She stopped and looked away, clearing her throat.

Kei's hand slipped around hers. Looking back at him, she smiled weakly. "Bo reminded me that's not who I am."

"Good." He turned and stared off at nothing. "He should have been punished though."

"He was, Kei. Roan sent him back to the Elves in chains." She told him what the Elves did, taking his power, scarring him, everything, and then she explained what Prince had done, binding him to her, about the runes around his wrists and neck and what they did.

"Wither me," he muttered, shaking his head. His brows drew together. "He truly can't harm you? Ever?"

"Not while he's bound to me. No." Kei didn't reply, so she continued, "Prince sent him to protect me. I think he will be useful."

Kei gave her a wry smile. "So, don't kill him?"

"So, don't kill him," she agreed.

His smile fading, he looked off at nothing again. "He's needed anyway."

"Kei?"

Leaning forward, he braced his elbows on his knees and put his face in his hands. She rested a hand on his back, unsure what to do or say, or what even was wrong.

"Is it about the prophecy?"

"Later, Aro. Later," he eventually replied.

He trembled under her hand, so she just let it be and rubbed his back.

Jen Wylie

Chapter 9

Breaking Bonds

Late the next morning, Aro found Bo before he headed over to the tavern.

"We need to talk. About if things don't go well. With the Were king," she clarified.

Bo rubbed a large hand over his face, but nodded.

"Can you come back home before dinner for a bit?"

He grinned. "I'm sure I can sneak away for a while." His face turned serious. "Are you going to let Baelan know?"

She wrinkled her nose. "Yes, he'll need to know eventually anyway."

Can we not tell him about me yet?

She looked down at Garen and raised her eyebrows. "Why not?"

He gave her a wolfish grin. *I want to see his face when I turn into a wolf.*

With a laugh, she agreed.

As always, the day went by quickly and before she knew it she was dragging Kei and Baelan to the kitchen. "Have a seat. Bo's on his way."

She'd already told Kei they'd be having a Were talk, but Baelan stared at her in confusion. "What's going on?"

"Family meeting."

Kei growled slightly. He didn't like her including the Elf in the family, she guessed.

Bo arrived shortly after, sitting next to her as Garen slipped under the table. Kei sat on her other side and Baelan across from her. She wished they'd been able to get a bigger table.

"We've a few important things to discuss. Hopefully it won't take too long. With Bo getting married in a few days," she sent him a big smile, "it won't be long until the rest of us head to the forest."

Kei sat up straighter. "How long?"

"Whenever you are ready. We have almost everything packed and set to go. Just a quick market trip for a bit of food is all."

The boy really did have the most beautiful beaming smile.

She caught Baelan staring at him in surprise. It looked like he noticed as well.

Clearing her throat, she crossed her arms and narrowed her eyes at the Elf. "So...what do you know about our Were problem?"

Turning his attention to her, his brows drew down in confusion and then he winced as her words sunk in. "You have a Were problem?"

From the higher pitched, almost whine, in his voice, she guessed nothing. Interesting. Apparently, the assumption he knew everything about her, that Roan had told him, had been wrong.

"How bad of a problem?"

"We can handle it," she answered firmly.

Kei snorted.

She shot a glare in his direction and then dove right in. "While in the forest, I accidentally on purpose made us a pack."

He stared at her, then looked at Bo, then Kei. His mouth opened and closed a few times before he blinked rapidly and shook his head. "You made a pack?"

"Yes. Me, Bo, Kei, Garen...and Prince."

"Oh, you did not!"

Bo chuckled. "Prince was none too happy about it."

Kei grinned wickedly. "Not at all."

She frowned. "We need to remove him. Before we leave."

Baelan didn't seem to know who to look at. "Why?"

"Because we aren't an official pack. We may never be. The Were king was rather furious about it. That's why we decided to winter in a city, where according to their laws, he couldn't touch us. Once we return though, Rhee-En said he'll make his decision. We'll either join with all the other Were, or he'll remove it."

"You've angered the Were king," Baelan hissed.

"I think Prince would prefer no one knew he was part of it," she continued, ignoring the increasingly agitated Elf.

"I imagine the Were have guessed, if they don't downright know already," Bo said.

"True," she agreed. "But not for certain. That's why we'll break the connection before we go."

"You've angered the Were king!" Baelan said, louder this time.

Really, she shouldn't be enjoying his reaction so much. "Yes, and believe me, I understand the severity of it. I have nightmares. But, I think things will work out. That at least he won't punish us for it."

"I hope so, pup," Bo said, not at all happy.

Leaning forward, she clasped his hand. "You don't have to worry. I'm taking full responsibility for this mess."

"That's not what I meant, and you know it."

She grinned and squeezed his hand again. "They want the Fey back to fight alongside them. They aren't going to jeopardize that. I'm pretty sure he won't kill me."

"Kill you!"

She glanced at Baelan, surprised Bay hadn't come out. But then, the threat wasn't currently present. "The other issue with Prince is that if the pack is made official, we will then be bound, and be subject, to the Were king."

Everyone frowned at that.

"For us," she continued quickly, "it shouldn't be much of an issue. If it becomes so later, we can always leave the pack. However, for Prince..."

"It is not at all acceptable," Baelan snapped.

"Exactly."

Bo nodded his agreement and rubbed at the scar on his face. "How do we deal with the Prince problem?"

"I'll ask Garen, or Rhee-En later."

"Next, if he dissolves the pack, we won't be able to talk anymore." She tapped her temple as Bo frowned. "But Garen and I still can. Talk to the Were, I mean. If it comes to that, we can send messages through Hale, or even Silas and Raythe." Before Bo could speak, she continued. "Same goes for if we happen to travel too far. But we'll just use other Were to bounce messages along."

Baelan frowned. "Wait. You can all talk to each other?"

They ignored him.

You are wonderfully evil at times, Garen said in her mind, laughing.

She held in her own laugh.

Bo continued, "You think that may be a problem? Finding some who will agree? Rhee-En seems to be on our side, but the other alphas..."

She grinned. "Again, we have the advantage. Healing the Fey, the Were won't have to fight the Vor alone anymore."

He couldn't argue with that, but still frowned.

"Besides," she continued. "I'm thinking we shouldn't have to travel too far north. Rhee-En mentioned most of the Fey hadn't strayed far from Furia. So, we should mostly be in his lands. We can heal the majority, then work on the stragglers."

Kei nodded enthusiastically, nearly bouncing in his seat.

"And if we are made a full pack? How will that work?"

She shook her head. "I've no idea. But I imagine it can only work in our favor. We'd have more support from the Were. I think." She turned to Kei. "Anything in the prophecies you can share?"

His smile faded. "Everything will be fine."

"That's a bit vague," Bo complained.

Kei ran a hand through his hair. "I can't..." He huffed out a breath and scowled at the table. "I can't interfere with most things. I am to just keep you on course. You all will just need to trust me," he finished softly.

Aro leaned over and wrapped her arms around him. "Of course we do. And we appreciate anything you can tell us."

From his weak smile, her words didn't really help.

"I need a drink," Baelan muttered, still looking stunned.

Do we want him in the pack?

Bo shrugged.

Doesn't matter to me, Garen replied.

Kei's eyes were hard. *No. It's not necessary at this time.*

Weird answer. *Then we won't. Not unless we all agree.*

"Well, that was it. Unless anyone else has something to add? I'll deal with the Prince part." When no one said anything, she stood. "How about we go to the tavern for dinner tonight?" She glanced at Baelan. "Someone wanted a drink."

∞ ∞ ∞

Baelan was quiet during their meal. She couldn't blame him. Once back in the house, she got Kei settled in bed to rest and then went down to the training room to get some practice in before she went to bed.

"I'm afraid to ask what other secrets you're keeping from me."

His voice startled her, but her dagger still hit its mark. Turning, she saw the Elf leaning against the door frame. "Ask all you want," she answered with a small smile. "Though I'll only tell you if I want you to know."

He chuckled and shook his head. "Is there anything else I *need* to know?" When she laughed, his face turned grave. "I'm serious, Arowyn. Is there anything I need to know in order to protect you?"

She looked up quickly at the change in his voice and noted his darker, stormy eyes. "Hello again. And no, nothing else is really important."

He nodded once and between one blink and the next he changed again.

"That is…" She didn't even have a word for it.

Baelan looked away. "I'm sorry, my lovely."

She shrugged and turned back to face her target.

"The house is back in order, except for Kei's door. I will work on it and see if I can fix any of the other furniture tomorrow."

"That is fine."

"Is there anything else you'd like me to do?"

She let out a slow breath and pushed back her irritation. "Did you find something to wear?"

"I will do that tomorrow, as well. If you are sure…"

Rolling her eyes, she turned to face him and put her hands on her hips. "Yes. I am sure."

"Very well." He hesitated again.

With a sigh, she collected her daggers and put them away. He'd bother her all night if he could. "I'm heading to bed. And no, I don't need anything."

He frowned slightly. "Very well. Good night, Arowyn."

She left him standing there and called to Garen as she headed to her room. *Are you busy? I'd like to talk to you about removing Prince.*

∞ ∞ ∞

Aro stood within in her mind, staring up at the handful of stars shining in her dark sky. Her boys. The stars symbolized her connection to them through their pack bond. According to Garen, as the alpha she could sever them at any time.

Concentrating, she rose off the ground, avoiding touching the faint strings that connected the balls of light to her. With a faint smile, she shook her head. She could do this here... Why had she panicked while in Kei's mind? Looking down, she saw the barren ground beneath her feet. Perhaps it had been due to all the darkness in his mind.

It didn't take long until she hovered amidst the balls of light. She named each, easily identifying them, though she wasn't exactly sure how she could. She just knew.

Considering how much trouble it caused her, it struck her then how little she knew about her pack, about being an alpha. She should have taken the time to learn more, especially as it meant so much to Garen.

She knew she could mind-speak with them, and that if she chose, she could use a controlling tone of voice to have them listen and obey. The thought made her cringe. Other than that, she knew the pack shared power. She just wasn't exactly sure how that worked.

Reaching out, she gently touched the light that was Garen. Warmth filled her, a gentle connection, similar, but weaker, than the one she had with Kei. Startled, she removed her hand.

After a moment's hesitation, she placed her hand on the light again. Unlike with Kei, she wasn't filled with various emotions. Instead, she merely received the general impression he was well and content. Strange, but interesting. If she were stronger, or their pack larger, or if she practiced, would she be able to feel more?

Stalling, she briefly touched the lights of Bo and Kei before turning to the one she knew as Prince. Shael. She extended her hand slowly, prepared for when it suddenly hit resistance. Stepping closer, she pressed her palms against the barrier and closed her eyes. Was it the wardwall? Or just how her mind manifested her inability to connect with Prince because of it?

Dropping her hands, she slid her fingers over the fine thread joining them. Unless he left Rivenward, he would never even know she'd cut him out of the pack. She winced at her choice of words. Would he feel something though? Perhaps at least a sense of loss?

Grasping the thread with both hands, she closed her eyes. "Shael, I remove you from my pack." Jerking her hands apart, the thread snapped.

Sadness filled her chest, weighing her down. Opening her eyes, she watched the thread break apart into sparks and fade away. The ball of light, the little star, quivered and shrank before it too gave one last little burst before disappearing.

"I'm sorry," she whispered.

Floating back down, she knelt on her barren ground. Hiding her face in her hands, she cried.

Chapter 10

Celebration

Aro smoothed the front of her dress down and winced as Baelan tugged too hard on another piece of her hair. "Are you almost done?" It felt like he'd been messing with it forever.

"Almost." Another tug. "There, let me see." He turned her around, his gaze flitting around her face as he studied his work before he stepped back and took in all of her. "You should have gotten a new dress."

Scowling, she raised a hand to her hair. "This one is fine."

He huffed, then stepped forward and swatted her hand. "Don't touch it."

It was going to be a long day.

"I'm going to check on Bo."

Before she could comment, the Elf was out the door. He remained quiet around her. Well, quieter than he had been. Considering she'd been cranky the last few days since she cut Shael out of her pack, she couldn't really blame him.

Losing that bond with her prince still bothered her. She had so little of him as it was.

Just don't think about it.

Bo and Elaina would marry at noon. Preparations for the marriage happily kept her busy.

She'd contacted Rhee-En, updating him on Kei's progress, the wedding, and that they'd be leaving in a few days. He assured her she and her family would be safe returning to the forest, no matter what the Were king decided, and told her he'd already brought their two horses from pasture and would only need a day's notice to get them to the ridge. Originally, she thought they would only need one horse, but now with Baelan joining them, and Kei not being well, they'd need both. Of course, getting Kei to admit he needed to ride would be interesting.

Glancing to the window, she saw they'd be heading out soon so went to Kei's room to make sure he was ready.

She found him sitting on his small bed, turning the hat she'd bought him around in his hands. She tapped her knuckles on the door frame and he looked up.

Handsome boy. She couldn't help but smile seeing him dressed up. "You look good."

He shrugged a shoulder, but a slight smile curved his lips for a moment. Looking her over as she stepped into the room, his smile grew. Standing, he tossed the hat on the bed. "You look beautiful," he said softly.

Her cheeks flushed.

His head tipped to the side, his brows drawing together. "Have I seen you in this dress before?"

Even though his lost memories broke her heart, she still smiled. "No. First time. First time in any dress actually."

His smile returned.

"The carriage should be here soon. Let's get that hat figured out." Her words made him grimace, but he couldn't argue. With no glamor to hide he was a Fey, he needed something to cover his pointed ears. His eyes didn't worry her as they once did. Hers were the same shade now, and she obviously had no pointed ears. The brother-sister story worked well for them in that regard, at least.

The carriage is here, Garen told her.

126

We'll be right down. "Time to go," she said to Kei, adjusting the brim of his hat once more.

He sighed, but then offered her his arm. She blinked at it for a moment before laughing and slipping her hand in.

"I don't think I'd ever get used to living like this."

Flashing her a grin, he agreed with a nod.

Smiling, she relaxed as they made their way down the stairs. Kei would be fine. Though still pale, the dark under his eyes had faded. He'd gained some weight. Even if they walked to the Registry Hall at the far north side of the city, she felt certain he wouldn't have any problems. She really did need to stop worrying about him.

"I'm fine, Aro," he murmured.

Stupid bond, he felt her worry. "I know."

Garen met them at the bottom of the stairs, tail wagging. *Don't forget to pay attention. To everything!*

I know, I know. Obviously, he couldn't come. At least to the actual marriage. He'd attend the celebration at the tavern, which made her feel better. She also promised to share her memories with him. He stopped sulking when she offered that.

Baelan walked out of the kitchen. "Go on!" He waved his hands at Garen. "You get hair all over that dress and you'll be locked outside for a month."

Garen snorted but backed away.

Aro struggled not to laugh. The Elf narrowed his eyes at her, hands on his hips. Her laugh faded, and she forced her gaze to the kitchen behind him.

Bo walked out, running a hand over his short hair.

"You all look so handsome," she said with a grin. They did, all in new pants, boots polished. Starched white shirts were crisp under their embroidered overcoats, Bo's blue, Kei's green, and Baelan's a deep red.

Stepping forward, Bo grinned and took her hands. "And look at you, pup. Such a beautiful young woman."

Her cheeks burned again. She squeezed Bo's hands. "Time for us to go meet another beauty." She bounced on her toes in excitement. "I can't believe you're getting married!"

If you don't want to be late, you should get going. Garen muttered in their minds.

Bo stole her arm and moved her quickly down the hall.

The carriage was fancy. Fancy and big. Bo helped her up and then slid in beside her, Baelan and Kei right behind him. The carriage lurched forward, moving slowly for a short while before stopping again. She peered out the window and saw the other carriage.

Bo had rented two. The other would take Elaina, her father, her brothers' widows, Venna and Cally, and their children.

After a moment, the carriage set out again for the long, and likely slow, ride to the Registry Hall.

They hadn't gone far at all when a thump startled them all. Hale leaned his head in the window, brows rising at the number of weapons currently pointed in his direction.

"I was going to ask if I could catch a ride…"

Sorry, I forgot I'd invited him along, Bo said sheepishly.

Aro tucked her daggers back into her boots. "Of course."

The carriage hadn't stopped, but the Were had no trouble swinging open the door and slipping in beside her.

He bounced a little and grinned around at everyone. "This is so exciting! I've never been to a human marriage before."

Well, that explained why he was here. She knew Bo had invited him to the celebration after. They became friends when she'd been taken by the Elves and was one of the few people who knew their dog was a Were.

Hale turned to her. "You look stunning, Arowyn."

Her cheeks grew warm once again. "Thank you."

Kei growled.

Bo burst out into his loud laugh.

Sometimes, she wondered what a normal life would be like.

On days like today, she doubted she'd like it.

∞ ∞ ∞

The carriages finally stopped. Kei, Hale, and Baelan got out first, but she waited. Partly because Bo had a death grip on her hand. Though Hale kept a conversation going on the ride, it hadn't been long before Bo's knee started bouncing and he began to clench and unclench his fists.

His knee started to bounce again, and she smiled slightly, turning toward him. "Bo, take a deep breath. This is going to be the best day of your life. You're going to have a family now."

His knee stilled, and his hand tightened around hers. He looked down at her, his face serious. "I have a family, silly pup. You and Kei and Garen. You'll always be my family."

Her eyes burned and she blinked rapidly. Her heart felt like it would burst out of her chest as a smile split her face. "You know what I mean."

He grinned. "And you know what I mean. Having a wife won't ever change what we have. After everything we've been through, nothing could."

She nodded quickly, leaning forward to wrap her arms around him and hide the tears blinding her. "I'm so happy for you." Leaning back, she wiped her eyes quickly and smiled again. "So happy, I'm even wearing a dress."

He laughed again, and she saw he'd finally relaxed. "Well, we better get this done then. Before you change your clothes."

Their group mingled as the carriages pulled away, parking until needed for their ride back to the tavern. The Registry Hall stole her attention, a huge sprawling three-story stone building. There were multiple entrances and she hoped someone knew where they were going.

Finally pulling her gaze away, she caught sight of Elaina. Dressed in a gorgeous embroidered dark green gown, her auburn hair piled on her head, she was a vision.

"Bo, look," she said, tugging on his arm.

Watching his face transform from a worried scowl into a love-struck groom nearly made her cry again.

"My bride," he murmured, his voice gruff with emotion. He strode toward her, stopping as he reached her to give a gentlemanly bow. When he straightened, he held out his hand. With her face flushed pink, his bride set her much smaller hand in his, laughing as he pulled her close for a kiss.

Aro let out a soft sigh. She felt so happy for them both she thought she might burst.

They all gathered together and entered the hall, Elaina's sister Verra steering them all to an area of desks on the right. Thankfully there wasn't much of a line and she occupied her time watching their group and the myriad of emotions playing on their faces. She only needed to swat Baelan twice for wanting to fiddle with her hair.

Once their turn came, Elaina and Bo were both directed to sit and the middle-aged man behind the desk plopped papers down in front of each. Bo stared at his, his knee bouncing again.

She moved forward quickly, catching the eye of the registrar. "May I assist?"

The man gave her a clipped nod. "Yes, but he must sign it."

She rested a hand on Bo's shoulder and squeezed before taking up the quill and dipping it in the ink jar. Scanning the sheet, she relaxed. All simple questions. First, name.

She began to write. *Just Bo?* It was rather embarrassing she needed to ask and she gave him a wry grin.

He nodded stiffly, and she continued with the list; age, parents, place of birth, occupation, Bo giving her the answers to any she didn't know.

Finally, he signed at the bottom, and then glanced up at her. "Will you be my witness?"

"Of course." She took the quill back and spoke quietly as she wrote, "Arowyn. Relationship...sister."

He grinned up at her. "Best sister there ever was."

She laughed. "Don't you forget it."

Papers returned to the registrar, he looked them over and they waited as he wrote something on both, and then on another smaller piece of paper which he handed to Bo. "Give this to the prince's man." He directed them to a door far down to the right.

Once there, Bo showed the paper to a man at the door, who then bade them wait. Luckily it wasn't long before a small group exited the room and they were ushered in.

"Bride and groom may each have two witnesses with them. Everyone else behind the rail, please."

The room was fairly small, so it didn't take long for her and Kei to follow Bo up the front. A raised desk occupied the center, with a shorter one at either side. Men sat behind each, and a few young boys stood near the back.

Bo handed his paper to the man in the center before stepping back next to his bride.

Aro glanced over at Elaina's guests, her father and sister Verra, and relaxed to see them both smiling.

The marriage itself she found uninteresting. Their information was read off again, confirmed, and then they were both asked if they were entering in to the marriage willingly. Before she knew it, the man was writing on more papers and pronounced them married. Bo and Elaina shared a quick kiss. The room filled with cheers and claps. Everyone signed more papers, Bo was given one to keep, and then they were ushered out again.

Your human marriages are rather boring, Baelan muttered in her mind.

Sadly, I must agree.

Though I will admit, Elven ones aren't much better.

That nearly made her laugh out loud.

However, I am quite looking forward to seeing how you celebrate.

They piled into the carriages once more, though this time Elaina joined them. The ride back wasn't any faster, but more amusing as they all tried to ignore the couples' quick kisses and murmured endearments.

Aro eventually stared out the window, trying not to think about her own future. With all the emotion and love going around, her thoughts couldn't help but turn to Prince. Would she ever see him again? Was it all just wishful thinking? Would she marry one day? Her heart twisted, knowing her missing brothers wouldn't be there.

A crowd met them as the carriages rolled to a stop in front of the tavern. Bo and Elaina exited first to shouts and cheers.

The crowd swallowed them and Aro paused at the edges, surprised at the number of people, the festive feeling nearly overwhelming.

Hale slipped by her, a big grin on his face. "This is more like it!"

Kei and Baelan hovered beside her as she tried to decide what to do. Just thinking of walking into the press of bodies set her heart beating quickly.

She started as Bo's voice spoke in her mind. *Our usual booth is reserved for you.* Looking over the crowd she saw him by the door to the tavern, watching her. He tipped his head for her to come inside.

He knew, of course, of her fear of crowds like this. Her heart warmed he'd thought of it, of her. She forced a smile and linked an arm into Kei's. "Our booth is waiting."

Even Kei seemed a bit wide-eyed at the amount of people and hesitated. Baelan huffed, took her other hand and pulled them along.

Once in the booth, her shoulders relaxed and she leaned back, finally able to enjoy the madness of her surroundings. Musicians played in the corner by the door, almost drowned out by the chatter of the people filling the tavern and courtyard. Bo had hired dozens to work in the kitchen and serve food and drink, and she watched the servers weave in and out of the crowd. Without even asking, ale was deposited at their table.

Kei and Baelan sat across from her, neither trying to talk over the din. A weight settled on her lap and she smiled down at Garen.

So? Tell me everything!

Sipping her ale, she did, smiling often at his enthusiasm. Eventually the crowds' excitement quieted and people began dancing, which gave her something to watch at least. Bo and Elaina stopped by a few times to check on them.

She snuck a look at Kei, checking to see if he looked tired or not. The sun had set, and it'd been a long day.

I'm fine.

Let me know when you want to go home.

He rolled his eyes. *I said I would.*

"You did well."

Glancing at Baelan, she tipped her head slightly to the side in confusion.

He gestured to Bo and Elaina, currently dancing. "Having him stay. He has found peace. Love." He turned to look at her. "He isn't…broken, like the rest of us."

Watching a beaming Bo, the way he held his new bride close and stared into her eyes, she couldn't argue with him. "But that could be us one day," she mused.

Kei choked on his drink.

She snorted and laughed at Baelan's wide eyes. "I don't mean us *together*."

She poked Garen to stop his laughter.

*The things you say…*he finally managed.

They ate, and drank, and ate some more. Bo pulled her out for a dance, basically flinging her around the room and leaving her laughing. Hale stole her away to dance some more, his commentary on the growing drunken state of the revelers leaving her more amused. She couldn't remember the last time she'd been so happy.

She didn't know anyone else, and refused to dance with a stranger, so he took her back to the booth. Sitting, she smiled at Kei and lifted her eyebrows. "Did you want to dance?"

He shook his head so hard his hat nearly flew off. Hunching in the corner, he fiddled with it, pulling and turning and playing with the brim.

He did look rather ridiculous wearing it while sitting in the booth.

"This is worse than my other one," he muttered.

Baelan turned and regarded him for a long moment. Finally, he pulled something from his coat and her eyebrows rose, seeing it was Kei's black knit hat. "Would you prefer it?"

"Wither me, yes!" The longing in the Fey's eyes made Baelan's mouth quirk into a smile.

Kei reached for it, but the Elf shook his head. Twisting on the bench, he blocked Kei from view and swiftly tossed off the felt hat and slipped the knit one on.

Baelan sat back slightly, yet his fingers lingered on Kei, slowly adjusting the hat. A thumb traced down the Fey's cheek.

Her eyes widened in surprise as they stared at each other for a long moment before Kei jerked back.

What just happened?

Her attention turned from the flustered Fey to Baelan, who now lounged back, sipping his ale as he watched the crowd once more.

She remembered a comment Roan once made to her about him flirting with anything with two legs. At the time she hadn't thought he meant that literally. *He flirts with everyone,* she told Kei. *Just ignore him.*

Kei drained his drink, eyeing the Elf warily. *I look half dead. He must be drunk.*

No you don't. Frowning, she caught Baelan's eye.

What did I do?

Really?

He grinned, his eyes crinkling with mirth, reminding her of the insanely happy Elf he'd been when they'd first met. *I appreciate beauty.* His gaze drifted back to Kei as he bit his lower lip and gave the Fey a smoldering look.

She snorted as Kei pushed himself farther into the corner. *I don't think he appreciates your appreciation. Don't play with him.*

He watched the wary Fey for a moment before shrugging and turning his back on him. *His loss.* He grinned at her. *Would you like to?*

Like to what?

Play?

Most certainly not.

He laughed at her sudden blush.

More drinks came, for which Kei was extremely thankful. She may have chugged hers back more quickly than usual as well as they went back to people watching as the night wore on.

Baelan slumped in his seat and sighed dramatically.

She glanced at him. "Is something wrong?"

He shrugged a shoulder, then craned his head, his gaze following someone else in the crowd. "You two don't want to have any fun." With another sigh, he set his elbow on the table and stuck his chin in his hand. "There are just so many beauties here tonight."

She had no idea what his problem was. Feeling rather tingly from the ale herself, she wondered if he'd drank one too many.

Glancing at her, he chuckled at her confusion. "I haven't had sex since before I," he waved his free hand in the air, "killed you. It's really rather frustrating."

Her cheeks burned so hot she raised her hands to cover them. Looking around quickly, she thankfully noted no one appeared to be listening.

Noting her discomfort, but not surprised by it, he raised his eyebrows, attempting innocence. "Us immortals don't have your issues, my lovely. We are quite fond of se—"

She raised a hand. It seemed, if nothing else, he'd drunk enough for his tongue to loosen. "I don't want to hear this." Closing her eyes for a moment, she shook her head and then gestured to the crowd. "Please, don't let me stop you."

He jerked up straight, staring at her in surprise. "Truly?"

Avoiding his gaze, she nodded, her cheeks burning again. "I just don't want to see it," she muttered. "Or hear it. Or hear about it. Or…" She gestured at the crowded tavern. "Just stay out of trouble," she added as Baelan rose and slid off the bench.

"I'll be home by morning." He leaned over and kissed the top of her head. "You are the best master ever!"

She swatted him away. "Ug, I hate you." She wasn't sure if he heard her, he'd already disappeared into the crowd.

Once Baelan disappeared, Kei pulled himself from the corner. His bewildered look made her laugh.

One of the hired girls stopped before them. Leaning forward as she set more ale out, she tipped her head toward the bar. "There is a man asking about you. I wasn't sure…"

Looking toward the bar, she was about to ask who, but the word died on her lips. She easily picked him out. He wasn't human. "Send him over."

Kei frowned, and Garen's quiet growl vibrated against her legs as the beautiful man approached. The Elves really needed to tone down the pretty with their glamors. It was so obvious to her now.

"I have an urgent message for Aro."

Her eyebrows rose as he quite clearly stressed the word urgent. She hesitated a moment before answering, "That's me."

Clear blue eyes looked her up and down quickly, but he hid any thoughts well. "The city is a dangerous place for a little tree. It would best survive in the forest."

A chill slid down her spine, but she forced a smile. "Understood. Thank you."

His eyes searched hers for a moment before he bowed his head slightly and then slipped into the crowd.

Kei frowned over at her. "What was that about?"

"A warning to leave the city. Trouble's coming." She looked warily into the crowd again. If it wasn't already here. Taking a slow breath, she forced herself to relax. They would have time. Tomorrow would be soon enough to worry.

However, the damage was done, the happy feelings of the day faded and now she just felt numb. Perhaps that was the ale, though.

"Aro?"

She looked up to meet Kei's worried glance. "You ready to go?" Thankfully he nodded in return.

It was late enough Bo didn't comment when they found him and Elaina to say goodnight. After making it home with only a bit of stumbling, she got Kei tucked into bed. Luckily, she remembered to have him undo her laces before he passed out.

"I love you, Aro," he said softly, his words slightly slurred.

She brushed her hand over his short hair. "I love you, too."

"I'm glad someone does. I won't be so lonely."

Her brows drew together. "What do you mean?"

His eyes fluttered closed and she sighed. Holding her loosened dress in place, she returned to her room.

Grabbing clothes to change into, she came across the pipe she'd bought for Baelan and then forgotten about. Setting it on her dresser, she stared at it while she struggled to get all the pins out of her hair. Should she, or shouldn't she? Would he see it as meaning something it didn't?

Deciding she was just thinking too hard, she left it on his bed and then found her own.

∞ ∞ ∞

Soft music pulled her out of sleep, though the pleasant sound kept her in an unmoving doze until it finally stopped.

Cracking an eye open, she groaned as her brain banged away at the front of her skull. Too much ale.

She found Baelan leaning against the wall by the window, watching her. As she sat up and rubbed at her aching head he walked over and sat on the edge of her bed. Her mouth felt horrible. She really needed a drink of–

He pointed to the bedside table with his pipe. "There."

"Thank you." Grabbing the water, she cast him a wary look. She never would get used to that.

Leaning back on his forearms, he tipped his head back and closed his eyes. "I must be dreaming."

Her eyebrows rose as she set the empty cup back on the table. "Why would you say that?"

Not answering, he shifted, pulling himself fully up on the bed to sit across from her. She barely had time to pull her feet up and out of his way. The faint dark circles rimming his eyes, and the fact he still wore the same clothes from yesterday, were the only clue he'd stayed out all night and not been to bed yet. And the smell of ale, though that may have come from her, too.

Rubbing sleep out of her eyes, she waited for him to answer.

"Well, my master who despises me let me go out, *and* gave me this delightful gift." He twirled the pipe around.

"I don't despise you."

He tipped his head to the side. "You should."

She shrugged a shoulder and looked away. "I'm not very good at hating people. Except Damon," she amended.

Baelan drew her attention back to him as he leaned forward. "But, my lovely, I killed you."

"Didn't we already talk about this?"

"Not really."

She struggled a moment with what to say. "The thought of dying doesn't bother me very much."

He gave her an incredulous look. "That's not normal. Even I don't want to die."

"I don't want to die," she said irritably. "I'm just not afraid of it. It's going to happen one of these days."

"Definitely not normal," he muttered.

"You're really going to talk to me about normal?"

His mouth opened, and then closed abruptly.

She waved her fingers at him to get off her bed. "There, you aren't dreaming. I'm the best. Now go to bed and try to get some sleep."

His eyes sparkled as he tipped his head to the side and chuckled. "You certainly are the most amusing human."

"See, the best. Sleep time. We've things to do."

Setting his elbow on his knee, he stuck his chin in his hand. His smile turned predatory as his smokey gaze locked onto hers. "The best at *everything*, my lovely?"

Her teeth ground together in irritation. "Are you still drunk? Go away."

Leaning back, he raised his hands. "Of course." He smiled again. "However, I would like you to know, should the...need arise, you needn't worry of the spell. I would be more than happy to come to your bed. At any time."

Her cheeks burned. She flung her arm out, pointing at the door. "Get out!"

He smirked and shifted backward. "Or I could offer kisses–"

"Out!"

"Or just to hold you in the night."

Her embarrassment and anger disappeared so quickly she couldn't breathe, only stare at him. She didn't need to be reminded how alone she was now. How she had neither Prince or Kei to keep her nightmares away. Rotting tears threatened. Her lips quivered. Snapping her head around, she clenched her fists, willed herself to calm. Thought very, very hard on how she desperately *needed* the stupid Elf out of her room.

"Aro? I was just–" His voice lowered, deepened. "Look what you've done."

The change in tone startled her enough she dared to look back at him. Her eyes met the dark, stormy gray she rarely saw. Jaw clenched, lips pressed tightly together, she leaned back, away from his anger.

He saw and relaxed slightly. "We are sorry, master. This stupid, selfish one gets carried away at times."

His eyes shifted again and then squeezed closed. Baelan smacked either side of his head with his fists. "It's not your turn! I know! Be quiet!" He hit himself again a few times before cracking open an eye. "I apologize. Very much."

Picking up the pipe, which had fallen to the bed at some point, he tucked it in his pants and stood in one fluid motion.

She had no idea what to say.

Walking to the door, he started banging on his head again. "Be quiet, already!" At the door, he turned to her, fingers curled in his hair. "So sorry, again." A brief bow and he slipped out.

"Wither me," she muttered.

"Quiet. Be quiet!"

Chapter 11

So it Begins

It shouldn't have been so difficult.

They managed to leave the house by dawn. Baelan had only been sent back twice for something they forgot.

And once to the market.

At least he hadn't thought it overly strange they decided to take the dog. Of course, the Elf also looked like he'd been run over by a carriage. After sleeping half the day after their incident, he then alternated between throwing up, apologizing, and helping them pack.

She now knew the Elf couldn't handle his liquor. Between that, his constant apologies, and the bit of crazy she'd seen, she forgave him.

At least their delays helped them avoid the earliest morning traffic of workers heading out of the city toward the fields and quarry.

The crowds near the city gates were still thick enough Garen kept close to them. Kei stuck to her side even closer. She wondered what he remembered but didn't ask. Maybe he just felt her growing unease.

Hands clenched into fists, lips pressed tightly together, she tried to ignore all the people pressing around her and concentrate on reaching the gates.

You don't like crowds?

Her eyes flicked over to Baelan. *No.*

But you go to the market.

The market isn't this crowded. Or hurried. It's different.

He kept glancing over at her, waiting for her to explain. She certainly didn't want to tell him how the press of mens' bodies terrified her, or why large crowds did. The second reason she didn't mind sharing. *Ever been in a crowd trying to escape a city under siege that just had its gates breached?*

His brows drew together, and a slight frown crossed his lips as he looked away. His next steps moved him closer to her.

Kei glared at him and growled.

Baelan shook his head in annoyance. "Really? You're more likely to hurt her than I am."

Eyes wide, Kei's head jerked in surprise.

"How many times do I have to explain how this rotting spell works," he muttered in annoyance. "I swear I'm surrounded by idiots."

A laugh sputtered out of her as she listened to his tirade, she couldn't help it. From the small smile on his lips, she realized he'd done it on purpose.

Adjusting her pack, she trudged onward. The weight bore down on her already. Yesterday when Kei wasn't looking, she replaced what she could to lighten his load. He could yell at her later, if he noticed. Her shoulders were already aching. Maybe she would need Baelan to rub them tonight.

He stumbled beside her and choked. *What was that?*

What was what? She kept her voice innocent and her gaze on the gates slowly drawing closer. Her lips twitched. He was so easy to tease. At least after telling him more than once to speak as he wished and "be himself" he'd finally taken her words to heart. She didn't regret it, for the most part. It was certainly better than his moping.

She shouldn't have been surprised when Silas and Raythe fell into step with them when they'd nearly reached the gates. Her evening talk with Roan had been short the night before. He hadn't mentioned anything in particular about her leaving, other than to be safe. She should have known better.

She smiled at the two Were as Baelan slowed his step and fell behind so Raythe could be next to her.

"Good morning, Miss Aro."

"And to you." When he didn't speak for a moment, she decided to just get it out of the way. "Should I be afraid to ask?"

Raythe grinned and winked. "Never."

"Roan being overprotective again?"

He chuckled and shrugged a shoulder. "Always. You know how he is."

"That I do." A quick glance showed he and his twin bore no packs of their own. "I'm surprised you're not coming with me."

"It was considered."

"Of course, it was," she muttered under her breath. Some days she rather wanted to throttle the pirate. "That's too bad. I wouldn't have said no to someone carrying my pack."

Even Silas grinned at that. "It can still be arranged, if you like."

With a tight smile, she shook her head.

"No Elves have come or gone within the last two days," Raythe said, getting to the point. "If that changes we'll let you know. I've men up the road today beyond the quarry. You won't be caught unawares. If you need assistance for any reason before you reach the forest, please don't hesitate to contact one of us."

"Thank you, I will." She wasn't sure what else to say and still be polite. It rather infuriated her how Roan had not mentioned any of this. She wasn't stupid. She'd planned on having Garen alternate running ahead or behind to keep watch.

The Were smiled and gave her shoulder a quick squeeze. "We are quite happy to assist, Miss Aro." He paused a moment and then leaned closer, lowering his voice. "Thank you, for talking with him again."

Clearing her throat, she fought the heat rising to her cheeks.

"Safe travels," the Were said together, and then slipped away into the crowd.

Kei's elbow bumped her arm. "I don't remember them."

At least this she could ease his fears on. "You wouldn't. I met them after Damon took you and haven't seen them since you've been back. They work for Roan."

He frowned before turning his attention again to the crowds around them. Her heart twisted, how different he was now. Quieter, unsure of himself. His shoulders curved in as he nervously fingered the straps of his pack.

Baelan stepped up to her side again, pulling her attention away. Unsurprisingly, he didn't remain silent for long. "You know, for just a friend Roan seems–"

She cut him off. "I already know what you're going to say, so don't bother."

He batted his eyes at her. "But you're quite beautiful when you blush, my lovely."

She glared at him, contemplating bodily harm.

"That rosy flush to your cheeks–ah!" He winced and smacked a hand to his temple. "I know... I wasn't..." His hand dropped and he straightened. "I apologize," he said quietly, his voice lower.

Well, she hadn't expected that. A wagon took her attention away and she glanced at Kei as they made their way around it. His glare at the Elf was part anger and part confusion. Usually how she felt, really, which brought a small smile to her lips.

Once close to the Elf again, she looked over and saw Bay remained. "Stay a while?"

His stormy eyes flicked to her for a moment before once again roaming the crowd. "I believe that is for the best."

"Unless he's…ah…giving you problems," she said quietly, not wanting to have to deal with an irritated assassin.

"I have no trouble ignoring him," came the quiet reply.

Finally, they made it out of the city and though the road remained crowded, it wasn't pressing.

Garen, I know the Were are watching, but roam a bit and keep your eye out.

Understood.

"The dog ran off," Bay said.

"He'll come back if we call him. He just wants to run."

She looked to Kei and saw his small secret smile. "Will be nice to have the horses to carry the packs," she said, trying to judge how he was doing without actually asking.

His smile dipped into an irritated frown and he looked away. "I'm fine, Aro."

"Well, my rotting shoulders hurt," she grumbled and was rewarded with a small smile.

A while later Garen informed her they were being followed by two men he was quite certain were Roan's. She thought for a moment before contacting Raythe.

You have men following us?

After a brief silence, he answered. *Yes. Two.*

Anyone else? When he didn't reply, she snapped out. *You do realize I've an assassin with me. Tell me now so your men don't get killed.*

Easy, Miss Aro. Can't really come to your aid all the way from the city. There are men randomly stationed up to the quarry road. Some will follow you down and then set up to rest where you head up the ridge to make sure no one follows.

You could have told me this, she said angrily.

Roan thought–

Roan's an idiot.

Feel free to tell him that. I'm certainly not going to. I'm just doing my job.

She snorted and then relayed the information to the boys. Bay frowned but didn't comment. She didn't ask what he was thinking. His silent presence was almost nice. Beside her, Kei relaxed slightly.

A short time later, Silas let her know of an Elf with a wagon coming by. He was known, with a scheduled shipment. Bay ordered them to the side of the road to sit and Garen kept an eye on him until he moved well passed them.

They'd nearly reached the quarry road when Raythe contacted her again.

One got by us. Not sure how, maybe while we were checking out–

Don't care how, she interrupted. *Where is he and what does he look like?*

Glamored. Brown hair. Workers clothes.

She passed on the information. Garen took off. Bay nearly flung her to the side of the road. Kei didn't even growl, just followed quickly.

The Elf shrugged off his pack and dumped it beside her. "Stay. Here."

She sat on her pack, Kei quiet beside her. Garen found him, she told Bay, even as she spotted the man herself. Close. Way too close for comfort. "Rot," she muttered, trying to appear as if she wasn't looking but still not taking her eye off the man.

Too pretty to be human, he walked with a slow but purposeful stride, eyes scanning the people on the road. *Are we sure he's–*she began to ask Bay. She certainly didn't want to be responsible for the death of someone innocent.

Yes. Bay appeared in front of him, slipped around him, and then caught the body before it fell, expertly moving it off to the side of the road with no one the wiser. Unless you'd been watching, then maybe you'd have seen the blood.

"Did you see that? He's good," Kei whispered.

"He's the best," she murmured in response before gathering her composure and contacting the Were. *He's taken care of. Body's off the road. Right side.*

Bay returned, picked up his pack, and started off again without a word.

Everyone remained tense and silent for the rest of the walk. Nearing the quarry, she grimaced, trying to remember where to break off the road to find the hidden trail up the cliff.

Do you remember where we're going?

Of course, Garen replied easily.

Another thought occurred to her. *Might not want to surprise Baelan while he's in this...mood.*

I absolutely agree.

Aro glanced over at the Elf, who still looked ready to kill anyone who looked at him, or her, twice.

Once they slipped off the road and made their way amidst the fallen rock and brush, they paused for a rest before starting the journey up.

"Roan's men are supposed to be watching so we aren't followed," she reminded everyone as she stretched her back, keeping her voice low. "But we still need to be quiet."

Bay eyed the not quite path they were to take. "You are certain we won't be seen?"

"The Were use it. I think they have the rocks and trees set up to keep themselves hidden."

They set out again, moving slowly. Garen, still glamored as a dog, bounded around them and led the way. Considering even she struggled in some of the steeper areas, Aro kept more of an eye on Kei than she did on where they were going. It was a decent distraction from thinking about the Were king.

They were nearly halfway up when she called another stop. Sweat ran down her face and between her shoulder blades. Bay appeared unaffected, but she'd seen Kei's hands begin to tremble. She sat on her pack, taking a long drink of water. Garen flopped down at her feet, tongue lolling. Cupping her hand, she poured water in to share with him, too.

Kei wiped his forehead on his sleeve and looked up. "Will we get there by dark?"

She pursed her lips, trying to remember how long it'd taken them coming down. Of course, down was also a lot easier than up. "We should," she finally answered. "We'll move into the forest a bit once we do and make camp."

"Will Garen be meeting us up there?"

She cleared her throat to hide her amusement at the Elf's question. "Probably sooner."

He nodded, blinked, and amused eyes met hers. "That sounds delightful, my lovely."

Her lips curved into a smile as she shook her head. Kei glanced over at him and frowned. *He's starting to wonder about you.*

It was bound to happen, the Elf replied. *I will tell him, if he asks.*

Does it bother you? People knowing now.

Looking over at her, he smiled faintly. *It would have before. They wouldn't have understood,* he explained. *However, you and Kei...*

He didn't have to finish.

Mention of Garen pulled her thoughts in another direction. *So Garen, what do you know about him?*

He's the only one of your pack who is actually a Were? The question in his tone let her know he had no idea where the conversation was going.

Yes. She paused, trying to think of what to say. *You know how the Were have two bodies they shift between.* His brows drew down, but he nodded slightly. *When he was young, Garen lost his human one. He can't...* She fumbled for words again.

He doesn't shift?

No, he doesn't. I just wanted you to know. We don't talk about it.

I see.

She hoped he did and wouldn't make some stupid comment at some point like he was prone to do.

They didn't rest for long. After taking some time to eat some cold food, they started back up the trail.

Garen bounded in front of her. *Soon?*

Holding back a laugh, she agreed.

The path forced them to walk single file most of the time. Aro followed behind Kei, with Baelan behind her, while Garen led them through the twists and turns and false trails.

"So, what are sleeping arrangements?"

Aro glanced over her shoulder. "What do you mean?"

"Are we staying with the Were most of the time?"

The Elf's question made her pause. "I doubt it. I don't think there are that many villages or whatever. Most nights we'll just set up a camp."

"I should have packed more blankets," he muttered. "And a pillow. Do we at least all cuddle?"

She turned again. "Cuddle?"

"It's cold at night," he whined.

"No, we don't cuddle."

"Well, there are other ways to keep warm," he said smoothly.

Kei looked over his shoulder at her, clearly irritated. *Want me to kill him?*

Baelan winked at him and a golden glow rose in the Fey's eyes even as his cheeks flushed.

She held back a laugh but shook her head. "Why did I say you could talk freely?"

"Because you like me as I am," Baelan responded happily.

"You're annoying."

They came to a break in the trail. *Oh, here, here. Stand aside.* She grinned at the excitement in Garen's tone as she and Kei both stepped back.

Baelan tipped his head slightly, wondering what they were doing, but then smiled as he saw Garen the dog running back toward them from up the trail.

He didn't slow as he approached. Just before he reached the Elf, he dropped the glamor.

Baelan screeched, throwing up his hands when the large wolf pounced him, pushing him back against a tipping tree, large paws on his chest.

Garen licked his face and dropped down, tongue out as he laughed.

She and Kei struggled unsuccessfully to hold their own laughter in as Baelan stared at them all with wide eyes, sputtering.

"You know Garen," she finally managed to say.

"Garen…the dog…Garen is the dog…" Shaking his head, he put his hands on his hips and glared at them all. "You are all truly evil."

His words set off another bout of laughter.

It was nice to laugh again.

∞ ∞ ∞

Baelan grumbled as they made their way higher, but didn't appear to be angry. As they neared the top, walking single file along one of the straight paths before another switchback, she tried to keep her thoughts calm.

They were doing this. They were going to heal the Fey. It wasn't just words anymore. The enormity of it all set her heart racing, but she kept her thoughts there.

She didn't want to think of the Were king, but the higher they climbed the more thoughts of his upcoming decision plagued her. Would he be waiting for her above?

She might die. He might not think her worth the trouble of keeping alive. She'd heard enough about him to know the Were thought him a good king, but he could be ruthless. He would have to be to control the tens of thousands of Were he ruled.

"Rot," she muttered, swiping a hand over her sweating forehead. She'd just have to convince him. She couldn't leave Kei alone. Not after everything.

She'd promised.

AROWYN MASON

She slammed her hands over her ears as the deep voice bellowed through her head, so loud it vibrated through her, stealing her breath from her lungs. A short cry of pain escaped before she bit down on her lower lip. Eyes squeezed closed, she felt rather than saw her boys gather around her. If they spoke, she couldn't hear them.

Hands pulled the pack from her back. A press to her shoulder bade her to sit.

"The King," she gasped out, wanting them to know what was happening.

He won't kill me. He won't kill me.

She wasn't sure if she spoke aloud or not, but someone's arms wrapped around her and hugged her tight.

AGAINST MY LAW YOU HAVE CREATED A PACK.

Why did he have to be so loud? *I'm sorry…*she began.

YET, GIVEN THE CIRCUMSTANCES, I WILL FORGIVE YOU THIS TRANSGRESSION. WILL YOU AGREE TO FOLLOW MY LAWS AND MY COMMAND?

Y-yes, she stuttered out through the ringing in her head.

For a moment, he remained silent and she forced herself to breathe.

THEN SO IT WILL BE. WELCOME TO THE WERE, ARO-EN.

She bit into her lip and jerked forward as something swelled inside her, wrapping around her and pulling her in. She could feel the pack bond she shared with Kei, Bo, and Garen grow and tighten around her. Their surprise. Panic. Relief.

From far away, she could hear the King speak to his Were, welcoming her into their midst, demanding they assist her in her quest.

The uncomfortable feeling of being somewhere else slid through her. She stopped listening and opened her eyes. Panic clawed at her chest. She had no idea where she was. Spinning in a circle, she found herself surrounded by everchanging images of people and wolves. Voices murmured in the background, too quiet for her to make out what they were saying. Yet she knew these were the Were, welcoming her.

Something pulled her, drawing her further into them, and she gasped as she felt herself dragged into something...bigger. Her entire being filled with the sense of belonging, of being whole, part of one great community. It wrapped around her, and sucked her in.

"No, Aro-En."

She looked up and froze, her eyes widening. A massive white wolf with pale blue eyes stalked toward her, heedless of the constantly changing images around them.

Something yanked at her hand, gently at first, then with a sharp pain. Suddenly she felt a tug inside of her, desperate, insistent. *Come back to me.*

"You shouldn't be here," the wolf rumbled, his words laced with power. "Go back."

Come back to me. Come back.

Between the command in his words and the tugging she had no choice. Immediately, she found herself back in the quiet of her own mind.

Apologizes, Aro-En. The King's voice echoed around her, and though still loud, it no longer boomed within her. *I suppose I should have known.*

"Known what?"

He didn't answer.

She wanted to go back, to feel the wholeness again, but something held her, pulling her back toward consciousness. A pain in her hand. A pull on her soul. Arms around her. A…kiss.

None of it made sense. Startled, she pushed herself from her mind.

Her eyes fluttered open.

"She's awake!"

Lips pulled away from hers and she blinked a few more times in surprise at the tortured face looking down at her. "Kei?"

"You came back," he whispered, his arms tightening around her, holding her close and tucking her head under his chin. "You came back."

"Of course," she said softly, and would have wrapped her arms around him but her hands were both occupied.

"I t-told you it would w-work," Baelan stammered out.

Kei released her, settling her up against the rocky cliff. To her right, Baelan knelt, holding her hand tightly despite his words. Looking to her left, she found Garen lying beside her, her hand in his mouth.

"Did you bite me?" His head lowered and ears went flat at her high-pitched question. Before he could answer, she pulled her hands free and wrapped her arms around his neck. "Thank you."

She kissed the top of his head and didn't comment when he scooted closer, pressing up against her legs.

Her attention turned back to Kei. He sat back, his face turned away from her, his lower lip between his teeth. She had no idea what went on inside his head, and worried about that.

"Kei," she said gently, leaning forward.

His head turned toward her, face pale and eyes glistening, breaking her heart. She didn't know what to say, if she should mention the kiss or just ignore it.

"I didn't know what to do," he whispered.

His whole body jerked on a sob and she threw her arms around him, holding him tightly to her for a long moment. Pushing him back, she held his face in her hands and pressed her forehead against his. They sat that way for a while, she didn't know for how long, until she felt him calm.

Her poor broken Fey.

Everything is fine. We're fine.

He didn't answer, just nodded and she sat back. When certain he wasn't going to break down again, she turned to Baelan who watched them in confusion.

She held out a hand and Baelan didn't hesitate to set his inside it. Giving it a light squeeze, she kept him from pulling back as she felt the dark wrapping around his wrist. Sticky. Wet. She let out a deep breath and looked up as she let him pull away. "I'm sorry."

He shrugged a shoulder, glancing away. "So you're a pack?"

"We are." Her eyes widened. "Bo." *Bo!*

It took a moment for him to respond and her heart nearly beat out of her chest. *All good here, pup. Was just a bit startling. Banged my head off a shelf in the storage room. Elaina is taking care of me,* he finished with some amusement.

We're almost up the ridge. All good here, too. Will talk later. Love you.

Love you, too, pup.

Chapter 12

Plans Gone Awry

Finally, they reached the top of the cliff. With a headache her power wouldn't cure pounding her skull with every step, it seemed to take forever. At least they made it before the sun set.

After moving quickly into the trees, Aro finally stopped and abruptly sat down. Squeezing her eyes closed, she pushed her fingers against her temples.

Kei crouched beside her, resting a hand on her shoulder. "Aro?"

"Just a headache. I'll be fine." Even though he didn't reply, she still felt his worry through their bond.

Hands lightly cupped her cheeks and she opened one eye to find Baelan's beautiful face intent upon hers.

She jerked back at the feel of him pushing at her mind. His admonishing look made her relax. He couldn't hurt her. She needed to remember that.

"Your mind is a bit...raw. Nothing serious." He nodded once, silver hair flipping over his eyes. "Some sleep and you'll be fine." Lowering his hands, he shifted back on his heels and brushed hair from his face. "Considering what was done, and the amount of power used by the king, I'm not surprised."

We have company, Garen interrupted.

Looking beyond the Elf, she saw a Were walking toward them and she pushed herself to her feet. "Our guide, I presume."

She didn't recognize him. Tall, broad shouldered, and attractive, he stopped before them.

He dipped his head in her direction, not meeting her eyes. "Welcome, Aro-En," he said quietly. "I have taken the liberty of setting up a camp. If you will follow me, it's not far."

"Thank you." They followed the silent Were as the sun set to an open area between the trees. A small fire crackled and she smelled something cooking. Their two Elven horses whinnied a welcome and a small smile crossed her lips, remembering Prince.

She dumped her pack on the ground. "What is your name?"

"Gillis," he answered, again quietly and not looking at her. Would she ever get used to how the Were would now treat her as an alpha? "Please, eat and rest. We will leave early to make it to Waycross before evening. Rhee-En will meet you there."

"Waycross is…?"

"East of here."

She didn't know what else to say and was too tired to try to carry on the awkward conversation, so moved to sit beside Kei. She worried about him, for so many reasons, but also knew her worry would only irritate him, so just sat and ate in silence.

"I'm fine," he offered after a while.

She smiled over at him. "Good." She turned back to her food. "Just remember if you ever aren't, I'm here."

"I know," he whispered. After a short while he shifted a little closer, his shoulder brushing hers. "I'm…confused. About so many things," he said, keeping his voice low and not looking at her. "There is…so much I don't remember. I don't know who I am."

His words came out painfully slow, twisting her insides. "You'll remember. It will just take some time. And I'll be here,

I'll always be here." She cupped his cheek. "That's one thing you never need to be confused about."

He nodded and looked away. "I shouldn't have kissed you. I..." His brows drew together as he shook his head. "I'm sorry."

Reaching over, she squeezed his hand. "I'm not angry. I understand. Besides," she leaned back and smiled, "it did bring me back."

His lips curved a little, but he didn't reply and focused on eating, the conversation apparently over.

She held in a sigh. At least he'd spoken about what he was feeling.

After eating she had a quick goodnight talk with Bo and then gathered her thoughts for a moment before contacting Roan.

Good evening, Roan.

And to you, Arowyn. How did everything go today?

I'm rather irritated with you, she answered after a moment.

Silence, until finally, *And why is that?*

All the men, guards. I'm not angry you did it, more that you failed to mention anything about it last night, she explained.

He chuckled. *Apologies. I knew you would argue with me about it.*

No, I wouldn't have. I'm not sure why you keep thinking I'm stupid.

I don't think that, Aro. But, you are stubborn and you don't like asking for help. Did you have any trouble?

Just the one Elf, which I'm sure you heard about already.

Yes.

She smiled. *It's going to drive you crazy not having everyone reporting back about me now, isn't it?*

He laughed. *Perhaps a little. You will be surrounded by Were though. You will be much safer now. I assume you made it to the forest?*

Yes, all settled in for the night. Tomorrow we travel to a place called Waycross to meet Rhee-En. She paused for a moment. *We're a pack now.*

So soon? Is everything good with you and the king now?

I guess so, she said slowly. *As long as I don't mess up. Which I will try very hard not to do. Gah, he was so loud in my head. Do you think that's a king thing? I thought my skull was going to break open.*

Hmm, I don't know. Perhaps. Are you hurt? Concern laced his voice and she hurried to reply.

No, I just have a headache. Baelan said I should be fine with some sleep. I'm not planning on talking to him again any time soon if I can help it though. He still rather terrifies me, she added quietly.

I wish there was something I could do to help you with your fear. You do understand he will not hurt you now? You are one of his.

I know, she mumbled.

Roan sighed. *Just remember the Were will help you, should you need it. You are pack.*

We'll be fine. At least we don't have to worry about Elves trying to kill us anymore.

Silence.

Roan?

Arowyn, he began slowly. *Elves may travel within the Were lands. There are no laws keeping them out.*

What? Why would they?

Some take what they call a Long Walk. Alone or in small groups, they will walk the forest. There are outcasts as well, and... Did Baelan mention–

That they are hunted? Yes. Do the Were not interfere with that?

Elven matters are not their concern.

It's wrong, she stated flatly. Worry gnawed at her stomach. So, they did still have Elves to worry about.

It's just how things are.

She didn't have to like it, but let the matter drop and changed the subject. *How is everything with you?*

Things are...honestly, they are difficult right now, he admitted.

What's wrong?

Nothing for you to worry over, Arowyn.

She didn't like the sound of that. At all. Or the fact he wouldn't tell her. But that, of course, wasn't anything new. *Be safe, Roan,* she said quietly.

Of course. There is no need to worry. Be on your guard as well. Get some sleep. Tomorrow your adventure begins.

Goodnight, Roan, she said with a laugh.

Goodnight, my Arowyn.

When she opened her eyes, she found Baelan staring at her, an amused look on his face. She refused to ask.

"The expressions on your face while you mind-speak are fascinating to watch."

"Go to sleep."

"Yes, master."

"I hate you."

"If you say so."

She plopped down on the ground next to Kei in an irritated huff, ignoring Baelan's quiet laugh.

"I'm still open to killing him," Kei said softly, looking over at her with tired eyes, but a slight smile curving his lips.

She huffed out a laugh. "I'll think about it. Goodnight, Kei."

"Goodnight, Aro."

∞ ∞ ∞

They didn't meet any other Were as they traveled the next day. After some protesting, she somehow managed to get Kei up on one of the horses. He still flashed her scowls during the day, mainly because she made him ride with Baelan. He not only needed rest, but riding with the Elf allowed him to work on his memories as well. He wasn't an accomplished enough rider to do so on his own horse.

Baelan didn't complain at all about his riding partner. She wasn't sure what to think of that.

Their guide remained quiet. Garen happily roamed around them, delighted to be without his glamor and out of the city.

For the most part, she walked silently, too many thoughts rambling through her mind.

Waycross was not what she expected. At first, they walked by the odd house or building. Paths appeared, and then turned into the dirt roads of a small town hidden beneath the trees. The town was loud with voices and the sounds of living; wood being chopped, the clanking of pots, slamming of doors.

The Were themselves nodded or gave their party short bows, always avoiding her gaze, before returning to whatever they had been doing. A few quiet "Welcome, Aro-En" met her ears, but her guide did not slow, so she didn't have the time to find the owners of the words to reply. The odd giant wolf wandering around amidst the people drew her attention. Though used to Garen, her brain still had trouble dealing with their size.

They finally stopped, dismounting and gathering their bags. After Gillis spoke with a man who led away the horses, they entered a large building which reminded her of the Westwind with its bar and tables set out, people eating a variety of foods.

"Is this an inn?"

Gillis turned in her direction as he led them through a door to the left into a hallway. "A waystation. Similar to a human inn, yes." Stopping, he gestured to two doors. "Rhee-En arranged for two rooms. Please settle in. You may dine in the common area," he gestured back to the first room they'd entered, "and baths are at the end of this hall. Rest tonight. I will meet you in the morning in the common area after breakfast to take you to Rhee-En."

"Thank you."

With another nod, he turned and left, leaving them standing in the hall and staring at the doors. Stepping forward she opened one and looked inside. Two beds. The other room appeared the same.

"I'll take this one," she told the boys, going into the first room and then closing the door behind her.

Dropping her bag on the floor, she took a deep breath. Alone was fine. She was an adult. She could do this.

∞ ∞ ∞

The common room was quieter in the morning. Or perhaps they were just early, it being barely after dawn. The night before they'd cleaned up and then ate, talking for a while about everything they needed to discuss with the alpha. With nothing else to do, they'd gone to bed early. They might as well get what rest they could.

She had nightmares. They were not, however, bad enough to bring any of the boys running in. She was pretty sure she didn't scream.

After eating a light breakfast, she looked around, watching the few Were. She couldn't help the sadness rising within her. She missed when they talked to her, when they didn't care who, or what, she was.

Gillis walked in, his shoulders relaxing when he saw them sitting at a table. Motioning for them to come, he didn't say a word as he led them quickly through the town until they stopped at a nondescript log building.

She turned, and then frowned as she saw Baelan and Kei farther back down the street, stopped and speaking to some Were.

161

"I will make sure they know where to go. Please go on in, Aro-En."

She smiled at Gillis and then closed her eyes for a moment, gathering herself. She was clean. Her hair was even brushed. Her clothes not only fit, but were of the highest quality. Thinking of Roan, she raised her chin and pushed open the door.

The room seemed dim after the brightness of the outdoors and she blinked a few times. The alpha stepped forward to meet her and she tilted her head up. His black hair was still a bit wild. His eyes still a strange mix of gold and blue. The scars marring one side of his face from cheek to jaw didn't frighten her this time, though perhaps she'd just gotten used to them.

"It is good to see you again, Aro-En."

Rot. She'd forgotten about his voice. His smooth, beautiful purr of a voice. A shiver ran through her and she clenched her teeth, trying not to let his effect on her show.

He chuckled, and she knew she'd failed. Giving up, she smiled awkwardly and took another step forward. "It's good to see you again as well."

They looked at each other until it grew awkward, which would have worried her, but he didn't say anything either and he was supposed to be good at this sort of thing, being a centuries old Were.

She cleared her throat but didn't lower her gaze.

An easy smile curved his lips. "I believe you will do well, Aro-En. You have learned much over the winter."

"Some things. Likely not enough. I was hoping you could help with some of it."

He laughed, the sound making her breath catch and her stomach clench, not in a bad way. She held in a frown. "Still bold as well. Yes, I will help you as I can." His head tipped to the side slightly. "You know things have changed now."

Her brows drew down. "Many things have changed. What in particular were you referring to?"

Raising a hand, a finger moved back and forth between them. "You also, are now alpha."

"Does that mean we can't be friends?"

"Were we friends before?"

"I like to think so."

He regarded her for a long moment before his stance relaxed and he chuckled. "Bold, and straightforward."

She forced herself to smile. "I need all the friends I can get. Things have…not been easy and I don't think they are going to get much better," she said quietly.

He nodded, solemn now. "You had a hard winter. I often wished…" Stopping, he shook his head. "Yes, we will be friends."

She didn't expect it, but when he spread his arms she didn't hesitate to step into his gentle embrace.

"You can do this," he whispered against her hair, giving her a light squeeze.

"I hope so."

Baelan walked in as she pulled away from Rhee-En's arms. The Elf raised his eyebrows and smirked.

She sighed. "Rhee-En, this is Baelan, the troublesome Elf I told you about a while ago."

The Were turned his attention to Baelan. "Ah, yes. The outcast assassin now bound to you."

Baelan's eyes widened slightly, his lips parting as he stared. "Wither me, you sound like sex. On a cold night, in front of a roaring fire with a couple of–"

Horrified, Aro gave him a sharp mental jab and his mouth snapped closed. Rhee-En simply seemed amused. For all she knew, he'd heard that before. Her cheeks burned, and she cleared her throat.

"It's fine, Aro-En. No need to be embarrassed." His gaze moved to the side. "Kei, Garen. Welcome." Turning, he gestured to a long table set up farther in the room. "Come, we have much to discuss."

The table was covered with a map, nearly the same length, and she paused, eyes flicking over landmarks she knew. Kei stopped at her side as her fists clenched.

"I assume you know how to read a map?"

Instead of the Were, her eyes met Kei's as she nodded. "It's not…"

Kei scowled then bit his lip, worry lines forming between his brows. "No, it isn't."

"Is there a problem?"

Clenching her jaw for a moment, she then turned to Rhee-En. "We had…plans. But this," she flung a hand out indicating the long map, "isn't what we were told." At the alpha's raised brow, she continued, "Prince drew us a map in the dirt once, the sea, the mountains, " she pointed from one end of the map to the other, "and the boundary between Were and human lands."

"He should not have done that," Rhee-En said crossly.

She shook her head. "He was *wrong*. His map was nearly square. The human lands not much less than the Weres."

Kei's hand slipped into hers. "It's fine, Aro. It will just take us longer than we expected."

Huffing out an angry breath, she forced a smile.

"What was your plan?"

Stepping down the table, she found the village on the map and then drew a line with her finger, north to south. "Work it like a grid. Down, east a bit, up, and so on. We'd spread out on each pass, cover as much ground as we can."

She turned to Kei. "Is that still doable?"

He paused for a moment, and then nodded. "Follow the Guide, Seek those who hide, Back and forth, again and again, Through the lands of Rhee-En."

She blinked a few times, then smiled faintly.

Rhee-En stared at Kei a long moment. "Very good." He cleared his throat. "The Fey like to hide. Their trails can also be difficult to follow. They know how to hide them, and even if not, they fade quickly."

"We're hoping to have a few Fey join us to track them down. A few others to help those we find. We'll set up camps here," she drew a line up the center of Rhee-En's lands, east to west, "moving them east as we go until we reach Furia."

He nodded. "That certainly would be more productive than dragging them all along with you."

"We'd have supplies delivered there as well, or to villages close by, if possible. We have Bo in Westport to gather what we need, it's just getting them here we need to discuss with you."

"Very good, Aro-En. That will not be a problem. We have Were working as night guards at the quarry. I can send my supply teams down and bring loads up."

Aro couldn't help but grin at that. "I'll pay you. And for help delivering them to us as we move."

Now knowing better than to argue, Rhee-En merely tipped his head in agreement.

They huddled over the map, working out specific routes, adjusting some so they could stop at villages, or ensure nearby water sources for the camps. After breaking for a quick lunch, they continued, and then discussed supplies. Rhee-En found a large notebook for Baelan to take notes.

"I believe we have missed dinner," Rhee-En finally commented. "You will still be able to eat at the waystation though."

She hadn't even noticed someone came in and lit lamps. Rubbing her stiff neck, she smiled and nodded.

"We will meet again tomorrow, though I am busy until noon. I will have Gillis bring you once I am free and we can finish up."

As they headed for the door, Rhee-En stopped them, placing a hand on each of her and Kei's shoulders. "I am proud of you. Well done."

With that he slipped out the door and she grinned at Kei, feeling some of the tension slip from her shoulders. They could do this.

∞ ∞ ∞

Baelan frowned when Gillis led them into the building the next day and Rhee-En wasn't yet there.

Aro rolled her eyes. The Elf had been in dream land since the night before and mentioned the alpha too many times. "Pay attention today." He'd also written almost nothing down.

"I am. Mostly."

"Just remember to take notes."

"It's not like I'm going to forget," Baelan muttered.

"You're not paying attention, so you might."

"It's not my fault his voice is so distracting."

She closed her eyes and took a deep breath. Rhee-En came in and she opened her eyes to see Baelan's cheeks flush and a beautiful smile cross his face.

Kei sighed.

Rhee-En glanced at the Elf with an amused smile. They looked at each other for a long moment and she wondered what sort of mental conversation they were having.

From the discouraged sigh Baelan finally let out, she decided she didn't want to know.

Rhee-En greeted them and got straight to business. "Shall we continue?"

After dealing with a few comments or questions each had come up with since they last met, the alpha moved to the map.

"I have spoken again with my Were. As far as we can tell, the Fey, at least those in my lands, are concentrated here." He indicated a good-sized area around Furia. "There are pockets,

166

here and here, which is unsurprising as the area has a number of caves. I believe there are also a good number in Alar-En's lands."

Her eyes slid over the map. "There are still some out this way though. Or are we wasting our time?"

"Some, yes."

"The closer we get to Furia the more we'll find," Kei said. "Even now, after all these centuries, it is our home and we won't travel far." His eyes met hers. "The more we heal and bring together, the stronger we will be. Others will be drawn to us."

"Such a unique society," Rhee-En murmured.

"What about the Vor? When will we need to worry about them?"

"Hopefully not for some time." His look turned sheepish, and he rubbed the back of his head, likely remembering last fall when some got far enough west they were attacked. "I will, of course, keep you updated."

"So, for now we've just Elves to deal with," she muttered to herself.

"Should my Were be near and you are attacked, you will be assisted," Rhee-En stated firmly. "You are now pack." His gaze slid to Baelan. "Unfortunately, you have no such protection."

The Elf shrugged a shoulder. "I am here to protect Arowyn, and I can take care of myself." He paused and then tipped his head to the side. "Will there be repercussions if I do?"

"No. We may not agree with the hunting of outcasts, but do stay out of it. Try not to damage my forest. If you start a fire, put it out. Bury the dead." A wry grin crossed the Were's lips. "If you do not leave a trail of bodies, that should keep the Elves off all our backs."

"Understood."

"Aro-En, our king will want to be kept updated."

Our king.

Oh, rot. She had a king. The Were king. How had that happened? No, how could she have never even considered it?

Rhee-En tipped his head to the side as she squirmed. "Do you still fear him?"

She shrugged a shoulder. Yes, yes she did, but wasn't about to admit it.

The alpha sighed. "That is partly my fault, I know. You need not fear our king, Aro-En. He is kind and just with his people. Until you, or he, decides otherwise, you are now considered one of us."

"Do I have to talk to him?"

"It is customary for us alphas to do so on a regular basis. He wishes to be kept informed."

Nodding once, she tried to hold back her rising panic.

She should have known she couldn't hide it from the Were. He let out a loud sigh. "Are you afraid to talk to me?"

"No, of course not."

"Then for now, if you promise to speak with me regularly, I will pass on the information for you." He leaned closer, making eye contact. "Just for now."

"Thank you," she said softly.

Leaning back, his gaze grew thoughtful. "However, I do think it would be helpful for me to send one of my betas with you, at least for a time. Terris, perhaps."

She nodded her agreement to that, remembering how Garen once mentioned betas were Were with alpha tendencies, and after the alpha, the strongest in the pack. Should the alpha die, the next would be chosen from them. They were a second tier in the hierarchy of the pack, often leading villages, or in charge of various military units.

"I am not sure if she can be here before you head out. If not, I will have her meet you."

"Thank you," she said.

"Do you wish to leave tomorrow?" At their nod, he continued. "The day is not over yet. Gillis will take you to our supply master."

It took them a while to choose, gather up, and then pack supplies. Though they had the two horses, Aro wanted room left for at least one of them to be ridden. They'd also be able to restock, but the time she and Kei had spent with nothing still influenced them and it was hard not to take more than was necessary.

By the time they finished, it was past dark. Walking back to the waystation, Baelan flirted with nearly everyone they walked by.

"I'm eating and going to bed," she finally said. "If you want to stay out for a while though, that's fine."

His eyes lit up and he bounced up on his toes as his enthralling smile appeared.

"Be back by midnight," she said firmly. "And don't drink too much."

"Yes, yes. Of course! Perhaps Kei would like to–"

"No," the Fey said sharply, eyes glowing.

"Or not." Baelan's smile became a bit forced.

"Stay out of trouble," she warned him.

"I'll be no trouble at all," the Elf promised with a smirk.

Jen Wylie

Chapter 13

Old and New

The birds were chirping too loudly.

She wasn't sure why she thought so, though she hadn't slept well. Since she usually didn't, the chirping shouldn't have annoyed her. Perhaps it was because they'd gotten up so early to pack up the horses and set out. She'd gotten used to sleeping past dawn over the winter.

Ahead of them, Garen shifted their direction slightly and they followed. After a few words of good luck and caution, Rhee-En had seen them off, sending one of his Were to guide them to the point they would begin their initial trek across his lands.

At least they didn't have to start right at the border of the human lands, but farther east within. The alpha kept extensive patrols all along that border to keep the humans out and assured her no Fey were in the area.

"When are we stopping to rest?"

She looked up to where Baelan rode on one of the horses, raising her eyebrows. "We just started. Probably at noon."

He let out a dramatic sigh.

Kei huffed in annoyance beside her.

"I'm bored," the Elf whined.

They both ignored him.

"We could play a game?"

"No."

"I could tell you about my night..."

She cast him an irritated look and knew she was blushing. She needed to find a way to stop doing that.

He smirked at her, but at least shut up.

Rotting Elf.

By the time they did stop to eat, he'd complained at least a dozen more times.

"This is a quick stop, stretch and eat. Check on the horses."

Baelan sighed. "Fine."

As she shoved food into her mouth, her gaze kept straying to Kei. Unlike Baelan, she hadn't been bored. Her mind whirled with a crazy, buzzing mess of thoughts and plans. And worries.

Kei hadn't asked her to run with him.

She would have thought he'd be more excited their quest to heal the Fey had finally started, but he didn't act like it. He hadn't complained either, about their delay, or even the early morning. He hadn't said much of anything. When she smiled over at him she was lucky to get a faint curve of his lips in return. Most of the time he didn't even notice her.

It was hard to keep the worry away, though at least she knew to keep it from *him*. Off her face and not felt through their bond.

The boy—no the young man—beside her wasn't the Kei she knew. More than once a bit of panic sped her heart. She just needed to keep reminding herself his faraway, lost looks had a reason. He too had been through much this winter. Perhaps he was even working on his mind and memories as they walked. Maybe he was thinking about the prophecy and what they were to do.

Her Kei was in there somewhere. He had to be.

He'd come back to her. She just had to give him time. The alternative stole her appetite away.

Garen walked over and pressed his large head against hers. *Everything will be fine.*

Looking away from Kei, she forced a smile and rubbed a hand over his soft fur. *I hope so.*

∞ ∞ ∞

From north to south, Rhee-En's lands were generally a three-and-half to a four-day journey, depending on terrain, how many times they stopped and for how long they stayed before moving on. Of course, this was at their more sedate pace. She imagined the Were running full out could make it in a day or less. She wondered if they could run that fast for so long.

Their guide left them in the early evening. Even though some daylight remained, they decided to set up camp and go over the small map Rhee-En had given her, and their plans.

Garen found them a good site. Baelan dismounted and then they all just…stood there. The awkwardness grew as they looked at each other in strained silence.

She'd forgotten.

This wasn't her old group of boys who had their duties memorized. Bo was gone. Prince was gone. Baelan was new and Kei apparently couldn't remember a thing.

She cleared her suddenly tight throat and then started giving orders. The resulting chaos made her head ache, but eventually everything got done.

It will get easier, Garen assured her as she set about cooking. Her teeth ground together in frustration. They'd literally been tripping over each other and it had taken forever.

I know. It's just…different.

Change isn't always a bad thing.

She snorted her disagreement.

Well, prepare for some more. Rhee-En's beta comes.

Do we know anything about her?

Garen let out a huff as he walked up to her. *I did not find out much in the village. No one was very talkative.*

She frowned as she glanced down at him. *I'm sorry.*

They will get used to the thought of us in time.

She hoped so, at least for his sake.

Baelan and Kei both turned toward the woods, also sensing the Were's approach. Giving the fire a poke with a long stick, she jabbed it into the ground before turning her attention to the shadows.

The lone wolf slinked into view, pausing as it reached the light of the fire.

Wither me, she's big.

Size is usually determined by status in the pack. Being a beta, she is one of the largest.

Rhee-En is bigger, she mused. Though they were similar in coloring, she too being mostly black.

As alpha, yes. He paused a moment. *The king is larger still.*

Of course, he had to say that.

Between one blink and the next the wolf disappeared, a tall woman taking its place. She was dressed to kill, clothed in thick black leathers over a dark shirt with a good number of weapons, considering Were mostly fought in their wolf form. Firelight glinted off her straight black hair, which was surprisingly short, not even reaching her shoulders. A strong jaw complimented high cheekbones and full lips. Pale blue eyes regarded them all slowly, no emotion showing on her face.

Finally, she strode forward, all grace and swinging hips, before stopping and meeting Aro's gaze.

She couldn't believe how awkward this meeting was and cleared her throat before speaking. "Welcome, Terris."

The Were kept eye contact, her chin up, though Aro wasn't quite sure if the woman was being defensive or just plain arrogant.

Garen's hackles rose slightly and she felt Baelan shift beside her.

She disrespects you, Garen snapped out.

I see that. She just didn't know why. Her muscles tensed as she waited to see what the Were would do.

Terris finally broke her gaze, glanced at Kei, Garen, and then Baelan. Her eyes narrowed before taking in their disorganized camp, the small meal cooking on the fire. She sniffed and her lip curled. "Glad I ate earlier," she muttered.

Aro clenched her teeth for a moment, fighting down her rising anger. "You are welcome to leave. I did not request your presence."

"No, but my alpha did."

At a loss for words, she just frowned. What was wrong with this woman?

Hearing her stray thought, Garen answered, *It could be any number of things. She could be testing you, or dislike you are human, or that the king made you an alpha. All of those, or something else entirely.*

The woman noticed the pile of packs and strode over, knelt, and began going through them.

When she noticed the Were leaving a mess in her wake, Aro strode over, her fury rising. "What are you looking for?"

"A pack for me was to have been sent with you."

Baelan moved forward, confident and in no hurry, easily picking out one of the bags and tossing it beside the Were.

Terris didn't acknowledge him at all, but grasped the pack, opening it and quickly going through the contents.

"Put everything else back as you found it," Aro finally said as the woman continued to ignore them.

The Were's head shot up and she opened her mouth to say something, but Aro turned on her heel and walked away.

175

Very good, Garen murmured.

I don't like this, Baelan grumbled, following her back to the fire.

I know, I don't understand why Rhee-En would send her, or why she's acting this way.

Perhaps all is not as it seems.

She glanced over at him, finding the assassin. *What do you mean?*

You think Rhee-En to be your friend.

She glanced back at the Were, frowning.

You think too simply and never consider the possibility of duplicity.

Not everyone is out to kill me.

Killing you is not the outcome some may desire. We don't know what Rhee-En is thinking, or wants. He sent his beta to watch us, under the guise of assistance.

Well, if he's trying to be sneaky he shouldn't have sent her. I don't trust her already.

Agreed. However, you don't need to trust her if her objective is something other than gaining your confidence.

With a small, sad sigh she just shook her head. How could she have been so stupid? She'd liked Rhee-En. She started as Bay lightly touched her elbow to gain her attention.

I could be wrong, Arowyn. Perhaps it is not Rhee-En at all, but the King's orders.

That doesn't make me feel better, she muttered.

Perhaps I am wrong, he said again after a long silence. *Trusting no one has kept me alive for a long time.* He glanced down at her and she met his stormy eyes. A faint smile crossed his lips for a moment. *Except for you. I don't believe you could deceive me if you tried.*

She shook her head at that. She knew very well she was too trusting… and forgiving.

It is something you will learn in time, he continued. His head tipped slightly. *And I stand corrected. Your deception with Garen being a dog was well done. Though I suppose it was more of an omission, a secret, than purposeful deceit.*

I... She stopped, unsure what to say.

You do not trust me, at least not fully. I do not blame you for your secrets, Arowyn.

Secrets. Yes, she still had a number of those.

∞ ∞ ∞

Terris did not stay with them that night, but shifted back into her wolf form and wandered back into the forest. Aro didn't complain and tried not to grimace when the woman returned the next morning as they finished packing up to leave.

"Good morning." She forced a smile.

Terris stopped before her, hands on her hips. "What are your plans for the day?"

She shrugged a shoulder. "We're travelling east. Going to spread out to cover as much ground as possible."

"Understood. I will roam ahead and inform you of any obstacles or dangers and water sources." Without waiting for a reply, the Were shifted and left.

Aro stared after her for a moment and sucked in a slow breath. Between the queasy feeling of not being liked, to the anger at the woman's attitude, she felt a bit nauseous.

"Is everyone ready to go?"

Baelan stepped close to Kei and leaned forward, sliding his cheek along the side of Kei's.

Kei froze. "What are you doing?"

"Refreshing my memory on what a Fey smells like."

The Fey scowled and pushed him away. "You know very well."

Baelan grinned.

Kei suddenly lunged forward, snapping his teeth in the Elf's face. Baelan stumbled back, startled.

Aro couldn't help but laugh. "You should be careful. One of these days, he's going to rip your pretty face off."

Kei flashed a bit of fang and then with a smirk, turned and headed into the forest.

Her laughter died. It'd been funny, but not like her Kei.

Baelan smiled wryly, but then the smile grew mischievous. "So, you think I'm pretty?"

She groaned. "I think you're impossible!" Frowning, she glanced over at him. "But really...Kei?"

"I appreciate beauty, in any form." His mirth faded, turning serious, thoughtful. "But not only that. I am not so shallow. Like that woman Terris. She is strong and beautiful, but I would rather sleep alone than with her."

"I see."

"Do you really, Aro?" The slight snappiness in his tone made her brows rise.

"I don't care who you take to your bed," she said honestly. "Just...please be careful with Kei."

The Elf stared at her for a long moment before making a surprised noise and shaking his head in amusement. "Very well, you are right, he doesn't need any games right now. I will try to leave him alone."

"Try?"

His face scrunched up in dismay as he turned away. "I forget sometimes," he said quietly.

She decided not to ask.

They did not come across any traces of Fey that day, or the next. Even though she knew finding them would be hard, and take time, and that the likelihood of many being this far west was low, a gloom still settled over her and the others.

Part of it she blamed on Terris. The unfriendly Were remained distant, but brought a bad mood with her whenever she did show up, and it seemed to linger.

Aro wished the Were would just leave. She wasn't particularly helpful anyway.

Putting away the cooking supplies, she frowned and looked around. Their camp was so quiet. She missed the sound of Bo's loud laughter, the talk of the men.

Music began to softly play, filling the silence. She turned, a faint smile curving her lips as she shook her head in amusement at Baelan, now playing his pipes. He gave a helpless shrug of his shoulders. Stupid spell.

When she returned to the fire she saw Kei with his arms around his legs, forehead against his knees as he rocked. Frowning, she moved quickly to his side.

"The Guardian is the key," he murmured. "The Guardian is the key."

"Kei?" She set a hand gently on his shoulder.

With a start, he raised his head. "The Guardian is the key."

"Of course," she said hesitantly.

He blinked and looked over at her. "Goodnight, Aro."

She forced a smile and struggled to speak beyond the lump in her throat. "Goodnight, Kei."

Morning brought gray skies and an unfortunate shift of the wind. While the others grumbled it came from the west, giving them little advantage to sniffing out the Fey as they traveled south, she shrugged and paid more attention to the darkening skies.

By late morning, a light rain began and they quickly set up one of the tents, using the tarp-like piece instead to make a lean-to. With their packs at the lower end, Garen then crawled in, leaving them free to sit against him and watch the rain.

Baelan frowned as he glared outside. "What do you plan to do now? This mess," he waved a hand dramatically at the rain, "will wash away all traces of any Fey."

"It depends on how long it lasts. We might be done for the day, though."

Kei nodded his agreement and then leaned back against Garen, closing his eyes. "Call me if we head out again."

She stared at him for a long moment before twisting to turn her attention to the Elf on her other side. "Shall we find something productive to do?" She paused. "One of us should still be able to keep watch, though."

They decided on working on her mental defenses. Baelan would attempt to invade or attack her mind and she would repel him.

As the rain turned into a bleak drizzle, she found she did well enough at pushing him out of her mind. However, when he attacked she didn't fare as well.

"You needn't hold back, my lovely."

"I'm not," she grumbled.

"You most certainly are." He regarded her calmly for a moment. "You don't see me as a threat, I believe. Which is true enough. And," he continued, nodding to himself, "you aren't angry. I've noticed your emotions are quite often tied into your powers, which is not ideal. We'll keep working on it. At least you are learning the correct techniques."

When they thought it was around noon, Aro poked Kei to get his attention.

His eyes snapped open as he startled. Blinking up at her, he smiled. "Aro." His brows then drew together in confusion as he looked around. "Where are we?"

She forced a smile and spoke calmly. "In the Were forest, looking for Fey." When he just stared up at her, still lost, she continued. "To heal them. We're just waiting for the rain to stop before we go out again."

He looked out into the forest and then nodded slowly. "Of course," he said quietly. She reached for his hand, but he shook himself and sat up. "Of course," he said more firmly, the confusion fading away.

Curling her fingers into a fist, she pulled her hand away and set it in her lap. She hated seeing him like this. Anger for Damon once again rose within her.

They ate a quick meal of dry goods. By the time they finished, the rain puttered out, but they sat and waited to see if it would start up again.

"Someone comes," Baelan whispered, sitting up straighter. His hand suddenly gripped her forearm. "Aro, they are Fey!" He turned to her, his eyes bright with excitement.

She grinned, having seen the four Fey as they emerged from the trees. "Yes, we have met them before. This is good." She stood, pulling him up with her. "You can meet a few other Fey who aren't wild first."

"Aren't wild?" He rose, following her and Kei as they moved toward their visitors.

"We met them some time ago, before we got Prince home." She smiled up at him. "I have already healed them."

The four Fey stopped before them, all giving a nod of respect. It struck her again how much they all reminded her of Kei, though her Fey was a bit taller now.

"It is a pleasure to see you all again," she said to them.

"As it is for us," the one man said.

"This is Baelan, and Garen. You remember Kei." She gestured to the Fey before her. "This is Cano and Lissana, their son Aron and his mate Meena." All but Meena had dark hair, the mens' short, and Lissana's in a long braid down her back. Meena's pale hair was just as long, but in a multitude of braids all bound together. All had the golden eyes and slightly curved ears of the Fey.

Baelan smiled brightly at all of them.

"You are back in the forest," Cano said, his voice raised lightly in question.

"Yes, we are looking for Fey." She grimaced up at the sky. "Unfortunately, we had to stop because of the rain."

"We had waited by the ridge for a time once the snows began to melt, but you never came. We had thought the worst." He bowed his head. "I apologize."

She shook her head. "There is no need. We were…delayed. Winter was not kind to us."

"I am sorry to hear that," the Fey said with a frown. It deepened as his eyes shot briefly to Kei, now noting his thinner frame. Looking back to her, he quickly smiled. "But you are here now. We have come to offer any aid we can."

"And we would be happy to have you." Somehow, she avoided doing a happy dance.

"The rain has passed," Lissana told them. "Will you continue today?"

She glanced at the others, and then nodded. "Yes. With extra people, we can cover the same amount of land well enough despite the wind and rain being against us."

As they took down the tent and loaded up the horses, she gave them a brief account of what befell them over the winter, and then explained their plans for searching for the Fey. Of everything, they seemed most surprised to learn the Were king had made her an alpha and did comment on how she smelled "more like a Were" this time.

At least the Fey were correct about the passing rain. As the afternoon wore on the sun even came out.

Chapter 14

Assassin's Arrows

She didn't see or hear the first arrow.

One moment she walked beside the horse, concentrating on the ground, looking for any trace of Fey, then the next she was face first in the mud with an Elf spread over her.

Another arrow thwumped into the ground near her face. She stopped trying to push Baelan off and froze.

The horses pranced and whinnied and then turned and trotted quickly back the way they'd come.

Elves?

Elves, Bay agreed, his arms wrapping around her, tucking her head safely beneath him.

She silently cursed as she elbowed him in the ribs. *How many?*

The wind is not working in our favor today, but I believe only one.

She let out a slow breath and relaxed. One they could handle. Another arrow landed too close and she jerked in surprise. *Why aren't they hitting?*

I don't know.

"Get up, outcast. I will let your human woman go."

Well, that answered that. *Can we trust him?*

Of course. We are not mindless killers. There is no reason for you to die.

She snorted. *They keep trying to kill me.*

It appears he is only hunting outcasts.

But…how does he know you're one?

His body tensed above hers for a moment. *You have seen all the runes on my body. One marks me as outcast. Elves can…sense it.*

But—

Not now.

She elbowed him again. *From how far? Do they—*

When they see me, they sense it, he snapped. *Now shush.*

Her eyes widened. Had he just shushed her?

Bay shifted, lifting her up to bring her face closer to his, cupping her cheek in one hand. "You have to go. Run."

She shook her head. *What are you doing?*

Using his mistake to our advantage. He believes you are my woman. "I need you safe. You have to go," he said again, his voice rough and firm.

Understanding, she nodded. "I don't want to leave you." It wasn't lost on her, this was also the truth.

His tense shoulders relaxed slightly as she played along. "I know, sweetheart. I'll be fine." Standing, he pulled her up with him, still shielding her body despite his assurance the Elf wouldn't kill her. "Go find the horses." *He is somewhere ahead of us. I'll find you when I'm done.* When she opened her mouth to argue, his eyes narrowed. *Are you…worried about me?*

She glared at him, but a slight, jerky nod answered him anyway.

His lips twisted into a frightening yet amused smirk. *I am your assassin, Arowyn. I'll be fine.*

She frowned and shook her head, irritated he was making her go. As she moved away, he didn't let go of her hand until he had to.

"Go."

She sprang into a run, but veered east, downwind, once she was out of sight. When far enough away she couldn't hear them talking anymore, she slowed a bit, moving as quietly as she could as she circled back.

There still only one?

Yes, my lovely.

She paused hearing Baelan was back. It couldn't be too bad if the assassin had retreated.

Drawing close, she crouched, using the trees and scrub for cover. The Elves weren't talking now, other than the occasional curse or taunt. The flashing lights of runes lit the area she'd left them in and she held in her own curses. She hated rune magic.

To be safe, she drew the dagger Prince had given her. She'd discovered one of the runes carved into it could break any runes thrown at her. After being hit by one once, she didn't ever want to go through that pain again.

Moving closer, she finally caught sight of the fighting between branches and leaves. Baelan fought with his sword in one hand as the other tossed runes at or around his opponent.

Grimacing as the foliage obstructed her view again, she debated moving closer.

Kei, Garen. We've encountered an Elf. Baelan is dealing with him.

Just one, Kei confirmed.

Yes.

We'll head back, Garen said. *No sense in us getting too far ahead.*

I agree. Be careful, Aro, Kei added quietly.

I will.

"Idiot! You don't use *fire* in the forest!"

Baelan's angry shout startled her out of her mental conversation.

It must have startled the other Elf as well. The lights disappeared and moments later only silence met her searching ears.

"You can come out now, Arowyn."

Wincing at the assassin's stiff voice, she rose and pushed her way through the brush into the newly made clearing.

"Rhee-En won't be impressed with this mess," she muttered.

His stormy gaze met hers as she reached him. "We will fix it, as much as we can."

She nodded once, before turning her gaze to the Elf sprawled out on the ground. Her eyes flicked away once she saw his blank, staring eyes. Curiosity made her look again.

"I've never seen an Elf like him." Where every other Elf she'd met had fair skin, his was a bit darker. Most shocking was his hair, an unnatural wine color. His eyes matched.

Bay glanced at the Elf and then shrugged. "Our creators seemed to like fair-skinned blondes, most of the originals were so. But some were different. His line. Mine." His fingers reached up to briefly touch his hair and then gesture to his eyes. "A few others."

She looked away again and then cleared her throat. "I contacted the others. They are headed this way."

"Good." He paused, staring at her. "You weren't supposed to come back. It wasn't safe."

She shrugged a shoulder. "We should get the horses."

He huffed out an irritated breath. "I will. They haven't gone far."

As he walked away, she called out, "Thank you!"

Turning slightly as he walked, he tipped his head. "I am to protect you, Arowyn. No thanks are needed."

"I meant thank you for not dying," she whispered as she watched him walk away.

Bay brought the horses back, ensured they weren't injured, and checked if the packs were secure. After handing the Elf's sword and dagger off to Bay, both beautiful Elven blades, she paced as she waited.

Kei caught her off guard when he arrived, bounding up to her and wrapping her in his arms. Her heart pounded in her chest as she held him tight. *This* was her Kei.

"Are you hurt?"

"No." She shook her head, holding in a sigh as he pulled away from her.

"You need to be careful, Aro."

"I know."

Garren arrived with Lissana and came up to butt his head against her thigh. Their worry brought a blush to her cheeks, and a bit of annoyance.

It is more than just your life at stake now, Arowyn, the Were reminded her.

Yes, she knew that, too.

Let's get the Elf buried. Do you want to camp here tonight?

"Oh, goodness no," she exclaimed.

Kei cast her a crooked smile and despite the fact they were about to bury a body, she smiled back.

By the time they finished and moved on a good distance to find a spot to make camp for the night, she was exhausted.

When Terris strolled into camp with a smirk on her beautiful face, Aro ground her teeth together, attempting to keep her fury in check.

"Where were you today?"

The Were raised an eyebrow as she poked at the empty pots from their recently finished dinner. "Scouting ahead, as I always do," she finally replied.

Aro set her empty plate to the side and rose from her seat by the fire. "Did you come across any trace of an Elf today?"

"I met him." Her eyes flicked to the side as Baelan also got to his feet.

"You didn't tell me."

"He was a simple traveler," she countered with a wave of her hand.

"No. He was not," Aro snapped out.

"Perhaps the alpha did not warn her," Baelan whispered.

"Of Elves intent on your life? He did. One young one travelling the forest was of no concern."

"He isn't now. He's dead," she said flatly. The Were froze. "Baelan killed him after he tried to shoot us full of holes. From now on," she continued sharply, "you will tell me immediately of any Elves."

"I suppose I can do that," Terris replied stiffly.

"That was not a suggestion."

The Were nodded once and then suddenly shifted and ran into the woods.

Baelan leaned in close, his voice a sultry purr. "You just reminded me a bit of Roan. Except you rather made my heart race. You are quite stunning when giving orders, my lovely."

Turning slowly, she glared at him, eyes flashing with the light of the fury within her.

He leaned away and swallowed quickly.

"Go clean the dishes."

"Yes, that is a wonderful idea."

Despite just wanting to go to sleep, she remembered she did have a number of people to contact first. Her goodnights to Bo and Roan, and it would be a good idea to contact Rhee-En and let him know about the Elf. Perhaps she would hint a bit at the issues she'd been having with his beta. She'd discussed the problem with both Garen and Baelan and found it to be a tricky slope since she didn't know if she could fully trust the Were. Speaking to him in person would be her best resort, but she didn't know when she would meet up with the alpha again.

∞ ∞ ∞

The morning brought a pain between her eyes as the birds once again sang too loudly.

She hadn't gotten a lot of sleep. Her chat with Bo had been sweet and short. Roan, of course, had a lot to say. He disagreed with their notion that the Were could not be trusted, instead pressing her first thoughts that Terris simply didn't like being pulled away to work with the new human alpha. His dismay twisted her insides, as she pointed out their thoughts and he shared his. Of course, his points sounded more valid than hers.

Rhee-En, when she eventually contacted him, didn't seem to catch her hints Terris wasn't working well with them. His alarm when he heard they'd already faced another Elf attack brought Roan's words to mind and she was left not knowing who to believe or what to think.

As they all set out together, Kei pulled her aside, his hand slipping into hers.

She looked at him, her smile both hesitant and hopeful.

"We got a bit ahead of you yesterday when you stopped." He paused a moment and then smiled. "Would you like to run?"

A grin split her face as she squeezed his hand. "Yes."

The answering boyish grin on his face made her heart soar. Sometimes the little things in life could make everything better.

It was the best morning she'd had in a long time.

They did eventually split up again, but even Baelan's stupid knowing looks couldn't take away her happiness. She didn't care what he thought, or what anyone else did, either.

To make the day even better, Terris contacted her shortly after they'd spread out again.

Caught the scent of a few Fey. Heading east.

Thank you, Terris.

She sent the information out to Garen and Kei and not long after she heard from them.

Found it, Kei said. *The Were was correct, heading east. Two of them. We'll keep on it. Anything, Garen?*

No, we will circle toward you.

When Baelan found the trail crossing their path they stopped and waited for Kei, Lissana, and Cano. They didn't have to wait long. The five of them continued on foot, leaving the horses safely behind.

"They aren't very far ahead," Kei whispered, his eyes glowing yellow with his excitement.

We're on their trail. Anything yet?

Catching scent of them now, Garen replied. *We'll hold back in case they make a run for it this way.*

Aro relayed the information as they quietly tracked the Fey.

"Tracks are gone," Cano suddenly said from ahead. "They've gone to the trees."

"They must have caught our scent," Kei grumbled as they all slowed, craning their heads to look up into the dark branches above them.

"We aren't here to hurt you," Aro said calmly, knowing this close the Fey could easily hear them. "I'm here to heal you, like I've done these Fey with me."

She waited, but the Fey didn't appear so they all continued slowly forward.

It shouldn't have surprised her they attacked her and Baelan, and not the other Fey. Still, being knocked to the ground by a growling mass of teeth and claws tore her breath away and sent her heart pounding. At least she didn't scream. Baelan did, and the sound would have been amusing if she hadn't been trying to keep herself in one piece.

She managed to avoid the snapping teeth. Not so much the tearing claws. On the ground, she tried to latch on to the Fey so she could draw out its power and protect herself, but that idea wasn't working well.

Too many cuts later the Fey jerked away from her, pulled off by the others. She lurched forward as Kei held the Fey down and slapped her hand to its head, pulling. She still didn't know if the Fey was male or female.

Power gone, the Fey slumped to the ground. Kei grabbed Aro's hand and pulled her to her feet. "Quickly!"

Cano and Lissana stood, holding the other struggling Fey by her thrashing arms. Aro slapped her hand on the Fey's chest, once again pulling fury into her. Neither were very strong. Once done, she stepped back and easily let some of the excess drain away.

"Well..." She heaved out a sigh and held in a wince. "That could have gone better." Dropping to the ground, she closed her eyes, quickly healing the gaping wounds on her arms and shoulders. "Still alive, Baelan?"

He groaned. "That was terrible. My shirt is ruined."

A small laugh escaped her, though he did have a point. Maybe they should have packed more clothes.

The two Fey were both women, Mayza and her daughter Gizine. Terris, once again helpful, directed Aro to a nearby stream where they could get cleaned up and the new Fey settled.

The most perfect part of the day though, was seeing the joy on Kei's face at having more of his people free of the fury.

∞ ∞ ∞

Days went by with a steady rhythm of searching, eating, sleeping. They reached the wardwall, traveled up it a short distance, and then began the trek north up Rhee-En's lands. They found another Fey, and then three more, another two, and so it continued as they turned and moved south again.

They traveled slowly. Some of the newly healed Fey required extra care, but some recovered quickly, helping those who needed it or with the search itself. By the time they reached the wardwall once more, they'd found fourteen Fey.

She sometimes found it hard to watch them struggle with their sudden normalcy. All but one had been born since the Queen's death. None of these could read or write, or knew much of their history. Some even had trouble with more than simple language. Her heart broke for them and all they'd lost.

Lissana told them how some Fey were wilder than others, locked into the red wild fury with little reprieve. It should have occurred to her they weren't stuck like that all the time. How would they find mates or raise children, otherwise? For most it was a cycle. If not provoked, the fury would slowly ease until their eyes turned orange, or rarely the glowing gold. The weaker the Fey, the harder it was to break from the raging red eyed fury. Strong Fey could more often, more easily, and she was told how it was said some, the strongest, never went wild at all. She wondered what happened to these Fey. She vaguely remembered someone mentioning it to her before. Would they come across them as well?

Aro spoke with Rhee-En about beginning the part of their plan where they would begin an eastward moving Fey camp along the center of his land. On this pass, they would go by the settlement she'd been to previously, which she learned they called Ridgeside. There they would restock supplies and meet again with the alpha.

Other than a few showers, the weather hadn't been bad. Spirits were high as the Fey reconnected with others of their kind.

She watched Kei now, as they all sat together around the large fire. His hair had started to grow out a little, short bits sticking out every which way. He'd put on more weight, more muscle, but his face still had a hollow look to it.

The darkness around his eyes bothered her. He smiled slightly at something another Fey said, but it didn't reach his eyes.

She still often caught him lost in quiet thought and a few times, lost in confusion. She didn't know how many more of his memories he needed to restore, and he didn't want to talk about it. She stopped asking, hating how such questions made him angry.

Moving to his side, she pretended to ignore his frown.

"I'm fine."

"I know," she answered. "I can't sit with you?"

He blinked rapidly at her and then looked away with a grimace. "Of course you can," he finally said.

They sat in silence for a while and she relaxed, content just to be by his side.

"What are you thinking about?"

Raising her eyebrows, she turned and smiled. "How I'm happy just to be here with you."

His hand slipped over hers, fingers entwining, as a faint glow of happiness came to his eyes. "Me, too."

They stared at each other for a long moment before he dropped his gaze and turned to watch the fire again. He didn't let go of her hand.

"I was thinking of Furia," he said after another long silence. "What it will be like."

"I've wondered, too. How long will it take to get there, do you think?"

"It's not time. We need to go, but it's not time."

She looked at him quickly. Her stomach twisted at the faraway look on his face. He wasn't really with her anymore.

Squeezing his hand, she forced words up through her tight throat. "Whenever you're ready."

"It's not time," he repeated softly.

Jen Wylie

Chapter 15

Dragon's Wrath

They'd hoped to reach Ridgeside by evening, but she doubted they would. After finding another Fey early in the morning, the tracking and healing of him had taken a good chunk of time from their day.

There is rain on the way.

She grimaced at the beta's words. *Is there shelter ahead? We only have two tents. Or can we reach Ridgeside before it hits?*

Not in time, no. I will see what I can find.

Thank you. She actually meant it. It surprised her how helpful Terris had become, though the Were still rarely spent any time with them. Perhaps that was a good thing.

A short time later, a shadow darkened the ground before her and she cursed. She'd thought they'd have more time before the rain came. Looking up to see how dark the clouds were, and how much they would get wet, she stopped. Sunlight struck her face and still she stood, eyes searching the bit of sky she could see through the trees. When the shadow fell on her again, she cursed louder.

Kei.

I saw him.

Rot!

Calm, Aro. It will be fine. We're doing what he wants. Just...try to not get angry.

Her fists clenched. Too late. *He hurt you! He took you from me! How can I not be angry about that?*

Aro, please.

The pleading in his voice startled her.

I don't want him to hurt you, he continued quietly. *He might not kill you, but he can hurt you.*

Grasping at her hair, she paced and cursed and tried to keep her fury in check.

"What is it?" Baelan, now taken to walking with her, leaving the horses with the Fey who followed them, had either seen or sensed her distress.

"Damon," she grated out.

The Elf glanced up, then around them. His lips pressed together. "What is your plan?"

"Plan? I don't have a plan!" She growled in frustration. "Not get eaten."

"I meant for everyone else. The Fey."

"Oh, rot."

"Yes."

She ran a hand over her face. Sucked in a deep breath. Thought a moment before sending out a message.

The Dragos Damon comes. Fall back. Protect the Fey.

Baelan gave her a brief, pleased nod. Terris and Garen both sent their agreement. Kei didn't.

I'll be there as soon as I can.

You know that's not a good idea.

Aro, just...trust me.

Even though he couldn't see her, she shook her head, but didn't argue. Turning on her heel, she started walking, putting more distance between her and the following Fey.

Baelan joined her. "What would you like me to do?"

A grin quirked her lips. "You're not going to go back and join them are you."

He made a face and shook his head. "You know I don't like to be far from you. Besides, I know better than to anger the dragon. Perhaps I can keep you calm, as well."

"Perhaps," she acknowledged. "Don't get killed."

He flashed her a brilliant, beautiful smile. "My lovely, keep saying such things and I might begin to believe you don't hate me."

"Haven't hated you for a while now, idiot."

He chuckled, and she smiled, too.

"Is my arrival amusing to you?"

They found him in the shadows, arms crossed as he leaned against a tree, watching them. She wondered where he had landed, how he'd gotten his monstrous dragon form to the ground. How had he even changed forms? Did he shift as the Were did?

He straightened, disrupting her thoughts, and moved toward them. Her fists clenched as he approached. He looked the same; tall, his short black hair curling around his slightly backward curving pointed ears. His eyes... Those terrifying eyes. With no whites and their vertical slits, the iridescent swirling colors held your attention.

She wanted to draw her daggers and stab them. Maybe that would kill him.

He frowned, his eyes narrowing as he stopped before her. "You never learn, do you, little human?" His gaze turned to Baelan and remained there until she heard the Elf back away. The Dragos turned his attention back to her.

"Hello, Damon." She did, at least, remember his anger if she didn't greet him properly.

"Such angry thoughts flying around in that weak little mind of yours." He grinned, teeth white and unfriendly. "That is enough. It is done, and as it should be. Your obsession with my death is a waste of time. You cannot kill me, little girl. I am not

197

human, nor Elf, Were, or Fey. I am Dragos. I am not of this world. Nothing, nothing in or of this world can kill me, Arowyn. Do you understand? Direct your anger elsewhere. It does you no good."

If he was right... She pressed her lips together, remembering stories she'd heard from the Were about the Dragos. The truth of his words settled in her very bones. Bitterness filled her, souring her stomach. She had failed before she'd begun. There would never be any vengeance for what he'd done to them.

"I am not your enemy. You don't seem to be able to grasp that simple fact. I am simply," he waved a hand, "ensuring the ending to this tale that I desire."

He'd said something similar before and she frowned, trying to remember.

"The Vor," Baelan said quietly from behind her.

"Of course the Vor," the Dragos snapped. "I cannot get off this rotting world until they are gone. I need the Fey back to get rid of them. It's simple."

He flicked his finger against her forehead and she jerked back.

"The problem—one of the problems," he amended with a sharp look her way, "is the ripples. Have you felt them? No, I suppose you have not."

"Ripples?"

"Of change. Within time. But they are unnatural, forced. Someone is trying to change what is to come. They are the enemy."

Her forehead wrinkled in confusion. "You want me to stop them?"

He snorted in amusement. "Of course not. They are a foe neither you, nor I, will face. That duty will come to another. But you must—" He stopped abruptly, his gaze going over her shoulder.

It's fine, Kei assured her, stepping up beside her.

"There you are. You heard?"

"Yes," Kei answered.

"Be aware of the ripples. Understand?" Damon spoke fervently, his eyes looking even more crazy than before. "You must watch for the changes and be prepared."

Kei's brows drew together as he bit his lip, but he nodded.

"It is unfortunate the Fey do not have a seer," Damon continued.

"The Were do," she offered, stepping closer to Kei as she felt his growing worry.

"Yes, but he is old. Nearly done. He makes little sense at all anymore. What he has spoken of in the past only concerns the Were."

"The Elven seer..."

"Very good. She is, I believe, the problem. Young, too strong... and in the hands of the queen. Vile, twisted woman." He waved a hand. "It is not your concern, Arowyn." Swirling eyes set on hers. "Why are you here?"

She blinked and struggled for a response to the strange question.

Don't fight him. Don't argue with him, Kei warned her.

"I'm...healing the Fey."

"So, you are. You should have started weeks ago. You should be half way through Rhee-En's land by now. Do you think this is a pleasure romp through the woods?"

Sweat broke out on her brow as her heart beat faster. "No. We've healed fifteen already. We were delayed because–"

"Because of your incompetence!"

She couldn't stop the anger from rising within her. "No! Because you nearly killed him!"

"Such a disobedient child." His rainbow eyes swirled in anger. "Do you need a reminder, Arowyn? You live on my sufferance because at this time I need you. Do not think, however, that you may do as you please, or disrespect me."

Aro, stop. Please stop.

Clenching her jaw, she straightened her spine and refused to back down from his stare. He may be a dragon, but she didn't belong to him. "You've done nothing to earn my respect," she snapped. "What you did to–"

"You should respect me, because I am so much more than you, little human. You are nothing. A speck in time. An annoying bug." His eyes narrowed. "You should fear me, and yet you do not. Perhaps I have been too lenient with you." The vertical slits in his eyes widened slightly as he took a step closer.

Apologize, Kei begged. *Say you're sorry!*

She held her ground, clenching her fists to keep a sudden surge of panic at bay. She'd gone too far…again.

One moment she was glaring at him, the next her back was slammed up against a tree, feet dangling as he held her there by the throat with one hand.

Her fingers scrambled against his hand, nails clawing to no affect before she simply clasped his wrist, trying to remove his hold.

"If you continue, I will destroy you," he said quietly. "But first, I will destroy those you love." She shook her head vehemently. "Because I need you does not give you any power over me. It merely allows *you* to live. Do you understand?"

When she didn't answer immediately, he slammed her against the tree. "Yes," she managed to gasp out.

His strange eyes narrowed. "You are too strong willed for me to believe you. Perhaps occasional reminders will be in order."

Spots danced before her eyes as she struggled to breathe. "No!"

"Still so disrespectful. Do you not understand how simple it would be for me to destroy those you care about? The human in the city, your Were, the Elf. I could break your Fey again."

Tears slipped down her cheeks. "No. Please no."

He dropped her and she gasped, sucking in deep breaths as she rubbed her throat. Rot, how she wished she could kill him.

Fingers gripped her face, smacking her head against the tree once more and she swore. Had he heard that?

Of course I did. "I think, right now. A reminder just for you."

She grasped his arm, trying to push him away. "No! No. I understand. Please, stay out of my mind." Would her fortress keep him out this time?

"You will never keep me out. No part of you is hidden from me." He paused, a slight, wicked smile crossing his lips. "Even now, you do not fear me, so what do you fear?"

No.

Sweat beaded her forehead. "Don't do this," she managed to whisper through a mouth suddenly gone dry.

"It is necessary, I believe," he said casually.

She winced when he entered her mind, every muscle tightening as she waited for the destruction and resulting pain.

Except it didn't come.

He knew right where to go, slipping through halls, moving deeper and deeper into the depths of her fortress.

No. No no no.

She followed, growing more frantic as he continued on.

He didn't slow or stop.

Deep within her mind, buried and chained and locked away, her most terrible memory hid. Out of sight, not quite forgotten. No, she could never forget, no matter how hard she tried. Even buried, it was one of the foundation stones for the person she'd become.

He slipped through stone, entering the deepest, most hidden room in her mind. He sliced through chains as if they were nothing, until only the heavy wooden box remained.

Don't open it. Don't open it.

Looking to him, breath coming in frantic gasps and eyes wide, she begged him not to. It was never meant to be opened again. Somehow, she'd overcome that part of her life. It had shaped her, changed her, and she eventually managed to move on, to mostly forget, except for the nightmares. But even those weren't as bad as the memory, were muted and easily pushed away in the light of day.

Don't open it.

He turned and regarded her solemnly. "You will remember my power, Arowyn. And from now on, you will do as you are told. You will show me respect. If you do not…once I am done with you, I'll lock you in with this memory for the rest of your life. I'll lock you in there and you'll be nothing but a screaming, tortured soul until the day you die."

"I will. I will." Her head bobbed crazily up and down. Right then she might have promised him her first born child, anything, to get him to leave. Just don't open that box…

His lips curved slightly. "I almost believe you. Yet, you have a habit of being forgetful. So, we will ensure you do not forget." Turning his back on her, he flipped open the lid…

A man grabbed her by the back of her shirt and jerked her backward so roughly she fell to the ground, her breath knocked out of her. When she looked up, they had surrounded her.

She scrambled to her feet, trying not to choke on the panic rising within her. The men were talking and laughing. She twirled around, counting. Six. A shuddering breath escaped her.

From their dress and speech, she was pretty certain the strangers were slavers, not other escaped slaves. "Rot it!"

One stepped forward. "Where are of the rest of you?"

She shook her head, afraid to speak, and certain she couldn't even if she wanted to. Terror held her frozen. She couldn't even breathe. Every muscle tensed, ready…even though she had no idea what to do…

"Arowyn."

She wanted to die. She couldn't stop screaming. Crying. Sobbing. The hands wouldn't stop. The pain just got worse.

"Arowyn!"

Then, the brief moment of respite, when suddenly gentle arms held her. Prince. Prince Prince Prince...

She couldn't stop crying, couldn't stop hurting. She still wanted to die, just to make it all stop, because *she* couldn't stop it. She wasn't strong enough and it was all about to start again.

"Arowyn!"

Kei killed them. Killed them all. The terror and the blood took her breath away and she choked on another sob. But...that voice. It wasn't right. It didn't belong.

Looking up, she saw Baelan struggling to push past...something in this little room in her mind. How did she get here?

Perhaps breaking from the memory helped him, as he suddenly surged forward, past her, and slammed the lid on the box closed.

Turning, he raised his hands as if to embrace her, and then dropped them, his gray eyes searching her face. After a moment, he simply took her hand and then they were flying, moving impossibly fast through the halls of her fortress until they broke free and she saw only darkness.

He tugged her hand again, gentle, but insistent. *Wake up.*

She did but didn't open her eyes. Arms held her tenderly and she remembered that, so curled into the warmth, resting her face on his chest as sobs choked their way out of her. He rocked her trembling body, pressing his cheek against her hair.

"It's over. You're safe. You're safe," he whispered.

Her crying slowed. The voice wasn't right. Even as she thought that, she realized nothing was right. She wasn't *then* anymore. It took a while to regain her composure, to stop the urge to scream and cry and wail, to settle her heartbeat and rapid breathing. She let him hold and rock her, whisper the soothing words.

Finally, she shifted and he stopped moving as she turned to look up at him. Baelan. Surprising, and yet somehow not. What surprised her was the lack of pity on his face. His glistening eyes, his brows drawn together, the downward curve of his lips spoke of sadness instead.

She took comfort in the man who killed her. Her life couldn't be more messed up than that.

She turned her gaze to a point over his shoulder. "How much did you see?" Her voice came out a raspy whisper, but he heard her.

"All of it," he answered after a moments silence. "It kept playing over and over..." Looking at him again she wondered why he now clenched his jaw and wouldn't look at her. "I couldn't get through it to you."

"He's gone..." It wasn't quite a question. Somehow, she just knew Damon wasn't there anymore.

"He didn't stay long."

Closing her eyes, she leaned her head against his chest again. "Did I scream out loud?"

"Yes, at first," he whispered.

Drawing in a deep breath, she sat up and rubbed her face. "Then we should go find the others. Before...before..." She cleared her throat and didn't finish, instead getting to her feet.

"They...were already here. Kei is helping set up a camp with them now." His voice softened, "Rest a while more."

"No," she snapped out. "Let's go." She smoothed back her hair and set her face. The memories were locked away again.

She was fine.

Rain began to softly fall.

She was fine.

∞ ∞ ∞

Only two tents did not make for a comfortable camp in the rain, though they rigged them up to make the most of them.

Terris came up to her, gripped her arm tightly, gave her a sharp nod of approval, and then left. She wasn't quite sure what that was about.

Kei pulled her aside and wrapped her in his arms, holding her tightly for a long time without saying a word. She could feel the anger within him though, so wasn't surprised when he later slipped away.

The rain stopped shortly after dark and they were able to all spread out again. Though she got a lot of looks, no one said anything to her and she was fine with that.

Hunting for dry wood for a fire, she ignored Baelan's quiet presence behind her. However, she didn't complain about the handful of little green lights floating around them.

"You truly haven't been with a man."

Baelan's sudden comment surprised her, and a bitter answer hovered on her lips until she looked at him and saw only sad contemplation on his face. "No."

He nodded once. "I apologize, for all my previous comments."

Her brows rose at that, and she didn't know what to say, so said nothing.

"I didn't know..." His voice trailed off and he cleared his throat. His gaze turned to hers and he smiled weakly. "I'm sorry."

She looked away, still unsure what to say. He'd seen her memory of the slavers attack. Many times. What they'd done. What they tried to do.

He remained silent for a while. "Many things make sense now." At her confused look, he continued, "You like to be held, it's a comfort to you. He held you when he pulled you away from them, when he made it stop. You don't like to sleep alone. You had nightmares, I would guess." He paused, ignoring her shocked face. "Someone close by would have helped with that. Made you feel safe."

"Yes," she answered quietly. "Both Prince and Kei did." Why was she telling him this?

He just nodded. "Would it upset you, if I felt your need, to offer such comfort?"

His words, all of them, rattled her more than they should have. "I… I don't know," she said honestly.

Strange, how things changed. Not long ago the idea would have repulsed her, but she'd seen a different side of the crazy Elf. After Damon forced the memories upon her, Baelan held her and she'd accepted it without a second thought. Even when she knew he wasn't Prince. Part of her wanted to say more, how she wouldn't need him, but she didn't know what would happen now, how being forced into the memories again might affect her. Affect her dreams. Nightmares.

Baelan gave her a soft, gentle smile before looking away. "I think I see some over there."

His gentleness confused her. She wasn't used to it, not from him. Not from most people. Anger and fury bubbled within her, just below the surface.

For some reason she felt no desire to unleash it on him.

She broke branches instead.

After they got a few good fires going and finally gotten everyone fed, Kei grabbed her hand and drew her into the trees. Her sight might have improved somewhat, but apparently was still not as good as Kei's. Another branch whacked her head and she cursed, pulling against his hand.

Instead of letting go, he stopped and pulled her close. His eyes glowed suddenly, startling her, and she remembered the first time he'd done that, long ago on a slave ship. It seemed to be the day for old memories.

His eyes searched hers for a long moment. "I'm so sorry," he finally whispered.

"It wasn't your fault."

His lips pressed together tightly, and he shook his head. "I wish you'd trust me."

"I do, Kei." She grimaced. "You know anger gets the best of me sometimes." She cupped his cheek. "And what he did to you, I can't forgive that."

"You have to let it go. Some things you just can't fight."

Dropping her hand, she turned her head away.

Taking her face in his hands, he turned her back to look at him and pulled her closer, resting his forehead against hers. Closing his eyes, he left her in darkness, yet still her heart lit at his attention.

"Come back to me, Kei," she whispered. "I miss you."

"I've been right here," he quietly returned.

"No, you haven't. I don't know where you've been, but it's not here."

His sigh blew across her face. "I'm trying. Everything is just so… It's hard, Aro. Sometimes I don't know who I am. I'm terrified I'm going to do something wrong. I don't want you to get hurt, or worse. Some days, I feel like I'm drowning under it all. But I *am* trying. I am. I just don't know what to do."

It was one of his longer speeches, and she appreciated that even as the earnestness of his voice made her breath catch. Wrapping her arms around him, she held him close. "I know. I know. I just miss us. How we used to be."

"I don't remember how we used to be." Tears filled her eyes and choked her throat. "I'm not the same anymore," he continued sadly, leaning back, his thumbs brushing across her cheeks.

"I'm not either," she admitted, brushing away tears.

"And you have someone else now."

Her brows rose at that. "Baelan? He's not you. He won't ever be you. *You* are my best friend. *You* are my brother."

A grin turned up one side of his mouth. "Really?"

She swatted his shoulder. "Forever beside you I shall stand."

"Together or apart, always I will be with you."

With a firm nod she smiled, too.

Leaning forward, he kissed her forehead and then drew away, slipping his hand into hers.

"Kei, if there's ever anything I can do, I will. You won't ever drown. I'll always be there to pull you free."

His eyes glowed brighter for a moment. He smiled and let out a long breath. "Thank you."

They walked silently for a while. She stepped to avoid a branch as they headed back to camp. "Were you jealous of Baelan?"

"That idiot Elf? Of course not."

She wasn't sure if she believed him or not.

∞ ∞ ∞

Are you awake?

She stared up at the stars and debated answering Roan. Finally, with a quiet sigh, she did. *Yes.*

I worried. I didn't hear from you tonight. When she didn't answer right away he continued, *You're up late.*

Can't sleep. She paused, forcing the words out. *Saw Damon today.*

It didn't go well.

No. It never does, she said quietly.

What did he do, Arowyn?

Since she never really kept anything from Roan, she told him of their meeting, and it wasn't as hard as she thought it would be. Except for the memory.

What did he make you remember? Tell me, Roan demanded softly.

She couldn't make the words come for a while. *The slavers,* she finally said. *That time they...found me in the forest.*

He knew what she meant, of course. She'd told him everything once. It'd been easier to tell, than to live it again. And again. And–

Ah, sweetheart, he murmured. *No wonder you can't sleep. I'll be fine.*

Yes, you will. I know you will.

She closed her eyes against the sting of tears.

But you aren't right now, the pirate continued. *I'll stay with you. As long as you need me. We don't even have to speak, just know that I'm here.*

Her heart clenched at his words. She wanted to tell him no. She didn't need him. *Thank you,* came out instead.

For a long time, she stared up at the stars, trying not to think. Not to remember. It wasn't like she was alone, with all the Fey scattered about their camp. Kei and Baelan slept near her, but neither very close. Kei hadn't offered to sleep beside her, and that broke her heart a little. Did he not remember how he used to? Or did he not want to?

Roan remained silent and she wondered if he'd fallen asleep, wherever in the world he was. *Are you still there?*

I am.

His words shouldn't have made her feel better, but they did. *Thank you.*

He chuckled. *Stop thanking me and go to sleep.*

I'm trying.

I would be there if I could.

It was a nice sentiment and she smiled slightly. *You have your own life to live, Roan. You can't drop everything to take care of me.*

*Yes, though I find lately…*his voice trailed off for a moment. *I would rather be there…with you.*

To keep me out of trouble?

Something like that. Another brief silence. *Now go to sleep.*

I can't close my eyes.

He was quiet for a while before he spoke again. *Then I will distract you.*

He started to sing.

She gasped, her eyes widening. She knew that song. She knew that voice. *It was you,* she blurted out, interrupting him. He'd been the mysterious singer while she was locked in riath dreams?

I thought you knew.

Emotion stole her words for a moment. *You sound so different. Don't stop,* she continued quickly.

As you wish, dear Arowyn.

He began to sing again.

Quietly.

His beautiful voice filled her mind until it was the only thing there.

Chapter 16

Grow Up

They reached Ridgeside by late morning, uncomfortable and wet from another bout of rain.

A Were met them at the edge of the settlement and Aro smiled when she recognized Cassia. When she'd been injured by the Vor and stayed at the settlement, Cassia had helped care for her. Deep brown eyes regarded her from a pretty face framed in short brown hair as she approached. The Were dropped her eyes and tipped her head.

"It is a pleasure to see you again, Aro-En."

"You as well, Cassia." When the woman smiled, Aro released a breath. They'd been friends once, but the whole alpha thing changed things so much.

"Come, let's get the Fey settled." Cassia motioned for them to follow. "We've the baths readied, and the supplies you've asked for. Things will be a bit cramped, but we can put them in the larger cabins. Do you mind staying in the room you had before?" Her eyes flicked to Baelan and Kei. "We can put a few more cots in if needed."

"That would be perfect, thank you."

"Would you like to bathe first?"

She shook her head. "I can wait."

"Very well. Rhee-En would like to see you now. If you'll follow me."

I could have used one now. I feel dreadful, Baelan grumbled.

I'm sure the Fey feel worse, she admonished him. *You'll live.*

She looked over at him in time to see his cheeks flush.

Of course. Apologies.

Kei and Garen went with the Fey. Another Were she didn't know took the horses, promising to care for them, have their things delivered to the cabin they'd use, and arrange for more cots.

Baelan followed her, strangely keeping quiet as Cassia dropped them off at another building before leaving with a smile.

Rhee-En waited inside, and Aro relaxed at the smell of hot food. As they entered he handed them each a blanket and gestured to the table set with food and steaming mugs of tea. "Welcome, again. Please, get comfortable and then we'll talk."

Baelan sighed wistfully at the alpha's beautiful voice, but thankfully didn't make any inappropriate comments this time.

"Have you talked with Terris?" She dried off her hair as best she could and then took a seat.

The alpha nodded, his lips pressed together, arms crossed, as he watched her.

She paused, suddenly sensing his anger. "And?" She spooned a mouthful of stew into her mouth.

"I have just finished speaking with the king."

Well, at least she didn't have to.

"We have much to discuss. Eat and we will start. You will stay the night." He raised his hand at her panicked look. "You need the rest," he said more softly, his sweet voice curling around her. "And there are many things we need to plan for you to be able to follow the orders of the Dragos." He spat the last words out, as though even saying such a thing repulsed him.

"I wish I could—"

"I know, Aro," he interrupted. "You have no choice in this. We are all quite aware of that fact." He frowned. "The king felt your pain. He is…unhappy."

She snorted. So was she.

Baelan tipped his head to the side. "Is that a pack thing?"

"Yes. alpha's, to some extent, feel the Were within their pack. The king does with all the Were, but more so with his alphas."

Baelan looked at her and she nodded. "I can get a general sense of how they are doing, and where they are. But I do need to *look*," she added.

"Yes," Rhee-En agreed. "Otherwise we would be bombarded with emotion. Something strong, however, such as fear or pain, is felt immediately."

"Fascinating," the Elf murmured.

Rhee-En cleared his throat. "The King has requested I accept volunteers of young Were to work with you." At her raised eyebrows, he spread his hands and explained. "You have Fey who wish to help, but the problem is communication as they can't mind-speak. Pairing them with Were, you will all be able to cover greater ground and move more quickly."

"We can give it a try," she agreed, unsure how well the young Were and Fey would work together.

They spent the rest of the morning and part of the afternoon going over ideas, discussing supplies they'd need, when the Fey not working with the search would begin camping and heading east, what supplies they would need, and so on. She spoke briefly to Bo and was happy to hear he had a load of supplies ready for them and worked out the details of getting them as well.

She liked to think neither man noticed her occasional bouncing leg or twitching fingers. For once not from riath, but from a growing sense of urgency to get moving again. To avoid Damon again. Avoid the memories. Avoid the pain...

Cassia popped her head in the door. "The baths are free. There is time for you two to wash up before dinner."

It was good timing, as they'd just been going over little details when she interrupted.

"Thank you," Aro said with a smile. She didn't begrudge the Fey getting cleaned up first, but she desperately needed a bath and clean clothes. Holding back a yawn, she added sleep to her list. If she could.

Baelan closed his notebook with a relieved sigh and she held in a laugh.

Rhee-En stood. "I will see you at dinner then."

"Thank you, for everything," she said sincerely as she headed for the door.

The alpha gave her a firm nod and then the door closed behind them.

Was it just me or did he seem...annoyed? Angry?

Baelan glanced her way as they followed Cassia to the bath house. *No, I noticed as well.*

She mulled that over. *It could have nothing to do with us.*

It could have everything to do with us.

She rolled her eyes but had to agree. *Maybe.*

The question is whether he is angry with us, or for us?

What?

Is he angry because of what Damon did? That you were hurt. Or angry the Were are being further dragged into this.

It was a good question, and one she didn't have an answer to.

Her bath was wonderful, even though the water wasn't all that warm. She scrubbed and scrubbed and scrubbed... When she realized what she was doing, her eyes flared red as her fury whipped out. Dipping under the water, she screamed.

Dinner brought back memories. The long tables set up with food, followed by music and dancing. The Fey seemed hesitant at first, but eventually ate and joined in.

The alpha did speak to them at dinner. However, she again noticed the conversation wasn't as friendly as it used to be. One shocking thing she learned was that Cassia was the leader of the settlement. She supposed she should have realized, it did make sense when she considered it.

Rain ended the evening sooner than expected, and she didn't mind at all. She didn't want to dance.

She paused as she stepped into their cabin for the night. For a moment a different view filling her vision. A single bed surrounded by chairs. The bed she almost died in.

A nudge from Kei made her blink and move inside. The room was cramped, the original bed moved over to make room for a bed beside it against the wall, another squished between the other wall and the feet of those beds. The chairs were gone. The few small tables pushed against the other wall.

Cassia stepped in behind them and lit a lamp. "I'm sorry it's so cramped. Do feel free to move things around." The woman frowned a moment, realizing there wasn't much moving that could be done.

"This is fine. Thank you, Cassia."

They said goodnights and Aro sat on the edge of the nearest bed with a groan and started taking off her boots.

"They do not seem at all surprised you will room with us," Baelan commented.

"It's…normal," Kei said quietly with a shrug.

She rubbed her temples. It wasn't so much she had a headache, her head just felt…full. Too full.

"Where do you want to sleep, Aro?"

Noticing she sat on her old bed, she sucked in a long breath. "Not this one." Standing up, she crawled over the bed and moved to the one against the wall next to it. Barely half an arm's length separated them. It amused her how they tried for some sense of propriety.

Lying down, she closed her eyes, listening to the boys move around and the rain fall on the roof. "Where's Garen?"

"It was crowded enough in here. He's with the Fey," Kei answered.

Yawning she rolled to her side, finding Kei sitting across from her, watching her with a worried look on his face. "You didn't sleep last night."

"I did a little. Eventually."

He nodded once and looked away, the worry fading to hardness. "We aren't children anymore, Arowyn."

Her brows drew down as she stared at him in confusion, wondering what exactly he meant.

"We must fight ourselves sometimes, to be stronger. To put aside the past and what we've been through."

She sat up straighter. "Are you telling me to just forget about it? Everything? *Everything* that has happened?" Her voice rose with each word as she clenched her hands in anger. Disbelief.

"Yes," he answered softly, still not meeting her gaze. "We need to grow up. Otherwise we'll never succeed."

"I don't control the nightmares, Kei!" She threw out an arm, indicating the room. "Do you recognize this? Do you?"

His jaw clenched. He wouldn't meet her gaze. "I do."

She wanted to scream. He'd crawled into her bed sobbing when he remembered what happened to her here. How could he be saying such things to her?

He straightened. "I am here, aren't I?"

"Are you serious!"

"I do not know everything you both have been through," Baelan interrupted from the bed at the foot of theirs. "But even what I do know, has been more than enough for one person to handle. A dozen people. That you have survived, that you find moments of happiness and to smile. That you are not insane."

He glanced over at her. "Is a testament to your strength. Both of you."

Kei glowered at the Elf. "It's not enough. We don't have time to—"

"You have each other," Baelan interrupted sharply. "Something you, I believe, have forgotten. Perhaps it is something you should remember again. Two is stronger than one, little Fey."

Kei's eyes flared gold. "I know that, *Elf*. But I'm not the one who can't sleep at night like a frightened little five-year-old."

Her head snapped back in shock. "How dare you..."

Baelan straightened, shadows falling over his face. "Arowyn has given up everything for you. For you," he said sharply. "She learned to use her rather frightening power. For you. She survived torture and riath addiction, so she could come back *to you*. All so she could heal the Fey, which are not her people. They are *yours*."

Kei grit his teeth, his mouth a firm angry line.

Baelan huffed a breath, shaking his head, and continued more softly, "And what have you done, little Fey. You are afraid of your own mind. She learned to walk in the minds of others to bring you back. You have not. Had I not been there yesterday, she would still be trapped in that horrific memory. Stop putting the blame where it doesn't belong." With that he closed his gray eyes, crossed his arms, and leaned back against the wall.

Kei stared at him, golden eyes flashing in anger, but didn't say a word.

Letting out a confused and angry breath, Aro settled back in bed. She couldn't think of what to say that wouldn't make things worse or start the argument again. She didn't want to say something in anger she couldn't take back.

She certainly hadn't expected Baelan to stand up for her. But then, she hadn't expected Kei's harsh words that started it all either. Tentatively, she reached for their bond to see what he felt and pulled away quickly. Anger. Shame. Fear. Confusion. At least under it all, she still felt his love. She didn't know what she'd do if she ever lost that.

For a long time, she just stared at the ceiling wishing she could just fall asleep and not think at all.

Apparently, it didn't matter how tired she was. Her eyes played a torturous game of close, snap open, close, snap open.

She heard Baelan rustle around, but still started when soft notes from his pipe met her ears. The gentle melodies calmed her, easing muscles she hadn't realized were tense.

"What song is that? I like it," she mumbled sleepily.

"Children's songs." Kei snorted from beside her but Baelan ignored him and continued, "Songs parents sing to their babes and tuck their little ones into bed with."

Thank you.

You are most welcome, Arowyn. I hope it helps.

So did she. She realized she hadn't spoken to Roan yet, and not wanting him to worry, contacted him before she fell asleep.

How are you today, Aro?

Tired. Better, maybe. She quickly told the general gist of her day, except her fight with Kei. She didn't even want to think about what he'd said.

You got much done. Very good. Do you think you will sleep tonight?

I hope so. I'm exhausted.

Would you like me to stay up with you again? I don't mind.

I think...I think I'll be fine. I'm so tired, and Baelan is playing his pipe. It's very soothing.

He chuckled. *I told you he would be helpful.*

His words brought a smile to her lips. *So you did. Good night, Roan.*

Goodnight, sweetheart.

Her thoughts drifted as she listened to Baelan's soft music. They turned to Roan. His words. How he had spoken. Where had the cold, bitter pirate gone? When had he started to speak so softly to her? She hadn't even noticed.

And when had he started to call her sweetheart?

∞ ∞ ∞

She woke from another nightmare with a gasp, chest heaving, and fingers clutching. Blinking in the darkness, panic pushed at her, heart racing, stomach clenching. Her eyes adjusted to the faint light in the room. Someone had left the lantern by the door on low.

Fingers squeezed hers and she blinked again, pulling herself fully from the nightmare.

Kei held her hand, his arm stretched over the short distance between their beds. He lay on his side facing her, his other hand under his cheek. A faint, sad smile curved his lips and he squeezed her hand again, tighter this time.

"Go back to sleep," he whispered. "I'm here."

She brushed hair from her face and then shifted closer to the edge of bed. Closer to him. Moving her other hand to rest over their clasped ones, she squeezed his hand in thanks.

"I'm sorry, Aro."

It was amazing how a few words and a gesture could change so much. Things weren't quite the same, but better. Her heart felt lighter.

When she woke again his absence was the first thing she noticed. Baelan shook her leg.

"I'm awake," she snapped, and then groaned. She still hadn't gotten enough sleep.

"The Fey has gone to get things moving." He paused. "I will go and find something for you to eat."

Yes, that stupid spell was annoying.

Sitting up, she rubbed at her face. "Wait."

He stopped before her and raised a perfect silver brow.

"Everything you said last night, it…helped, I think. Thank you, for your wise words."

He shook his head and laughed. "I might be old, and have the silver hair, but I never said I was wise. I'm not human."

"And that makes a difference?"

"Of course. Just because you're old doesn't make you wise." He leaned toward her. "Do you know what makes you wise? Two things: mistakes and having the time to think about them. When you're young, you make many mistakes, but you run off to your next adventure, not thinking about them at all. When you humans get old, your body fails you. You slow down, and you then have time to think. To understand. That is what makes you wise. Immortals, we are forever young. Some will slow down, some will think, but many of us just keep on running through our lives from one thing to the next."

Shaking her head in amusement, she grinned. Silly Elf. "And you said you're not wise? Hmm?"

He frowned at her, paused, and then shook his head. "Not in so many things that matter," he said softly. He bowed his head and retreated. "I will be back shortly."

Getting up, she fixed her clothes, put on her boots, brushed her hair and teeth, and checked her pack.

After Baelan returned and she'd eaten, they gathered up their bags and headed to find the horses.

The sun had barely risen but the settlement bustled with activity as Were and Fey ran about preparing for her people to head out once more. She didn't see Kei but didn't ask his whereabouts.

Once the horses were loaded, she and Baelan led them through the village, collecting Fey as they went.

Rhee-En approached, with Cassia a step behind and four young Were following.

"Good morning, Aro-En."

"And to you, Rhee-En. Cassia." She hated politics. Greet the alpha first, slight nod. None for her friend. It was difficult to force a smile when she turned back to Rhee-En. "Thank you all again, for everything you have done. It is most appreciated."

"I will pass your thanks on to the king as well," the alpha replied, slight admonishment in his tone. He turned away before she could reply. "These are our young volunteers. They are from the area, so we will change them out as you move. If that is acceptable."

"Yes, of course." None of the Were, two girls and two boys, looked older than her. The youngest she guessed to be maybe fifteen. She pushed back the unease in her stomach. They were only to be scouts. Nothing would happen to them.

She gestured them to come forward and made a short show of looking them over. "You have been told what is expected of you?"

The oldest nodded. "To assist in your search for the wild Fey. We are to also help with communication along the line."

She crossed her arms. "Yes. You are scouts only. If you come across a Fey, or a trace, you pass the information along and do not engage. Others will do that." She looked at them all. "Do you understand?" They shifted slightly, but all nodded.

"Perhaps they should be shown why," Kei said suddenly from her side. She turned to look at him and he raised a pale brow.

Returning her attention to the young Were, she thought of her brothers, how they'd once taught her. "The Fey are quick. They often hide up in the trees." She paused to let that sink in. "They will attack from above." She gestured to Kei, "And be armed like so."

Claws sprang from his fingertips and fangs from his mouth. The Were jumped, a few taking a step back.

She gestured them forward. "Come. Look. Those claws are strong, a sword won't cut through them. And deadly sharp. As are the fangs."

One of the girls came forward and gingerly touched one of Kei's claws. Jerking her finger back in surprise, she wiped off the blood. "Wither me."

"They can do a lot of damage," Aro continued. "They can kill," she said softly. "You are not their enemy, but they will know they are being tracked. You will appear to be a threat. They will attack. They can't help it, they won't be able to reason through the fury."

Stopping before them again, she held out her hands. "We don't want anyone hurt. You or them. Agreed?" She waited until they all nodded quickly. "Good. You understand. Track. Do not engage."

Well done, Aro, Garen said.

Thank you.

"Kei will give you a place on the line. It's time to head out."

Kei, claws and fangs once again gone, gave her a faint smile. People moved around her and she let out a slow breath.

Looking up, she saw Rhee-En watching her. A smile crossed his face and he gave her a slow nod of approval.

Chapter 17

Deadly Mistake

Weeks went by in a wet blur. She didn't remember last spring being so rainy, but they hadn't been so far south either. Between storms, showers, swollen rivers, and flooded lowlands, she felt permanently waterlogged. Despite the growing heat, and bugs, she heartily welcomed the arrival of summer.

They had found seventy-four Fey and covered more than a quarter of Rhee-En's land. It wasn't enough. Despite pushing everyone, pushing herself, to exhaustion, an obsessive fear still choked her. He would come back, eventually. It didn't matter how tired she felt, how she knew they traveled as fast as they possibly could, she knew it wouldn't be enough for the Dragos.

"Aro, wait!"

Grimacing, she stopped her pacing at Lissana's call. Sunlight barely brightened the area of their camp. Shortly, they'd all head out for another day.

The Fey jogged up to her and held out a wrapped package. "You forgot food," she said, pressing it into her hands. "You keep forgetting to eat," she admonished softly.

She nodded and forced a small smile at the Fey's concern. They didn't stop at noon any more but ate as they moved.

Something the others weren't overly happy about, but no one complained too loudly. At least not to her.

She'd been getting a lot of strange looks. She knew her push to move caused many to think she wasn't right in the head, even those who knew about Damon. Perhaps it was a reason why the Fey and Were shifted out in the rotation so often though.

Baelan walked up as Lissana left to find the Were she paired with. Rubbing at his tangled hair, he muttered quietly.

She ignored it since he did that now and then. Mostly just around her, but she'd heard quiet comments about the Elf who talked to himself. Since he quite literally was, she ignored the gossiping whispers as well. She'd become quite good at ignoring things.

"Kei was muttering nonsense again this morning," he finally said.

She snorted a bit and then rubbed her burning eyes. "We're all crazy," she said quietly, more to herself than the Elf.

Stepping closer, he brushed a lock of hair from her face, a wry smile crossing his lips. "We make good company then."

She huffed out a tired laugh. Straightening her shoulders, she glanced around the camp. "Looks like everyone's ready. Let's go."

Baelan sighed but followed her into the trees.

They moved along at a slow jog throughout the morning, silent except for occasionally checking in with the others. Sweat tickled the back of her neck as the day warmed.

Stop. An arm shot out across her chest, forcing her to do so.

Freezing in place, she looked around, trying to find out what the Elf had seen or heard. Finding nothing, she looked over to him.

Head tipped slightly to the side, his gray eyes scanned the forest ahead of them.

What is it?

I thought I caught the scent of– His lips pressed together suddenly and he grabbed her arm, pulling her back behind a large tree.

She dropped into a crouch, muscles tense. Not a Fey. They didn't hide from them. She pushed a rush of panic down. Had Damon returned?

He tapped her shoulder, gaining her attention. *Elf. Stay here.*

One?

He nodded once, and the dark, dangerous eyes of her assassin met hers. *Stay.*

Between one breath and the next he was gone, lost to the shadows. Impressive really, considering the brightness of the day.

She waited silently, the sound of her heart thumping in her ears. Shifting position, she peeked around the tree. Where were they?

Movement to the right caught her eye and she saw the Elf just as he spotted her.

The Elf began to raise his hand. A jolt of panic sped her heart. She hadn't drawn the blade Prince gave her and wouldn't have time to block his rune. She let loose the dagger she did hold, hoping it would distract him. His eyes widened in shock as his body jerked. He blinked, eyes dropping to the hilt protruding from his chest before rising to meet hers, brows drawing together in confusion.

"Why–?"

Words cut off as Bay appeared as a shadow behind him and swiftly snapped his neck.

Her body tensed as the body dropped to the ground.

"Nice shot, Arowyn. A bit more to the left."

"Something's not right," she whispered, her mouth suddenly gone dry as she replayed what just occurred in her mind.

225

Bay tipped his head to the side slightly, regarding her growing unease, before kneeling beside the body.

Panic rose within her as she moved to join him.

Terris! You forget to tell us of another Elf?

The Were chuckled. *Of course not. Heshel isn't a threat.*

Her breath froze in her chest, sweat suddenly beading her forehead. "Heshel."

Bay looked up at her. "Yes."

"Terris just said..." Her voice gave out and she tried again. "Said he wasn't a threat."

He nodded once, his lips set in a grim line.

"Oh rot. Rot rot rot." Hand on her forehead, she started to pace, her breaths coming in quick, harsh gasps. They'd just killed an innocent person. She'd killed...

She wrapped her arms around herself as nausea twisted her insides. Her vision swam and she squeezed her burning eyes closed as she bent over. "I can't breathe."

Bay's arms wrapped around her and he pulled her to his chest, holding her so tight it was almost painful. "Such things happen, Aro," he murmured against her hair.

"I killed him. I killed him." She choked on a breath, her fingers curling into his shirt. Pressing her face into his neck, she tried to keep control of herself and failed. A whimper started and turned into a silent wail as she clutched at him, her legs giving out under her.

Aro? What's wrong?

She couldn't find the words within her to answer Kei.

Bay held her more tightly, an arm around her waist, another her shoulders as he dropped to his knees, pulling her onto his lap. His raised his hand, cupping her head and holding it to him as well. His cheek pressed against her hair as he held her shaking body tightly and rocked.

"No, no. It was I who killed him," he whispered. "It's not your fault."

Tears burned her eyes but wouldn't fall. Perhaps because she shook so hard, or because she couldn't seem to get enough air.

"It's not your fault," he said again, and then began to softly hum as he continued to rock them from side to side.

Other hands pulled her away, and for a moment she met Kei's worried gaze before he tucked her against him and too, began to rock. She wanted to complain, to tell him she wasn't a child, but the words wouldn't come. She felt too terribly small and inadequate, as though she'd been trying to play an adult and failed.

After a time, the shaking stopped, her breathing slowed. The lump of guilt remained heavy in her stomach and clogged her throat.

"Bring her here."

She pushed away from Kei, though his hands guided her as they stood. She rubbed at her blurry eyes and then ran her fingers through her hair, forcing herself to just breathe.

"Come, my lovely." Baelan held out a hand to her, and without hesitation she took it, her fingers closing tightly around his. Kei's hand rested against her lower back as the Elf led her into the trees.

Her own feet stopped her as the giant tree came into view. The ancient rose high above the surrounding trees, its trunk so wide, even the three of them wouldn't have been able to circle it. Near its base, laid out amongst the rolling twists of roots, was the Elf.

The Elf she'd killed.

Heshel.

Her lower lip trembled and she sucked it between her teeth, biting down to keep it still.

"I will give him a proper burial. Unlike the others," Baelan added.

His gaze remained on her until she nodded. He turned to face the tree and raised his hands. Runes floated in the air as his hands gracefully moved around. Some landed on the trunk of the tree, others the roots, some settled on the body.

She watched as all began to softly glow and then jerked backward into Kei as the loops of roots began to writhe and move, some even looping over the body as it slowly began to sink beneath the ground.

Her heart pounded in her chest, and continued to do so even after the body disappeared and the lights faded away.

"Arowyn?"

She blinked, and looked up from the now empty ground to find Baelan watching her with a worried frown.

"He rests beneath the tree now."

Managing a nod, she forced herself not to look again. Kei rubbed her back and she closed her eyes. Rot, she was tired. So tired.

"We should stop for the day," the Elf said, his voice quiet and weary.

"I agree," said Kei.

"Yes," Baelan said again, his voice deeper.

Opening her eyes, she caught the assassin's stormy gaze before he disappeared once again.

Kei frowned at the Elf, his brows drawing together.

The familiar panic started to rise within her. *She needed to move, stopping was bad, the Dragos would come...* But for once the thoughts weren't loud enough, so she pushed them away.

Kei took her hand and pulled her through the trees. Her mind numb, she followed, not paying attention.

"Sit. We're going to make camp here. The others will be here soon."

She dropped onto her butt and pulled up her knees, wrapping her arms around her legs.

Kei crouched before her and took her face in his hands. "It's not your fault, Aro. Sometimes, things like this happen."

Pressing her lips tightly together, she nodded sharply. His words didn't help. Guilt ate at her insides like some hungry starving beast. Kei sighed and backed away. Closing her eyes, she dropped her forehead to her knees and concentrated on just breathing.

Camp sounds grew louder as the Fey and young Were returned. Even trying to block everything else out, she heard the confusion of everyone wondering why they had stopped.

"Where is she? Where is she!" Terris' increasingly shrill voice broke her out of her guilt-ridden thoughts. Clenching her fists, trying to hold in her sudden anger, she rose.

The beta strode through camp, and once spotting her, increased her pace. "What did you do? Where is he?"

Aro moved forward to meet her, squaring her shoulders. "Dead."

The one word froze the Were in her tracks, her startled face paling in shock.

Closing the distance between them, Aro didn't try overly hard to stem the rising fury within her. Red and black. Anger and rage. "What did you think would happen?" Terris' mouth opened and closed. "I told you," Aro ground out angrily, her voice rising, "to tell us if you came across an Elf. All you had to do, was tell us he was safe!"

Gathering her composure, the Were snarled. "You should have known!"

"How? How? Stop and have a talk first? Every Elf we've come across has tried to kill us! I've been kidnapped and tortured by them!" She sucked in a breath. "When he raised his hand," her own hand went up, "I thought he was about to cast a rune. I've been hit with rune magic before. I wasn't going to experience that again."

"You are a menace, you freak! You shouldn't be here!"

She clenched her fists again. "Well, I am. *Your* king approved it. I know you don't like me, and I don't rotting care. This is just as much your fault as it is mine."

Terris got in her face. "Don't you dare blame this on me, you despicable human!"

"Stop being so petty." She was pretty sure her eyes were glowing now as the anger continued to flare within her. "Take responsibility for your...your inaction."

The Were snarled and lunged, but Baelan quickly stepped in, yanking her back.

"Don't touch me, outcast."

"Get out of my camp," Aro snapped.

Terris raised her chin. "You forget this is *my* land," she said haughtily.

"I may not be *your* alpha, but I *am* alpha and I outrank you. Leave. Now."

"You will regret this."

Regret. Yes. She would for all of her life.

"Pups, come."

The young Were looked from her to Terris, eyes wide. Grinding her teeth, she gave a slight nod, letting them go. She wouldn't drag them into this.

The Were left. The Fey stared. The sudden awkward silence calmed some of her anger, but not all. Rot. Now what would happen?

Clutching at her hair, she spun away from everyone and let out a scream of frustration. Arms wrapped around her, and after a moment she let out a long breath, tired. Defeated.

"I'm so sorry, Kei."

He turned her in his arms before embracing her again. "Everything will be fine. Don't worry."

She looked up at him. "Are you sure?"

"Yes. I am." His glowing golden eyes stared into hers for a long moment. "Let's get something to eat. We'll rest and figure out what to do next."

Taut muscles relaxed. She trusted him. He had to be right, he just had to be. Everything would be fine.

∞ ∞ ∞

Aro-En.

She knew it was coming, that Rhee-En would find out sooner rather than later and she'd have to deal with him, but her mouth still went dry and her heart began a frantic beat when the alpha snapped out her name.

Tell me. Tell me what happened. Right now.

She did, tripping and stuttering over her words in her haste and panic.

It was her fault. She knew it was her fault. But it wasn't *only* hers. It had been a mistake, an accident.

When she finished, silence filled her mind and she wondered if that was it. If he'd say anything at all. *I...I suppose I should speak with the king,* she finally said quietly.

No. His angry voice snapped out, startling her. *I will speak with him. I will tell him what you've done. Perhaps he will see some sense now.*

She didn't argue. Taking a shuddering breath, she opened her eyes. One thing for certain, Rhee-En's voice was not as beautiful when he was furious.

A relieved sigh slipped out when he said nothing else. From his anger, she assumed he also had been friends with the Elf. She rubbed at her face, wishing she could rub the guilt away.

"What's wrong?"

"Rhee-En is not happy," she answered Kei.

He frowned, but then shrugged. "He will have to deal with it." Gesturing to the map on the ground before them, he continued, "Let's finish."

With Terris gone, they'd lost their forward scout. They debated sending Garen ahead, but decided it wasn't worth it. They had the map, which was fairly accurate. The loss of the four young Were caused more problems. They were left with no choice but to shorten their line, spreading Kei and Garen between the Fey of the group so they could still all communicate.

Aro's leg bounced as she sat on a fallen log, waiting for dinner to finish cooking. Guilt still clung to her insides and the thought of food made her nauseous. Despite that, panic and restlessness kept creeping up on her. Too much time wasted.

Kei kept her busy with plans, going over their supplies, checking their gear. He even sent her off to the nearest stream to get cleaned up.

Thump thump thump. Her foot just wouldn't stop.

"Baelan, watch the food."

"Of course."

She looked up at Kei, then at his hand held out to her. He wiggled his fingers and a small smile curved her lips as she took his hand and let him pull her up. He led her away from camp, not letting go of her hand. Somehow, it made her feel better.

When he stopped and turned to her she squeezed his hand, not wanting to let go.

"I'm sorry," he said softly, his eyes searching her face.

"Did you know? That this would happen?"

He looked away, his brows drawing together, before shaking his head. "No."

She let out a slow breath and nodded.

"It will get easier."

Lips pressed together, it was her turn to look away.

"It will, Aro. I promise."

Clenching her teeth, she jerked her head back around, angry words on her tongue. The look on his face stopped her cold. The guilt. The pain.

"You..." Words failed her, but she didn't need them anyway. Sometimes she forgot about Kei's past, how he'd spent years wild before her father found him.

Kei nodded, and then pulled her close. "Unfortunately, it's something I have remembered," he murmured. They held each other tightly, heads pressed together. Understanding.

Eventually he pulled back. "After you eat, try to get some rest."

"I don't think I could sleep." She didn't want to imagine what her nightmares would contain now.

He tucked a lock of hair behind her ear. "You need to slow down, Aro." When she shook her head, he grasped her face, holding her still. "I'm serious."

"Kei, I can't."

"Use the arrow to heal the Fey. Push too hard and it will break. Not enough and be too late. Understand?"

Rotting prophecy. "I understand," she whispered.

He rested his forehead against hers. "I can't lose you, Aro. Don't break."

Her breath caught in her throat as she wrapped her arms around him again. Warmth filled her. Even though the guilt wasn't gone, or the fear of Damon, she still had Kei. Though she worried a little, that she'd already broken.

∞ ∞ ∞

Insects chirped away as she stared up through branches, watching the odd star she could see. The fire popped and crackled, and murmured voices rose and fell, too quiet for her to make out any words. She wondered if the Fey spoke of her. Of what happened. What did they think of her now?

It didn't matter, really. After healing, she didn't have much to do with them all. The others, Kei and Garen, and even Baelan, dealt with their growing group of Fey. She was usually too exhausted to wander through the camp to speak with them. That was her excuse, anyway. She thought it a rather good one, and partially true. The looks they gave, awe and adoration…they made her so uncomfortable she just wanted to hide.

She pulled her cloak closer and shifted on the hard ground. Once the sun set, it took the day's warmth with it. Her eyes burned with fatigue. Tired, so tired.

She rubbed at her forehead. She should contact Roan, he'd worry if she didn't, but dreaded doing so. Dealing with a lecture, or worse, would be more than she could handle. Rot, he might even have known the Elf she killed. Her hand moved to her stomach as another wave of nausea rolled through her.

A wet nose nudged her hand. *You think too much.*

I know.

Talk to Roan. He makes you feel better. Then you can get some sleep.

She couldn't disagree with Garen. *It's irritating when you're right.*

He chuckled. *I'll be here.*

As the large Were settled down beside her, she took a deep breath to calm her nerves and closed her eyes. Maybe the pirate wouldn't notice how early it was. *Are you busy?*

After a brief wait he replied, *I'm never too busy for you, Arowyn.*

His words made her smile.

What's wrong?

Her smile faded. She should have known. She struggled to find words. *I suppose you already know.*

I've heard some things.

That was unexpected. She'd only been teasing. Also, a bit unnerving. So, he did have spies within the Were? She'd considered it a possibility, but for him to have already heard… either he had more than she thought, or the news spread quite quickly through the pack. *Then I don't have to tell you and we can leave it that I had a rotting awful day.*

You know that's not how it works. Tell me what happened.

She opened her eyes, startled at the anger in his voice, and cursed out loud.

Garen raised his head, his ears flicking toward her.

She grimaced but closed her eyes again. Sometimes she wondered if this was his own form of torture for her, always making her speak again of the horrible things that befell her. Gritting her teeth, she did as he asked, letting it all out in a jumble of quick words as he listened silently.

By the time she finished, she'd clenched her teeth so hard her head hurt. Keep control. If she broke down now she would never survive it.

She lay there, eyes closed in the dark, waiting for him to speak.

To say something. Anything.

Finally, *It was not entirely your fault.*

She had no response to that. His words certainly did nothing to lessen the guilt still clawing within her. He said nothing else and she wondered if that was it. His tone had been matter-of-fact. Neutral. Perhaps he'd finally had enough of her and her stupid mistakes. She couldn't blame him.

It hurt her heart though, because lately he'd lost his coldness. He comforted her when she needed it, and a part of her hoped for that again tonight.

The silence dragged on and finally she couldn't take it anymore. *Goodnight, then*, she said hesitantly.

I'm not done with you yet, his voice snapped out. *You said Baelan knew the Elf. Did he recognize him before or after he was dead?*

I...have no idea. Confusion filled her from his question, his tone of voice.

Details are important, he admonished. *Heshel has not been back to Rivenward for decades. He could not have been sent by the Elven queen. He is also well known as a gentle soul. He would not hunt outcasts. Baelan would have known all of this, so why did he kill him?*

235

Jen Wylie

I don't know, she began, flustered. *Maybe he didn't recognize him. Or maybe he saw me attack and thought I was in danger.*

Or perhaps he killed him intentionally.

Why would he do that?

To cause problems. To become closer to you. There are many possible reasons. Do not fall for his trickery. He is old, and smart, and a survivor.

You said I could trust him. You insisted. It took a while, but now that I do, you're saying I shouldn't?

He is your servant. He will not harm you and will protect your life, that you can trust in. Anything else is not real, Arowyn. He does not care for you. You are his master and stand between him and freedom.

Everything he said made her more and more confused. Worry knotted her stomach. She *had* been getting closer to the Elf lately. Was it all a lie? She didn't know what to believe.

I swear I can hear you disagreeing with me. You never see the bad in people. Always so trusting, he said, irritation evident in his voice.

It's not a bad thing, she said defensively.

For you it is. You are destined for more, Arowyn. Do you understand?

No. Because no one told her anything. She wanted to throttle the man.

I don't know why I bother sometimes, he muttered. *You are such a frustrating child.*

His words were like a smack to the face. A punch to the gut. The fury within her rose quickly, protectively. *Don't bother then. I don't need you! Obviously, you don't care about me either.*

Don't be ridiculous. After all I've done for you—

Oh yes, I know, she interrupted scathingly. *You remind me often enough.*

What is that supposed to mean?

You have no problem keeping me in the dark, not telling me things, but telling me what to do, what to say, how to rotting feel! Maybe I shouldn't trust you either!

The silence echoed in her ears after their shouted words. *How can you say that?* His tone was softer now, but still cold, angry. *A relationship is built on trust. I thought we had that.*

What relationship? You're just a friend, if that, she snapped out, still furious with him.

A friend? A friend? Is that still all I am? The disbelief, the absolute anger in his words, shocked her silent.

He let out a frustrated yell, startling her. She easily imagined him stomping around his room, maybe throwing or hitting something in his anger.

I can't deal with you right now, he spat out.

Then there was once again, only silence.

Jen Wylie

Chapter 18

Inner Pain

Aro flung herself at the Fey, pinning her body to the ground as Kei grabbed the girl's hands, preventing the Fey from slashing her into pieces.

Hand on the girl's chest, she pulled, and pulled, and pulled. Her vision swam with black and red. Raw, wild fury vibrated within her so strongly she needed to clench her teeth to keep them from knocking together.

She should have let go of what she'd taken from the other two first, but there hadn't been time...

Finally, there was nothing more to pull, and she collapsed onto the Fey, breaths coming in fast pants as her entire body trembled. "Kei..."

Hands rolled her to the side, off the Fey, and she closed her eyes. She needed to get up, to let it all out, but couldn't find the strength to move. "Rot, she was strong," she muttered.

The girl started sobbing.

"Shh, you're safe," Kei whispered. "What's your name?"

"A-ava."

"You'll be just fine now, Ava. Cano!"

Hands pressed against her cheeks and she opened her eyes to Kei's worried face. "Come." He helped her up and hooked his arm around her waist as she stumbled through the trees away from the chaos of the new Fey being helped by those she'd already healed.

She stumbled and fell to her knees. Leaning forward and bracing her hands on the ground, she started to dry heave.

"Rot, Aro," Kei whispered, running a hand over her back. "Let it out, you'll feel better."

Opening her eyes, she stared at her hands. Blinked. Faint smokey tendrils slid around her fingers. Were they really there? She was going rotting insane. Insaner? Wonderful.

Sucking in a deep breath, she closed her eyes, harnessing the wild power ricocheting through her. Curling her fingers into the dirt, she pushed it out.

The force of it threw her backward, landing awkwardly on Kei as dirt rained down on them.

"Haven't done that in a while," she wheezed out, wondering how big a hole she'd left in the ground this time.

Kei grunted and shifted out from under her until he rested beside her instead. "Better now?" His golden eyes searched hers until she nodded. He let out a faint sigh and a small smile curved his lips. He leaned forward, pressing a light kiss to her dirty forehead. "Good."

Smiling, she closed her eyes, feeling giddy. He was back. Her Kei was back. She could handle anything now that she had him with her once more.

He brushed hair and dirt from her face, until laughing, she smacked his hand away.

"Rest a bit. I'll send the Elf over to deal with the hole."

Staring up through the trees, she saw not much of the day remained. "I'll have Garen look ahead for a good campsite."

"Good." He sprang to his feet and ran off as she contacted the Were.

"My lovely, what a delightful mess you've made."

Craning her head, she looked over to see Baelan standing with his hands on his hips, head tilted to one side as he looked at the ground before them.

She pushed herself up and walked over to him, brushing dirt from her clothes. Her nose wrinkled at the size of the hole. "Can you fix it?"

He flashed her a saucy smile. "Of course."

She stepped away, crossing her arms and leaning against a tree as she watched him send out runes, pushing dirt back into the large hole.

"What happened the other night?"

She glanced over at him and then away. "Nothing."

"Something did," he disagreed cautiously. "You've been acting...different toward me the last few days."

Had she? Roan's words bounced around in her head again. He confused her so much, she didn't know what to think anymore. "Did you know Heshel?"

He paused for a moment before continuing to work. "We had never met. I'd known of him."

She remained quiet, thinking his reply over. He walked up to her, his brows drawn together. "So, it does have something to do with the Elf. I'd thought so at first, that you were angry I killed him, but...something wasn't quite right. What is it?" He awaited her reply, gray eyes regarding her calmly.

She met his gaze. "Did you know who he was, before you killed him?"

"No." When she continued to stare at him he continued, "I saw his hand rise. I saw you attack. I killed him."

"Why did you wait until then? You were gone a while."

He frowned. "I wanted to see if he was a threat. I *do* understand not every Elf is trying to kill us," he ground out.

Looking away, she nodded. His words made sense. But then they would. If he was playing with her, he'd have this sort of conversation already planned out.

He huffed in irritation. "You don't believe me. You think I did this on purpose."

"Roan said–"

"Roan doesn't know anything," he snapped. "I cannot cause you harm, Arowyn. This whole rotting disaster has put you in distress. It's slowed us down, causing you worry. The Were are now an issue. There is no way I would have intentionally caused this. It is impossible."

She rubbed her forehead. Her brain was going to explode. His words made sense, but Roan's had, too. Maybe Baelan hadn't done this on purpose, but what else might he have done? Or do?

Turning on his heel, he walked over to her hole, now covered in loose dirt. He began stomping it down angrily. "You don't trust me now. That is the issue."

It wasn't a question, but she whispered her response anyway. "No, I don't."

He shook his head, silver hair flying from side to side. "That Roan causes you more problems..." He didn't finish, just kept stomping out his anger.

"Well, we had a fight. I don't think we're talking right now." Maybe. She hadn't heard back from him since that night. Perhaps she'd hear from him tonight? She wasn't sure if she wanted to or not.

"Speaking of someone not to trust," he muttered, putting his hands on his hips and looking away. He suddenly clapped his hands together once. "They will still be a bit. Lesson time."

Her mouth opened and closed in surprise at his sudden change. "What?"

"We need to talk." He strode over to her and then dropped to the ground. "Sit."

Still confused, she sat in front of him. He held out a hand, palm up. She ignored it.

With a weary sigh, he shook his head. But left his hand out. "When you invite someone into your mind, or go into another's, it is a form of intimacy. You are vulnerable." He leaned forward slightly. "Which is why you don't *ever* do either if you don't trust them. *Really* trust them. Or know you are way more powerful than they are. Understand?" She nodded quickly. "Good. One reason, is that if you pay attention, if you know how, you'll find that you can know if they are lying. You can feel it here." He tapped his chest with his other hand. "So...come."

Still, she hesitated. She'd just said she didn't trust him. He said not to do this if she didn't.

"Arowyn," he said in exasperation. "I can't hurt you. Trust that at least."

She looked down at his outstretched hand, his fingers wiggled, urging her to take it. She supposed it didn't really matter. How many times had she gone into his mind, and him into hers, already?

Setting her hand in his, she noted the blood-stained bandages around his wrist. Had she been causing him pain again somehow?

"When you're ready."

Entering his mind, she immediately froze. Where was the little field of flowers? She spun around, finding herself surrounded by dark dead trees with grasping limbs. "Baelan?"

Spinning again, she suddenly spotted him between the trees and ran toward him.

He turned around as she approached, and she froze, her voice catching in her throat. The scar on his cheek bled. Bruises darkened his face and eyes. And his eyes... they were so empty. Yet, most horrifying of all were the runes on his neck and wrists slowly dripping blood.

"Have you come to punish me?"

His voice startled her as much as his words. Low and raspy, as if he'd been screaming for hours, days.

She didn't know this Baelan, but she could guess what part of him he was.

243

He continued speaking as she struggled for words. "Would you like me to scream?" He took a slow step toward her, his head tipped slightly to one side in question. "Cry? Beg?"

"Baelan," she whispered, tears catching in her throat. She didn't know what to do. "No. I don't…"

He nodded once and straightened. "Ah, I am to take it like a man."

A tear slipped down her cheek as she moved forward, the desire to just hold him overcoming her.

"Go on now."

She turned to find another Baelan, who gave her a weak smile, though she didn't miss how it wavered, just a bit.

"So sorry, my lovely. You shouldn't have had to see that."

Her head swung around quickly, just in time to see the other Baelan limp off into the trees. She watched until he disappeared, trying to gather herself and failing.

"You're breaking my heart," she whispered, finally looking at him as he stepped to her side.

He regarded her quietly for a moment, his usual happy face solemn. "That has never been my intention. This," his waved his hand around them, "you were never meant to see."

"I don't know how to help you."

A faint smile crossed his lips as he shook his head and then looked away. "Don't even try, Aro. I am well beyond any kind of help. I am what I am." Clearing his throat, he looked back at her and held out his hand. "Come, we've things to do."

Slipping her hand into his, she nodded, remaining quiet. She didn't know what to say.

They walked for a short while before he suddenly squeezed her hand. "It is…nice. That you would think to help me. I…appreciate that."

Heat burned her cheeks, so she kept her gaze on the ground. Crunch. Crunch.

Finally, they reached his safe place and her tense muscles relaxed as they stepped into the flowers. "I'm sorry, I don't know how I ended up over there."

He shrugged, not meeting her eyes. There was a brief, awkward silence before he turned to her again. "How are you doing?"

"Fine."

His lips pressed together at her lie. His gaze flicked over her shoulder and he huffed out a breath.

"I worry," the assassin said from behind her and she whirled around in surprise. "I worry you will hesitate now. To kill." He stepped closer and grasped her chin in his hand, forcing her gaze to remain on him. "You must not, Arowyn."

Heart beating quickly, she swallowed the lump in her throat and nodded. He dropped his hand and stepped back.

"Wait!" When he paused, she scrambled for something to say. "Do you feel no remorse?"

His dark gaze turned...haunted, before he looked away. "One becomes...numb, after a while."

Numb. She wished she felt numb.

"Arowyn." He paused. "I am sorry that I cannot protect you from everything. I would, if I could."

"I know." For some strange reason, she did.

"Don't hesitate," Bay said again and then turned and walked away.

Baelan cleared his throat and she turned around.

He forced a smile. "Now. This won't take long. Close your eyes and just...feel. Listen. Ready?"

Eyes closed, she nodded.

"My name is Baelan. I am human. I am twenty years old. The sun is purple." She smiled slightly. "Can you feel it?"

Frowning, she shook her head.

"Concentrate. On me. You know me. Listen to my voice. How I speak. Feel my words as you hear them. Listen for the truth. Listen for the lie." Her brows drew together as she concentrated. "I have ten sisters," he continued slowly. "Carrots are my favorite food."

A strange whisper of something came over her at his obvious lies. An unsettling feeling in her chest. It wasn't strong, but if she paid attention she could sense it.

"I am an Elf. My hair is brown. The Queen is insane."

"I feel it."

"Good."

She opened her eyes. "Does it work with mind-speech too?"

"Unfortunately, no." He grinned. "Feel free to lie all you like."

She laughed, shaking her head, though his comment made her a bit uneasy.

His smile faded away. "I killed him to protect you. No other reason."

Nothing in her chest, not even a twinge. She nodded.

"You can trust me," he said softly. "I will never hurt you."

Also truth. For some reason though, the words send a shiver up her spine.

His gaze flitted around her face for a moment and then he relaxed, leaning back and running a hand through his hair.

"You know, if I was going to cause trouble, I'd seduce you away from Shael," he said with a sudden wicked grin.

Startled, she looked over at him. His words made her frown. "I thought you said he'd never come, that I wasn't good enough for him. Why would you bother?"

"That doesn't mean he doesn't care for you in some way. I am here, after all. It would most certainly make him angry."

"You told me that you and Prince were friends."

"We were. And then we weren't." He smiled faintly and then looked away. "Some days I hate him. Most days... I'm just angry, because things could have been different. If some things hadn't been said, hadn't been done. Some days I'm just sad, when I think of how it was before and how it could have been if we both weren't such arrogant idiots."

She snorted at that, but sobered when he turned to her with such sad eyes. They reminded her of Prince, and she wondered if sometimes, his eyes had been so sad because he'd been thinking of his lost friendship. "Maybe you can be friends again one day," she said.

His laugh was sharp and brittle. "Some things you can't forget, Arowyn. Some things can't be undone...or unsaid. They just fester and the best you can do is try not to think of them too often."

"I'm sorry," she whispered.

"What's done is done, as they say. Sometimes what is broken can't be fixed." He grinned and waved a hand around. "What might have been won't ever be. And all that nonsense. Come, the others should be ready to head out by now."

She wanted to ask him more questions, but saw the shadows of past hurt still on his face so held her tongue and just returned to her own mind.

Though she now believed Baelan hadn't killed the Elf to cause trouble, other doubts rose in her mind. Meeting the other him, the way he directed their conversation, left her suspicious. Had he wanted her to pity him? If so, then why? What would he gain? She had too many questions without answers. The only thing she could do was pay attention, not let her guard down, and be careful. Eventually, he'd slip up or she would figure it out.

∞ ∞ ∞

Kei and Baelan walked quietly beside her as they approached the village. Being so close to a Were settlement, she'd called in the Fey and a crowd of them now followed behind her. Garen roamed around them, ensuring no stragglers got left behind or into mischief.

Rhee-En had finally spoken to her again the night before, instructing her to meet with him when they arrived at the village of Hollowbrook.

Though originally, she planned to collect supplies and head out immediately, he told her they would stay the night. She didn't argue. It'd been four days since the incident with the Elf.

Heshel. She closed her eyes for a moment. His name was Heshel.

Rhee-En hadn't spoken to her since his original rant until the night before. His tone hadn't changed much. She wasn't looking forward to this meeting.

She still hadn't heard from Roan, either. Which set her stomach in knots for an entirely different reason. She tried to send him an apology twice, but he never responded. Since she doubted he'd been asleep at the time, he was ignoring her. It hurt. She wanted to make things right. Regret for what she said filled her more and more every day. She hadn't meant it. He *did* mean something to her, was more than just a simple friend, but she didn't know how to put her feelings into words. Thinking about what he was to her just left her feeling confused, which was why she avoided it.

Were came to meet them and she helped get their large number of Fey settled at the edge of the village. The stiffness in her shoulders eased somewhat when the Were gave them no problems. They weren't overly friendly but were courteous enough and ensured they were comfortable.

Looking over the growing group, she rubbed at her forehead and nudged Kei. "It's getting a lot harder to move. We're finding a lot more now."

He understood her unspoken question. "A few weeks. Then we'll go. It's not time."

Of course it wasn't. He kept saying that but would never tell her when it would be time for them to go to Furia.

Nerves fluttered in her stomach, but she smiled, excited he'd finally given her something. A few weeks. Soon they would make their way to Furia. City of the Fey.

"Rhee-En has sent for us," Baelan said, walking up to them.

Her stomach churned, but she followed him into the village, Kei trailing behind her. A Were met them and led them to a small log cabin. He left them at the door and she paused a moment, gathering her courage.

Kei's fingers briefly brushed her lower back. "It will be fine," he whispered.

She met his golden gaze with her own and then nodded once, before opening the door and walking inside. It took her eyes a moment to adjust to the dim room. It was small with a table and a few chairs. The alpha sat in one, a mug of something in front of him.

He didn't rise as they entered.

Gesturing them to sit, she did, Kei and Baelan to either side of her.

He didn't offer them anything to eat or drink. Which rather relieved her, she didn't know if she'd have been able to hold it down. However, both inactions spoke of disrespect, and she wasn't quite sure what to do about it. Rhee-En was not Terris, but a strong alpha.

"You look ill, Aro-En." His voice was still delicious, but contained a slight biting edge.

Straightening her shoulders, she raised her chin. "It's been a difficult few days."

His blue and gold eyes regarded her calmly from his scarred face. "So it has," he finally said. He shifted forward. "Well, then. Update me on the Fey and your plans."

Relaxing slightly, she cleared her throat and did so, watching his face carefully as she spoke. He didn't give anything away and she wondered again how old he was. Centuries at least.

When she finished he glanced down at his mug and then took a long drink before leaning back and giving them his attention again.

"We have word from our people in the human cities of growing unrest within Rivenward."

Her brows rose at the topic. Why was he telling her this? The reason nearly stole her voice. "I...see. The Queen is getting even crazier?" Inside, she held back her panic, barely. Was Prince in the middle of it? Was he even still alive?

The alpha frowned. "It would seem so." He paused.

"Is he dead," she asked quietly, eyes going to her hands.

"No, Aro-En. No," he said, his voice suddenly softer. "I'm afraid I have few details, but I do know that."

She nodded, relief letting her breathe again.

"In the north," Rhee-En continued, changing the subject, "The Frans have now taken four cities and are marching on a fifth."

Shock nearly knocked her out of her chair. She'd heard they were attacking in the north, but to have moved so quickly... "Wither me. How big is their army?"

"Quite large and growing with each new city they take. Most of those they don't kill are forced into it."

"They're not going to stop," she whispered, the sickness in her stomach rising again.

"At some point, they will have to. For winter surely. They barely have supplies for the army they have now. They are only surviving from pillaging as they move. Once the snows come, many will die."

She frowned. The Frans weren't stupid. "The crops have been planted. If they stop in the fall and use the slaves and army to harvest they won't be in nearly as dire straits."

Rhee-En stared at her for a long moment before cursing under his breath.

Guess he hadn't thought of that.

"Are the Were going to do anything?"

"We've offered our assistance and it was refused," he said, his voice nearly a growl. "The most we can do now is move refugees south through the forest when a city is attacked."

"The Were are monsters, so are the Frans," she continued quickly, "But I guess they are keeping with the enemy they know. Someone is bound to accept."

"I hope they do before it's not too late."

She bit her lip, mind whirling. The Frans had already attacked the northern Were. If they took all of the coast... "They'll go after you next." It would be a slaughter...

"Probably, and it couldn't be worse timing."

Or maybe not. She sat back, grimacing. By the time the Frans took the entire coast, the Vor would be all over them from the east.

"The King has plans in place," the Were continued more lightly. "I just wanted to keep you informed."

"Thank you." She bit her lip, worried about Bo. She'd have to make sure he knew what was going on. And get him and Elaina out of Westport if she needed to. The way things were going, it would be best to send them across the sea.

"Is there anything else you would like to discuss?"

"No." She pushed her chair back, but then stopped and looked up at the alpha, uncertain if she should speak or not. His head tilted to the side, noticing her hesitation. "I'm sorry," she finally managed to say, her voice barely a whisper.

"I know," he answered quietly. "However, you will speak with the king directly from now on, rather than going through me."

He was still angry. She couldn't really blame him. Forcing a faint smile, she nodded her agreement.

"I'll give you back the young Were. But Aro-En, if something happens to them, I'm holding you responsible."

She opened her mouth to agree, but then paused as his words sank in. "No. Keep them." At his frown, she continued, "The prophecy did not mention Heshel. It doesn't mention them." She wasn't sure about that, but anyway... "I can't control if we are attacked by Vor. Or Elves. Or if they'll get too close to a Fey." Her voice rose. "And I certainly can't control whatever Damon might do. So, no. I won't be held responsible for things I can't control."

His brows rose and for a moment, she thought a smile twitched at his lips. He bowed his head toward her slightly. "You are correct. Very well."

"The Were are my friends," she continued, her voice soft and earnest, wishing he'd believe her. "I would never let anything happen to any of them if I could prevent it."

"I believe you. As I said, very well. They are yours again."

Oh. She hadn't realized that's what he meant. She stood and concentrated on pushing the chair back in to hide her embarrassment.

Walking back to where the Fey camped, she ran the conversation over in her mind and worry suddenly clamped around her chest, making her stumble. She'd never realized how she possessed so very little control over her life.

Kei grabbed her elbow, keeping her upright. "What's wrong?"

Everything. She shook her head and forced a smile. "Just tired."

Baelan gave her a solemn knowing look. At least he knew when to keep quiet.

Chapter 19

News From Home

She shouldn't have been surprised the Were set up a huge dinner near the Fey, bringing out what tables they had and serving food and drink. They'd known they were coming, and she felt a bit guilty how she thought the Were would ignore them because of what happened.

Sitting on a bench near the end of a long table, jammed between Kei and Baelan, she tried not to think at all as she ate. She wasn't hungry, but eating was easier than dealing with their annoyance if she just picked at her food.

Baelan, sitting at the end of the bench, reached by her to grab another slab of meat. Her brows rose, since it was at least his fifth, but then she saw him hold it out to Garen, curled up around the end of the bench with his large head nearly in the Elf's lap.

"You should give him some vegetables, too."

Baelan's brows rose as he looked down at the Were.

Don't you dare, Garen responded, his ears flicking back, and they both smiled.

She turned to Kei, but he was turned away from her, in an energetic conversation with the Fey beside him. Well, the girl talked away, Kei nodding every now and then. How…cute.

Her gaze darted to Rhee-En who sat on the other side of the table, but closer to the middle. She'd been relieved when he hadn't sat near them, yet a twinge of sadness still echoed. Things changed so quickly. The constant blanket of sorrow that seemed to smother her thickened. His gaze met hers and she forced a weak smile before turning her attention back to the half-eaten meal on her plate.

Grabbing a slice of bread, she took a bite and forced herself to chew.

Aro? You busy?

She stopped mid-chew, startled. *Bo? No, we're just eating. Is something wrong?*

Panic seized her chest. Bo rarely contacted her, and if so never so early. It wasn't even dark out yet. Her head jerked around, looking to see if he'd contacted the others as well, but they continued on as they had been.

We're fine, pup.

Swallowing the lump of bread in her mouth, she tried to calm down. *Good. Good. We are, too. Rhee-En gave us back the Were. I have to talk to the king directly now, though. He's still rather angry with us, I think.*

Could have been worse. A bit of time will calm everyone down. He knows it was an accident.

I know.

Kei's hand brushed her arm. "What is it?"

"Bo," she said quietly, glancing up from her plate she'd just been staring at. She shrugged as his head tipped to the side in confusion.

So... I've news but I don't know how... His voice drifted off. *Heard a rumor a few days ago. But Silas was by today and...*

What was it he didn't want to tell her? Her thoughts drifted back to what the alpha told her earlier. Were the Frans closer to Westport than they'd all thought? Her heart starting thumping harder in her chest. *What, Bo?*

I suppose it's best just to say it. Roan is dead.

Her heart missed a few beats. Her lungs forgot how to work. "No," she whispered. *He can't be,* she finally said, desperation lacing her voice.

I'm sorry, pup. I trust Silas, though. He certainly wouldn't lie about this to us, to you.

But...no. How? He can't be... But she hadn't heard from the pirate in days. He'd not been answering her because...because...

I don't have any more information than that. I wish I did. I truly am sorry. I know you were friends.

He might have said more, but suddenly all she could hear was a rushing sound in her ears as Roan's words echoed in her head. *A friend? Is that still all I am?*

Nausea flipped her stomach around and she pushed her forearm across her waist and pressed her fingers to lips.

Don't scream.

Don't cry.

Emotions surged through her and she didn't have the strength to stop them. The fury within her rose up, wrapping her in anger. Why? *Why?*

She wanted to throw her plate across the table. She wanted to throw everything, toss the rotting table itself end over end.

Pain pulled her away for a moment and she looked to her side, finding Kei gripping her upper arm tightly.

"Aro, what happened?"

She couldn't answer him. Couldn't breathe enough to say the words. Couldn't say the words at all.

His gaze grew distant and she pulled away, pushing back into Baelan and ignoring his quiet question as well. Somehow managing to get out from between them and over the bench, she walked quickly toward the nearby trees.

"Wait!"

She ignored Kei's call, walking faster.

Rhee-En called sharply for the Fey, and she moved even faster, stumbling into the trees and away from everyone else.

Alone. She just needed to be alone.

Light and dark flickered across her vision. Sunlight and shadows.

Life and death.

For a moment familiar darkness stole her sight, complete silence filled her head. She stumbled, blinking as the memory, the reminder, faded away.

Why did he have to die? He shouldn't have, he'd been so strong. Untouchable. How could it have happened? Why?

"The strong always have many enemies," Baelan said from behind her.

She stopped, closing her eyes, clenching her fists.

"You're not guarding your thoughts well right now."

No, with the mess her head was in, she probably wasn't. Anger at his invasion still rippled through her until she pushed it aside. "You think someone killed him," she said quietly. "That it wasn't some accident."

"Probably," the Elf said, a little bit closer.

"I wish I knew..." Grief clogged her throat. There were so many ways to die. Like with her brothers, the not knowing twisted her stomach. "I hope he didn't suffer."

"He might have. Unless he was caught unaware. A quick strike—"

"Stop it!" She spun to find him right behind her. He didn't look upset at all Roan was dead.

"I'm not."

The fury roared. She swung, her fist cracking into the Elf's jaw. "Did you do this?"

"Of course not, silly girl. I've been with you."

But he could have been behind it. Was it coincidence Roan died shortly after he warned her about the Elf? Twisting ribbons of red and black tightened within her as she hit him again.

Baelan barked out a sharp laugh. "Who would I send? The Were were his allies. Humans are too weak, and to the Elves I do not even exist."

She faltered a moment, his words making sense even through her anger and pain. Her lips trembled, and she clenched her fists, not ready to stop. Wanting to punish something. Hit something. Try to pound the feelings overwhelming her away.

"But, if I could have, yes, I would have killed him."

Her fists flew, again and again until he stumbled back a step, wiping blood from his mouth and nose on the back of his hand.

"You can do better than that."

His words fueled the anger inside of her until she felt a brief throb of pain across her knuckles. He hadn't defended himself at all. What had she done? All the wild emotions within her just...died. Faded away, leaving only sorrow and regret and an aching empty hole inside of her.

"Rot. I'm so sorry."

He shook his head and stepped closer. "You're allowed to hit me." He spread his arms out, inviting her to do so again.

And he broke her. Just like that.

Tears slipped down her cheeks as she shook her head vehemently. She moved toward him and he didn't even flinch. Her fists hit his chest, but there was no force to them. Then she was pressed up against him, her forehead on his chest as her hands fisted in his shirt.

Wrapping his arms around her, he stroked her hair. Placed a soft kiss on the top of her head. "Shhh."

Her tears immediately disappeared, drying on her cheeks. She stayed in his arms, breathing against him as her heart settled into its normal rhythm once more. He continued to hold her, his hand still stroking gently down her hair. Another kiss ghosted atop her head, and he placed his cheek there.

"Baelan."

Kei's sharp voice startled her, but she didn't move. The Elf raised his head, his hand stilled, but he didn't speak.

Hands gripped her shoulders, pulling her away, turning her around. She blinked up at Kei, her eyes feeling hot and dry. He frowned as he cupped her cheek, his thumb moving over dried tears. "Let's go back. Rhee-En has a cabin for us. Sleep will do you good."

She didn't agree but didn't argue. Kei didn't know, he didn't understand, how close she and the Elf had been.

Taking her hand, he pulled her through the trees. Garen bumped into her other side. His head rubbed against her arm until she rested a hand on his back as she walked. Baelan trailed silently behind them.

Aro-En.

She stopped abruptly, a choked sound escaping her at the loud, echoing sound of the king's voice.

Yes? Her voice sounded so weak she wanted to smack herself.

I feel your distress. What is wrong?

"What's wrong?"

She glanced over at Kei, "The king."

He grimaced and squeezed her hand tighter.

I...I just had some bad news from home. Someone I...cared about very much died.

I am sorry to hear that. Neither spoke for a long moment until he continued, *Would you like to talk about it?*

Her eyes widened slightly at the thought. *No! Thank you,* she added quickly. Sweat beaded her brow as a headache started to form.

I am here if you need me. That is how the Were work. We support each other.

Rot, was she going to get a lecture? *I know,* she said quickly. *I just can't...right now.*

That seemed to mollify him, as after another silence he changed the subject. *On another matter, since we are already speaking, the one you call Garen, his family is aware he lives.*

What did that mean? She looked down at Garen in confusion.

Does he wish to send word to them?

Ah...just a moment. I'll ask.

Garen flicked his ears forward as she continued to stare at him.

"The one you call Garen. What does that mean?"

The Were looked away with a snort. *I changed my name when I left. I'm not that Were any more. I haven't been for a very long time.*

Kei squeezed her hand and she nodded. "The king said your family knows you're alive and he asked if you wanted to send word to them?"

No.

She ran her fingers through the fur on his back, noting the tense muscles. "Then that's what I'll tell him." Garen turned back to look at her. "It's your choice."

His body relaxed under her hand. *Thank you.*

Taking a breath, she spoke to the king again. *He doesn't wish to.*

Why?

I don't know. He didn't say.

Then ask–

No.

She could sense the king's irritation zapping through their connection. She didn't want to deal with this now. She couldn't. *Thank you for your concern. I need to go now.*

Very well. I am here, if you need me, Aro-En.

She didn't reply, though she probably should have. Pain poked at her eyeballs and she gritted her teeth. "He's gone. I told him no. Can we go?"

Kei nodded, and pulled her along once more. It only took a few steps for her thoughts to return to Roan. To death. He was dead. Gone. She'd been dead. Partly dead? Was there more than the darkness and the silence? He'd always carried such an interest in it. Now he knew. Knew if that was all or if there was more. Maybe he was with his lost mate now.

Lost again in her thoughts, she barely registered entering the cabin, the four small beds lined up, or the boys' mutterings as they directed her to stand to the side as they shoved three of them together.

Baelan took her hand and pulled her to stand at the foot of the center bed. "Go to sleep."

Her brain didn't seem to be connected to her body, but she managed to sit on the bed and remove her boots and weapons.

The next thing she knew she was on her side, staring at nothing. Soft sounds met her ears, the boys and Garen moving around. If they spoke to each other, they didn't use words she could hear.

Her chest hurt.

Closing her eyes, she went inside, into the darkness of her mind. Leaning against the walls of her fortress, she waved her hand and a memory appeared. Her and Roan.

She had months of memories. Knowing she would never lose them, that she would never forget, eased some of the pain in her heart. So, she watched, memory after memory.

Baelan's voice suddenly echoed around her. "I don't know how much more of this she can take." A hand slid down her hair, brushed hair from her face.

Kei growled.

"Don't start that with me," the Elf snapped.

Kei didn't respond with words, but he shifted closer, wrapping his arms around her and tucking her head under his chin, holding her tight.

He'd never done that before had he? But she didn't think anything of it, just breathed in his scent and held on to the feeling of safety and love as she pulled another memory from her mind. A rare one of Roan smiling. Yes, he'd become more than a friend to her. She just wasn't sure what he was.

Not that it mattered any more.

∞ ∞ ∞

"I am sorry for the loss of your lover."

Feet spread, arms crossed, Aro clenched her jaw and tried not to glare at the alpha. She kept her gaze firmly on the mass of Fey before her as they readied to once again head out.

Stand tall. Push everything else away. Keep the fury firmly locked inside. Think of the cold. Make everything numb.

"Thank you," she finally managed to say, avoiding his searching gaze. There was no point in correcting him. No one ever believed her when she told them Roan wasn't her lover anyway. Had the Were brought him up to hurt her, or was he being polite? Her lips tightened as she struggled to hold in a frown.

Things used to be so much easier.

"You seem to be doing well, compared to last night."

She glanced over at him, noted how closely he watched her, and raised her chin. "He would have wanted me to be strong."

"True," Rhee-En replied vaguely.

Her thoughts churned as they stood in silence for a while. Did he realize he'd admitted to having her watched, or had it been a slip? She knew the young Were reported back to him, as did Terris, but how many other eyes were in the forest she hadn't known of? It was important, more than ever, for her to be in control. Strong.

Or at least appear to be.

"I will contact you when I will be in the area and we can meet again."

"I will keep you updated of anything of importance."

He frowned. "You are to report directly to the king now."

Turning to look at him, she raised her brows innocently. "Of course. I assumed you would also like to be kept informed."

After a moment, his lips quirked into a slight smile. He knew what she was doing. "Yes, I would. Until later then, Aro-En."

Baelan stepped to her side. *So it begins.*

I hate politics.

Whether you like them or not doesn't matter.

I know that!

Just making sure.

I hate you.

Of course you do.

She shot a glare in his direction and huffed at the grin on his face. Rotting Elves.

He's been watching us, she thought, instead of swatting him.

Yes.

You knew?

You didn't?

Terris, the young Were, yes.

He tipped his head toward her, brows furrowed. *I forget you have not been brought up in this life. I will make sure to point out such things in the future.*

She didn't quite know what to say to that.

I may not be your prince, Aro, but I was raised in the same court. The Were are not much different in general. Politics are politics. I understand this world and I will do my best for you.

Thank you. She wondered if she should be alarmed at how often the Elf surprised her. Her gaze found Kei as he moved among the Fey. *I don't want to fail him.*

He laughed out loud, startling her. *I don't think you ever could. Silly human. He adores you.*

She shook her head. *There are so many more Fey to heal.*

You don't have to heal them all, he said softly. When her head snapped around to look at him, he continued, *They just need a Queen.*

Her mouth opened and closed. She hadn't thought much about that. *He hasn't said how that will be done.*

I imagine he knows. Hopefully he does. Perhaps a certain number of women are needed to choose from, or one from a certain lineage? Maybe it has to do with their strength.

She stared at the Elf. How could he seem so unconcerned?

My point is, if you were to leave now, right this moment, he would find a way to still save his people. A queen would still be chosen. Eventually.

Shaking her head, she frowned. *You don't know that.*

No, he admitted. *But he would still let you go. He would find a way. That's how much he cares for you.*

She crossed her arms again. "It doesn't matter," she said out loud. "I'm not leaving him."

They watched the Fey in silence for a while before he chuckled and shook his head. "Have you never wondered?"

"About what?"

"Kei." She gave him a blank stare. "That perhaps he only bound himself to you so you would stay with him. Love him. So all of this," he waved a hand around, "would happen because of that. Because you would then never leave him. Because you want to help him, make him happy. Because–"

Her fury rose with every word. "If you ever say such a thing again, I will gut you."

He laughed, ignoring her anger. "You are so very innocent."

"And you don't make any sense!"

His head tipped to the side, contemplating. "Hmm. Sometimes, I suppose." His lips quirked into a smile again. "Wipe that anger off your face, my lovely. I never said he didn't care for you now. You are surprisingly likeable."

Narrowing her eyes, she frowned at him before deciding whatever this conversation was, it wasn't worth continuing. "I'm going to go help with something," she muttered, leaving the crazy Elf and his laughter behind her.

Chapter 20

Coming Storm

A bead of sweat trickled down the back of her neck. The day had turned into one of the hottest so far of the summer. With no breeze, even the shade of the trees didn't give much relief. Though many now wore sleeveless shirts, or none at all, Baelan remained covered. Hiding the wrappings around his wrists and neck. Hiding his scars. She told him no one cared, he hadn't listened. She didn't have the energy to argue with him.

Wiping sweat from her forehead with the back of her hand, she trudged forward at a steady walk, back straight, chin up.

She wasn't sure how many days had passed since she heard Roan died. A week? More? She stopped caring since it didn't matter. Over a hundred Fey followed behind her, their chattering a constant buzz she didn't pay any attention to.

It was easier, just to ignore the things that didn't matter.

Not very much did anymore.

She hadn't cried any more tears over Roan, though she still thought of him, especially at night during the times he would have normally spoken to her. She wasn't new to death, yet struggled in dealing with his. His death left her…lost.

The others cast her the occasional worried glance, would squeeze her hand or give some other brief sign of comfort. They didn't ask how she was doing. She probably would have hit them if they had. Perhaps they worried she'd break down into tears or that the constant fury within her would bring forth more irrational anger, snapped words and angry glares. Her solemn silence was certainly easier to deal with.

Healing the Fey kept her going. Gave her a purpose and a goal.

Kei hovered the most, even more than Baelan who stayed at a wary distance. She coveted those moments with her Fey after being so long without him. Even if she was a mess and not quite who she once was, even though he did it in worry, he was *there*. By her side.

"You need to slow down," he said.

"No."

"Aro," he said in exasperation.

"You can barely keep your eyes open," Baelan added.

She liked it that way, when she was so exhausted she fell right to sleep at night.

"You're going to get hurt," Kei added quietly. He bumped her shoulder, seeing if she was paying attention.

"No." Getting hurt wasn't a worry. They had so many Fey with them, it was no problem for many of them to hold any new Fey they found so she was in no danger. The growing number of Fey they came across…that worried her a little. The amount of fury moving in and out of her body was starting to make her feel ill at times and just…strange at others. None of that mattered anyway. She wasn't stopping, not with an insane Dragos liable to stop by at any time.

Her gaze flicked upward, and worry pulled at her chest. He'd not been back since the time he locked her in her mind with her nightmares.

Aro-En, a storm approaches.

She grimaced at the alpha's words. *When?*

It should hit you tomorrow evening. He paused. *It comes from the mountains, which is rare. Such storms are quite violent, and normally last two to three days. I would suggest you move everyone to the caves.*

We will. Thank you, Rhee-En.

She frowned. They were nearly to the main group of Fey now and would reach them before noon. They had planned on dropping off those they'd healed, pick up supplies, and then carry on south, while the main group continued east to set up yet another camp to wait for them.

The young Were had already told her of the cave system they would reach late the next day. Many Fey had been seen there and she'd been told some had made various caves into a permanent home. Since they assumed they would be a few days searching all the caves, at least the storm wouldn't cause too much of a delay.

Moving everyone there and into them would certainly be a headache though. "Slight change of plans." She related what Rhee-En had told her to the others.

Baelan scrunched up his nose. "Moving so many Fey, this is a nightmare. Are we sure there is room in the caves?"

"Rhee-En seemed to think so," she answered.

He pulled out his now worn notebook and began quickly flipping through pages.

She turned to Kei to find him staring off into the distance, his brows drawn together. "What is it?"

He blinked and then shook his head. "Just thinking."

The young Were assure me there will be ample room for all of us, Garen told them. *We will be broken up though. There are many small caves, some connected, but there are only a few larger caves.*

"We've nearly seven hundred Fey now," Baelan said, looking up from his book. "Supplies were delivered to the main group yesterday, so we will be good in that regard. Water, of course, will not be a problem."

She rolled her shoulders, trying to loosen the growing tension. "Good. So…just firewood will be an issue? We can gather as we make our way there."

"I'll go ahead," Kei offered. "Let the main group know what is going on. And get them moving."

"Take some Were and Fey and move on to check out the caves. We can see what we have to work with and if there are Fey already there."

I'll go with him.

She smiled over at Garen. "Good enough. Anything else?" When no one had anything to add, she continued. "Let's get moving then. Keep in touch."

When Garen and Kei were gone from view she huffed out a breath.

Baelan grinned as he tucked his notebook away. "There's always something, isn't there?"

She grimaced. "Sure seems like it."

∞ ∞ ∞

Aro stared up at the shadows flickering along the cave ceiling. A fire crackled to her left, warming her side and face though her back seemed to suck the damp and cold right up out of the stone despite the blanket under her.

In the distance, echoing through the connecting caves, came the sound of pipes and singing. Baelan, entertaining the Fey in the largest cavern. She was quite certain they didn't know quite what to make of the Elf. His music kept everyone in high spirits though, despite the cramped quarters.

The storm still howled on in the darkness outside. After nearly two days, she hoped it would end soon. Though they had enough wood, food, and water, there had been issues with flooding and crowding the hundreds of Fey into tighter quarters.

Click, click, click.

Closing her eyes, she sighed. Weariness pulled at her, but she couldn't sleep, even though she had her own little cave to herself. They found thirty-four Fey in the caverns. She'd just healed the last of them earlier. Though she released much of the fury, it still hummed within her. Winding threads of red and black.

Click, click, click.

Groaning, she pushed herself up and stood, turning toward Kei.

He stood along the back of the cave, shoulder against the stone. Head tipped down, his wild hair shone gold in the firelight around his face. It'd grown out, nearly to the length it'd been before Damon took him from her. He stared off into the shadows, lost in his thoughts. A knot of worry twisted her stomach when she saw his eyes glowed. Gold, nearly orange.

Click. Click, click.

Her gaze shot down to his hands. The claws gently clicking together. Through their bond she felt his agitation.

"Kei," she said softly, moving toward him. He didn't move, and she gently touched his shoulder. "Kei."

He looked up at her. "They come—"

"With the storm," she finished. "I know."

He kept saying those words, over and over, the past two days. They discussed it briefly the first day. The phrase was one of the few lines seemingly randomly noted in the book of prophecies. He didn't know what it meant, neither had Damon. Kei suddenly thought it was important, and not knowing who "they" were was driving him crazy. *They* could be anyone; assassins, Fey, Elves, humans, Vor...or someone else entirely.

They took what little precautions they could, placing extra guards at all the entrances to the caves.

It worried her, how the prophecy still had such a hold over him. He'd been doing so much better. She'd thought, she'd hoped, all of his mental torment was over now.

"I don't... I can't..." His gaze dropped, and he shook his head.

She placed her palms on his cheeks, holding his face for a moment before stepping closer. Her fingers moved, gently soothing, over his face, pushing back his hair. "We'll find out soon enough."

"I know." Sighing, he closed his eyes. A hand settled over hers, stopping it as it cupped his face. He pressed his cheek against it for a moment, before stepping away.

Her hands dropped, but her worry lessoned. His claws were gone. When his eyes opened, she found the light gone from them as well.

"I can't lose you," he whispered.

"You won't." He looked away, but she didn't know what else to say.

"You're supposed to be sleeping," he finally said, changing the subject.

She shrugged a shoulder, still watching him carefully. "Can't sleep."

"The Elf needs to learn some new songs. Those are getting old."

She smiled a bit at that. "The Fey don't seem to mind. I think a few have been trying to teach him some new ones."

Aro-En.

She held up a hand as Kei opened his mouth to speak. "Rhee-En."

Good evening, she answered the alpha. *Is the storm almost done?*

Yes, it should be passed you later tonight. How are you all faring? Are there any issues?

No, we are doing well enough.

Good, good.

"The storm should be done later tonight," she quickly said to Kei in the lull that followed.

I need you and the Fey to stay at the caves, Rhee-En finally said.

Her brows rose as she darted a glance at Kei. *Why?*

I...We...made an error. We were not vigilant enough. We didn't think... His words trailed off. *A large number of Vor have made it deep within my lands.*

They came with the storm, she said.

Yes, he agreed, surprise coloring his beautiful voice. *Hidden in the heart while we all took shelter. Even as the storm passed, we did not know. It washed away their tracks and scent.*

Where are they now?

The swollen rivers are at least keeping them contained to some extent, he said, ignoring her question.

Rhee-En.

He paused, and then started naming off landmarks.

She waved her hand at Kei. "Map! I need the map!" *Are they still moving?*

Kei dropped to his knees and began frantically digging through their packs. Once he pulled it out, she joined him as they flattened it out.

"What is it?"

"Vor."

He let out a deep breath and nodded as her fingers danced over the page, finding the spot Rhee-En mentioned.

Yes, the alpha answered. *Heading for the wardwall as usual. The river is keeping them from turning right now, but they will soon enough.*

Have you engaged with them?

Just outliers. There is an unforested stretch of land by the wall. We will strike them there.

When?

Late morning.

Her eyes flitted over the map. *We aren't far from there. We could make it on time.*

Aro-En... He let out a mental sigh. *We could use any assistance you can provide. I'm uncertain how many of my Were I can gather there by that time. And...I was not expecting such numbers.*

How many?

Thousands. There are thousands of them, Aro-En.

"Wither me." She met Kei's eyes. *I'll bring as many Fey as I can.* She paused, thinking. *Not all of them. Some aren't ready and—*

I understand. Any help will be appreciated.

I'll get back to you.

Thank you.

She sat back on her heels, looking up as Baelan rushed into the room.

"What did you need?"

She blinked up at him in confusion, before remembering the map. "Sorry." She grimaced and gestured at it.

He relaxed but then frowned. "What's happened?"

Leaning over the map again, she quickly told them what the alpha said to her.

Baelan ran a hand over his face. "Thousands?"

She nodded grimly. "If we leave at first light, we can make it there on time."

The Elf's voice rose. "Thousands as in two...or eight?"

"Ah, I didn't ask." Rot. She should have.

Kei leaned forward. "What kind of Vor? Those big ones? The crab things? Something else?"

Hadn't asked that either. "I told Rhee-En I'd contact him about what we're doing. I'll ask then."

Kei's eyes were glowing again. "We need to decide who will stay and who will go."

"You better mean in regard to the Fey," she said sharply. "Because I'm going."

His gaze lowered. "I know."

"Well, if she's going then I'm going," Baelan said, though he didn't look too enthused by the idea. He frowned. "Is it a good idea to bring the Fey? You just found them, and it's not like there are a lot left."

"We were created to fight," Kei said firmly.

The Elf rolled his eyes. "I know. I'm just saying perhaps giving your people time to increase their numbers might be wise."

Aro frowned. He was right, in a way, but unless they weren't going to fight at all during this rising...it still didn't matter. They didn't have years for the Fey to mate, have children, have those children grow up... Yet, he made a good point. "Well, let's talk this out."

Garen joined them, and then Cano and Lissana. Eventually it was decided they would ask for volunteers to fight. However, those who were uncertain of their control over their fury, or healed in the last few days, would stay behind. As would the few children and pregnant women. The main argument revolved around mated pairs, whether they should fight or not. In the end, Baelan's concerns won out. That, and there were not many pairs among the Fey. They too would remain behind. However, a compromise was made. All the Fey would travel toward the battle, those staying behind stopping a safe distance away. The young Were would stay with them, giving them warning if the battle went badly or Vor approached so they could run. The mates would protect the pregnant women and children. Once the battle ended, the Fey left behind would join them to help with the wounded.

It was a sound plan. Aro wondered how much of it would go wrong, and then bit her tongue.

She contacted Rhee-En again, letting him know she had around six hundred Fey who would fight, and he answered her questions.

"Well?" Baelan rubbed at the back of his head and yawned. "Do we want to know?"

"They estimate around six thousand."

"Wither me," Kei muttered.

"He said he should have close to three thousand Were gathered by then. Hopefully."

"That evens things out," Cano said. "What kind of Vor?"

"Not the ones we have seen. They are the size of a small Were. Long bodies, claws, a long face with lots of teeth. They slink in the shadows and are fast. Why he doesn't want to engage in the forest."

"Any Vor-ai?"

She shook her head. "Not that they've seen. But we need to make sure everyone knows the Vor bindings."

Though they'd found several older Fey, not all remembered the words to the bindings. Luckily, they eventually finally found a few who did.

Vor-ai bind, still and blind, moving not, until death it finds.

Shorter than the bindings she had done with Kei, though she did worry it still seemed a bit long. Kei assured her it was fine. What was important was the Fey's intent. What he did worry about was if she would be able to cast the binding. Though she had bound with Kei, she wasn't Fey.

She looked to Baelan. "You know what to do once they are bound?"

He nodded, a hand going to his side, and she remembered some of the runes there. "All ready to go."

If not killed by an Elven rune quickly, a Vor-ai could possibly escape if the binding wasn't strong enough. If it was, and there was no Elf to kill them, they'd remain bound until they starved to death.

Then we have our plan, Garen said. *Time now for some sleep. Tomorrow will be a long day.*

Cano and Lissana left, intending to speak to the rest of the Fey again. She would be leaving them in charge during the battle. At least she didn't worry about that, she trusted them and knew they'd protect their people.

Kei added more wood to the fire. Garen curled up in the small cave entrance. She shouldn't have been surprised everyone was spending the night in her little cave.

"So, prophecy boy," Baelan said into the quiet. "We all going to survive tomorrow?"

The silence was deafening.

"Probably," Kei finally answered, his voice low and quiet. "I don't know."

"Next time I ask, just say yes."

She and Kei snorted at the same time, which made her laugh. It was a little bit hysterical. Kei laughed quietly at her, shaking his head. Even Baelan laughed, a soft chuckle. For some reason, it relieved some of the tension in her body.

"Good night, boys."

"Good night, Aro."

,

Chapter 21

Behind the Wall

They left at first light. A small army of Fey with a few Were, one Elf, and one human. Or whatever she was. Some days, she wasn't quite so sure.

The storm passed in the night as Rhee-En said it would. The sun shone brightly, not a cloud in the sky. The temperature rose as they walked, slowly drying the rain-soaked ground and turning the air sticky with humidity. She hoped the battlefield would be dry enough by the time the Vor arrived they wouldn't be fighting in mud.

She and the boys led the way. The murmur of hundreds of quiet voices behind her was oddly soothing. She spoke to Rhee-En a few times as the morning progressed, keeping him updated on her location and discussing battle tactics. Their chosen battleground was a long stretch of open ground in the river valley. With the river to the east and the wardwall to the south, they planned to box in the Vor. Were would attack from the north, behind the approaching Vor, pushing them forward, and then a line of Were and Fey from the west.

Later that morning they stopped briefly to settle those who would stay behind. Kei stood before them all, with Cano and Lissana at his side, discussing the care of possible wounded.

When they finished, she uncomfortably moved forward to speak with them all.

"Good morning." She cleared her throat nervously and looked to Kei as they quieted. He gave her an encouraging smile. "As most of you know, I'm Arowyn Mason. Aro." She held back a grimace. They probably all knew who she was. Stupid.

"So, a few things." She rubbed her hands nervously against her thighs and glanced at Kei again. "As you may have noticed, I can take your fury. The power of it. Enough for you to regain control. I…uh…" Hundreds of Fey watched her, giving her their full attention. She felt a bit nauseous. "I can also give it back," she finished quickly. They stared at her. "If you need it. To…ah…heal." Their gazes remained locked on her silently for a moment before they broke out in quiet, shocked whispers.

Feeling her unease, Kei quickly turned the talk to the fighting ahead and gave final instructions to those going on with them. After preparing for battle, they set out again.

She had every weapon she owned strapped on her somewhere. Swords, daggers. Baelan pulled her hair back into a tight braid. Her fingers danced from weapon to weapon as she walked. Garen roamed ahead of them. Kei and Baelan walked to either side of her, quiet in their own thoughts.

She felt Kei's skittering emotions; unease, worry, excitement. Glancing at the Elf, she thought he looked at bit pale. He'd never fought the Vor. As far as she knew, he'd never fought in any sort of large battle. Would Baelan remain once the fighting started, or would the assassin come out?

He glanced over at her. "We will protect you," he said softly, his voice more serious than she'd ever heard it.

"That's not what I'm worried about."

His lips curved up slightly. "No, of course not."

"I'd rather you didn't die."

He chuckled and shook his head. "You needn't worry about me."

"Fine. I'll worry about Kei."

The Fey snorted. When she turned to look at him, she briefly caught his small smile before it disappeared.

"Well, then." *Garen, I'm going to worry about you.*

The Were laughed as he trotted into view. *We're almost there.*

Another Were joined him, tipping his head to her as she noticed him. *Aro-En. If you would follow me.*

She nodded and picked up her pace to follow the Were through the trees to where Rhee-En wanted them positioned.

Once they reached the tree line, she sent the Fey off in either direction, spreading them out. Kei, Baelan, and Garen remained at her side as she surveyed the long stretch of river valley. The wind that brought the storm hadn't shifted and it teased her hair, blowing loose strands around her face. At least they were downwind and the Vor wouldn't scent them.

Short grasses and flowers filled the valley. Though there were a few dips, it was mostly flat. "Where is the river?"

Just beyond the far trees, Garen answered. *You can see where the wardwall is to the right. The valley ends at it.*

"Why?" That didn't make any sense.

"We keep the valley clear of trees for the deer."

She turned, unable to stop the smile forming on her face at the sound of that beautiful voice. "Rhee-En."

"Aro-En." He tipped his head slightly. "You brought more Fey than I thought you would."

"They wanted to fight. It was hard to keep the young and the mated pairs back."

"That was wise."

"It was Baelan's idea, actually."

The alpha looked to the Elf, who stared up at him almost...adoringly. Yes, Baelan still couldn't get over the Were's sultry voice.

She tried to hold in her amused grin.

Rhee-En shook his head, his lips turning up into a faint smile, twisting the scars across this cheek.

Don't embarrass me, she reminded the Elf.

He blinked a few times before lowering his gaze. *I apologize. I just...*

Oh, I know. I've gotten used to it. Mostly. Catching his gaze, she smiled so he knew she wasn't angry. She turned her attention back to the Were. "What's the word?"

He tipped his head to the side in confusion and her cheeks flushed with heat. He figured out what she meant before she could explain it was a phrase her brothers used to say.

"Ah. They are still on course. It will be a little bit until they arrive, but not too long."

Clearing her throat to get over her embarrassment, she nodded.

His face softened. "I trust you will take better care of yourself this time, Aro."

She noted he'd dropped the En, but wasn't quite sure what that meant. His tone didn't indicate disrespect. An endearment? "I will," she answered. "Would rather not go through that again."

"None of us would," Kei muttered.

She felt his worry and unease increase through their bond.

A low growl came from the alpha and her gaze quickly returned to him. He wasn't looking at them though, but beyond toward the wardwall. "Rotting Elves."

She turned to look, but didn't see anything. "What is it?"

"Elves at the wardwall."

"This side?"

He snorted an unamused laugh. "No. Of course not," he said bitterly. "Rotting bastards like to watch sometimes."

She frowned, and her gaze shot to Baelan. However, he didn't seem the least bit offended.

"Well, that is...interesting." Rhee-En looked to her. "It appears your presence has been requested. By their prince."

Her breath lodged in her throat as she stared at the Were with wide eyes.

His smile turned soft. "Go on, then. Be quick about it."

"I-I will," she managed to stammer out.

He was *here.*

Her prince was here.

∞ ∞ ∞

She raced along the tree line, her eyes searching along the wardwall. Her boys followed her, somewhat discreetly. Her heart raced in her chest. She felt...light. For the first time in a long while joy filled her.

How long had it been since she last saw him? Since they parted ways at the gates to Rivenward? It'd been early fall then, was midsummer now. Nearly a year then. It seemed so much longer. She didn't count the two dreams they shared. Those...weren't quite real.

Her heart was singing, but it was a sad, painful song.

Even this time, she'd see him, but not be with him. The stupid wall would separate them. She wouldn't be able to touch him, to have him hold her in his arms. To kiss her.

She spotted him by the wall, beneath the trees on the other side. He stood straight and still, hands at his side, watching her approach.

Darting across the field, she looked once down the length, checking for Vor. Seeing no sign of them, she pushed the beasts, and the battle to come, from her mind. She'd have a little time and she wouldn't waste it.

Kei, Baelan, and Garen stayed by the treeline, giving her some semblance of privacy.

Shael's eyes remained trained on hers as she reached him, slowing as she neared the wall, struggling to calm her heart. He was beautiful. Healthy. Strong. Powerful. His black hair hung past his shoulders. Fair skin shone with health. His eyes, those beautiful blue eyes, caught her gaze and held it. Her breath hitched in her throat. Rot, she wanted him so much.

He reached out a hand, pressing it against the wall so she knew where it was. She stopped before him, unable to stop herself from raising her hand and placing it up against his.

She smiled so wide it hurt her face. So much emotion crashed through her for a moment her eyes burned until she pushed the unwanted tears of joy away.

He stared at her for a long moment, his gaze flickering over her from head to toe before focusing on her face once more. A rare soft smile crossed his face. Her beautiful prince.

"Prince."

He stepped closer and moved his free hand to his ear, shaking his head.

Anger flared up within her. Of course. Of course, he couldn't hear her.

His fingers moved to his eyes, and then his mouth. She sighed but nodded. Reading lips it would be. Those distracting lips she wanted to kiss so badly it hurt.

At least she could see him. It wasn't such a bad thing she'd have to concentrate on his lips. The thought brought her smile back.

"My Arowyn," he began, sending her heart fluttering again. His gaze roamed her face once more. "I have missed you."

She stepped closer, placing her other hand on the wardwall. "I've missed you, too. So much."

His free hand rose, matching hers, and they stood there for a long moment just...looking. His eyes were full of so much emotion. She wished she could read him better, know what thoughts and feelings made him look at her in such a way.

With a sigh he closed his eyes for a moment and she dropped her gaze. Beneath the cuffs of his shirt, she saw runes encircling his wrists. Not chains like Baelans, but thick bands.

Her gaze met his again. "It's true?"

He saw her looking and with a grimace, nodded. "Yes."

Her stomach clenched, and her emotions flew everywhere. Anger. Sorrow. Worry. "I'm sorry."

"You were not the one to do it."

He seemed so calm, but then he was an expert at hiding his emotions when he wanted to.

He looked to the side, and then back to her. "Is he taking care of you? Protecting you?"

"He is," she answered, nodding.

His lips flattened into a grim line for a moment. "Good."

Fingers curling against the wall, she shifted closer. She didn't want to talk about Baelan. She wanted to press through the stupid wall and be with him. Her lips trembled for a moment before she pushed the sadness away. "I wish…"

Their eyes locked together again. "I know, Arowyn. I know."

They both leaned forward, heads pressing against the wardwall. She tried to imagine his skin against hers. The feel of him. He shifted back and she raised her head. Lifting a hand from the wall, he traced a line with his fingers, as though stroking them down her cheek.

"I wish things were different."

His face filled with sadness. He sighed and dropped his hand. "I as well, Aro, I as well. You are…" He shook his head.

"I love you," she whispered. "I've never stopped."

A faint smile crossed his lips. "Oh, my sweet girl. There is so much I wish I could say."

Why couldn't he? She dropped her hands and took a deep breath. For another long moment they just stared at each other, faces shifting with emotions neither of them wanted the other to see.

Movement tore her gaze from his face and her brows drew together as she looked beyond him into the trees. Scattered through the forest behind him Elves stood, all watching her.

She counted four, but didn't doubt there were more than that, which brought forth a number of questions.

"Why...How are you here?"

He let out a heavy breath, as if he knew she'd ask and hoped she wouldn't "Our Seer spoke of a Vor attack at the wardwall. She suggested archers be sent." He paused and smiled slightly. "She told me you would be there. I did not argue when the queen ordered me to come."

She stared at him, blinking rapidly, as his words crashed into her brain. "When," she asked quietly, "when did she see this?"

His head tipped to the side. "A few weeks ago."

She pressed a hand to her stomach as it twisted, her fury rising. "And you didn't think to warn us?"

Confusion crossed his face. "It is not–"

"We're on the same side! We didn't know! And now..." She sucked in a breath through gritted teeth. "You could have sent word to the city. Rot, you could have found a Were patrolling along the wardwall. You could–"

"Arowyn, stop. Why are you so upset? It is not something we do. The Were–"

"Didn't know," she interrupted, her voice rising. "They weren't ready for–"

"That is not my problem."

Her eyes widened. How could he say such a thing? Red and black, the fury whipped around within her. "How can you say that!"

An Elf stepping closer caught her attention and she narrowed her eyes at him. It struck her then, how much emotion Prince had been showing, something he rarely did as it was, but in front of others, other *Elves*... Her gaze moved to the Elves behind him, of course...they couldn't see most of it. Did he hide his words as well? Moving his lips yet making no sound?

Prince turned his head to speak to the other Elf, but she didn't catch what he said until he faced her again. "They do that sometimes. Especially when she's…emotional."

Her eyes were glowing. Not surprising with how angry she felt right then.

"No. She won't hurt me."

She glared at him. Right then she rather wanted to. Did he not have any idea how a warning could have saved lives? Allowed them to be ready for such an attack? People were going to die. She held no delusions all the Were and Fey would survive the battle to come.

His eyes closed for a moment, as though he had to compose himself to deal with her. "I have to go."

Of course he did. Her fists clenched. She lifted her chin. "So do I."

He shook his head, frowning in annoyance. "Don't be like that. There are Vor near. I need to find–"

He couldn't be serious. She stepped closer to the wardwall. "They are *here*," she said, interrupting him. Turning she pointed at the faint dark mass of them now visible at the end of the valley and then turned back. "Why do you think I'm here?"

"No." Eyes wide, he stepped closer, placing a hand on the wardwall again. "She did not say…" His gaze flitted between her and the approaching Vor a few times. "You need to leave. Now."

"Idiot." She shook her head. "I'm here to fight them."

He looked beyond her for a long moment before looking back at her, his face tortured. "You cannot fight that. There are so many. You will not…"

"Survive," she finished for him, raising her brows mockingly. "I'm not alone. Fey and Were wait in the trees." Her eyes searched his. "Come. Fight with me. Not this battle, but the next."

"We do not…" He shook his head and stepped back. Away from her.

"Fight? Risk yourselves? I shouldn't be surprised. There are thousands of us here to fight. Do you know that word?" She shot her gaze behind him at the other Elves. "I suppose not. You're a bunch of cowards hiding behind a wall."

Her words gained the desired effect. His jaw clenched in anger. "Arowyn–"

How could he not understand? Her voice rose with her growing anger and frustration. "Are you here? No. What good are you? Go home. Buy some skirts and dance around your pretty fountains. Drink wine in your fancy halls. Hide away like the cowards you are."

"You do not–"

"Understand? I do perfectly. You are all there. We are here. You didn't even bother to warn us! We will fight and we will die. And you… What are you doing? Nothing!"

Though we are quite enjoying listening to you, I would suggest you take your position. Now.

She didn't miss how the alpha's suggestion was more of an order, but didn't say anything about it. He was right.

Prince slammed both of his hands against the wall, regaining her attention. "Listen to me. You need to leave. This is not your fight."

"Of course it's my fight!"

The fury within her rose higher. How could he say that? He knew who she was, what she could do, how she helped the Fey. How was this not her fight? Even if she were a normal human, she would still fight to keep her family safe from the Vor.

She pounded a fist against her chest. "I fight because I can. I can't just wait for someone else to do it." She pressed her lips together angrily as she shook her head. "Of course, you don't understand, that's exactly what you Elves do."

Her rage melted away. He didn't know her at all, to say such a thing. Apparently, she didn't know him either, to have thought he'd agree to come and fight with her.

Disappointment filled her. In him. In herself. She should have known better. She should have listened to everyone who told her he didn't care. He didn't love her or want her, and she should stop wasting time and just move on.

He wouldn't fight for his people against the Vor, how could she have thought he'd fight for her? She'd been so wrong. So very, very wrong...and it broke her heart.

His anger melted away, brows drawing down in confusion as he watched her. He stepped forward, eyes widening in panic as he suddenly realized he was losing this argument. Losing her.

"Goodbye, Shael," she whispered, meeting those beautiful eyes one last time.

"No! Do not do this! Do not leave like–"

She turned her back on him. Spine straight, chin high, she walked away, her steps quick but sure. She had no reason to stay.

Her boys joined her side quickly as she continued down the middle of the valley. Her fury thrummed higher within her as her gaze focused on the quickly approaching Vor.

"He's dancing about trying to get your attention. Looking quite frantic really," Baelan said with quiet amusement.

She glanced to the side to see the Elf looking over his shoulder as he walked. "I don't care."

He looked to her and then faced forward again. A faint unnervingly wicked smile crossed his lips for a moment before quickly disappearing.

The Vor sped toward them. Thousands of paws creating a growing thunder with every moment. Kei looked over at her. "We aren't moving to the side?"

She shrugged a shoulder. "Doesn't really matter, I don't think."

His golden eyes met hers before looking away. There was so much in that one look. The past. The future. The gold turned to red. "I suppose it doesn't."

Always by your side, she reminded him, because in the end, that was all that ever mattered.

His lips curved into a smile. *Always by your side.*

She turned to the Elf. "Ready?"

"You are too excited," he grumbled. "And they call me crazy." With a shake of his head, he composed himself. "Yes." He held out a hand, showing fingers curled around a glowing rune. "Just let me know when."

Aro-En, really?

She smiled at the alpha's exasperation as she drew her blades and quickened her step.

Sometimes I think you want to die.

Not today.

You better not, he muttered. *Ready?*

Yes.

A long moment passed. *Now.*

"Now."

Baelan immediately threw his hand in the air. The rune flew high above them before exploding into a ball of blue light. Before it had even faded, the Fey rushed from the trees with a wild roar nearly drowned out by the growls of charging Were.

Jerking her fury forward, she ran headlong at the Vor with Baelan, Garen, and Kei by her side.

As it should be.

Chapter 22

The First Battle

She fought. She fought and fought, blades swinging and blood flying. Claws and fangs tore at her, adding her own blood to that of her enemies. Running down her arms. Splattering her face. The power of the fury healed her. It heightened her senses, it sped her reflexes as it urged her on.

Fight. Kill. Destroy. *Destroy them all.*

The Vor threatened to overwhelm with their sheer numbers. Masses of darkness laced with teeth and claws on every side. Their previous encounter with them had been nothing but a skirmish. This was the first battle in a war.

Flashes of rune magic teased the edge of her vision for a time. She saw Kei. Wild in his fury. Claws and teeth rending any Vor in his path. Now and then, he would find her. Touch her arm or side with a whispered, "Take," before bounding off again. Once his power depleted, Baelan gave way to the assassin. Bay circled around her, graceful in his silent, deadly dance.

All she saw was blood and the dark horde of Vor falling upon her blades. The battlefield screamed with the shouts and cries, the roars, of those triumphant…and those in pain. Death screams. Howls of loss.

Until nothing more stood before her. She heard nothing but the pounding of her own blood in her ears. Her feet slid on blood and gore as she turned, eyes searching, blades ready.

Only the dead surrounded her. In the distance, here and there, Were and Fey pounced and tore apart the remaining few Vor.

Her chest rose and fell quickly, her blood still rushing through her, ready, waiting to fight. The fury though, what remained, simmered. Content. No longer screaming for death. The enemy was defeated.

She was alive.

Tipping her head to the sky, she sucked in a deep breath and closed her eyes. Her body sang with the knowledge. *Alive, alive, alive!*

She wanted to scream, to roar out and share her victory with the very sky. *I am alive!*

"And she stood so beautiful," a deep voice spoke reverently.

Lowering her head, she turned to face Bay. The assassin.

"Fierce and wild and strong. Victorious. Bathed in the blood of her enemies."

Did he quote a poem? A song? Or did he perhaps, just speak what he saw. She stared at him, the blood dripping from his hair, smeared across his face. So very terrifying. So very beautiful. So very...alive.

Alive, alive, alive...

She stared into his eyes. Became lost in his storm. He was wild and fierce, vicious and strong. Alive, so very alive.

Blades tumbled to the ground. His. Hers. Did she move forward or did he?

Lips crashed together. Fingers tangled in bloody hair. There were no words, just frantic kisses and touches. He jerked her body closer. She pulled his hair and opened her mouth under his. He moaned against her. She pushed against him. Closer. More. More, more, more.

"Aro. Aro!" *Arowyn!*

She opened her eyes, startled. Gray eyes met hers. Bright and vibrant. Baelan's lips slid over hers once more before he pulled back, his arms relaxing around her, but not yet letting go.

"Well, that was certainly something. Wasn't it, my lovely," he whispered.

Blinking rapidly, she tried to gather her scattered thoughts.

"Aro," Kei snapped.

She tore her gaze from Baelan and found Kei beside them. Bloody, eyes golden…and irritated.

"There are a few Fey stuck in the fury." He frowned. "We need to start looking for wounded."

Guilt punched her in the stomach and she jerked back, out of Baelan's arms. What had she been *doing?*

With a sigh, Kei turned and began walking away. "Let's go."

Scrambling, she picked up her weapons and quickly followed him, wiping them off as best she could on her pants before sheathing them.

Baelan joined her, humming as he walked.

She had no idea what to say. Guilt knotted her stomach as they walked. She tried to think of something else. Concentrated on where she put her feet. Watched as more and more Fey and Were began to walk the battlefield, searching for wounded. For their dead. Flies began to gather. A few carrion birds cried above them. It didn't help.

Kei stopped suddenly and turned to face her. Various emotions flitted quickly across his face. "Stop, Aro," he said softly. "It wasn't…" He glanced away, frowning. "I feel your guilt. Just…stop. It was battle lust. It happens."

Her brows drew together. Beside her, Baelan's head cocked to the side, questioning.

"It's when…" The Fey's hands moved around awkwardly. "You fight. For your life. Your body is all about surviving.

291

Living. Then suddenly it's over. You're still all wound up. You're alive. Now *that* is all that matters." He touched his chest. "It's instinct. You're not thinking. You survived death and now, well...instinct directs you toward life." He waved his hands in front of him again.

"Sex," Baelan supplied with a huge grin.

Her cheeks burned as she shot him a glare. "This actually happens?"

Kei cleared his throat as his own cheeks flushed. "I've seen it. In the army. Sometimes we'd fight and then..." He made an embarrassed, frustrated sound. "So, don't feel guilty anymore. See?" With a jerky nod, he turned and started quickly walking again.

She could only follow and try to wrap her head around what he'd said. It made sense, in a way. But she wasn't that kind of person, instinct or not, was she? Rubbing a hand across her forehead, she shook her head. Apparently, she was. How had that happened? With her past and...

Kei stopped again. He stood for a moment, staring ahead before turning and closing the distance between them in a few quick steps.

She froze, her thoughts scattered, wondering what she'd done now.

His gaze darted over her and she glanced down, seeing the dirt and blood and rent clothing. When she looked up at him again, his eyes met hers, softer this time.

"I'm sorry," he whispered. He cupped her cheek, the blood on his hand sticky against her skin.

She felt then his worry. His love. Relief. Her lips trembled, and she lurched forward, throwing her arms around him. He held her tightly, pressing his face into her bloody hair.

Something pressed into her side and they pulled away to find Garen pressing his head against them. A small laugh escaped her as she bent and hugged his head.

They'd all survived. But she'd already known that, deep down she could feel the bonds she shared with her small pack. Her family.

Kei cleared his throat and she straightened. No other words were spoken as they followed Kei. They didn't need to be.

∞ ∞ ∞

She bent over another Fey, pressing her hands to his mangled chest and pushing power into him. The wound was bad, but with her help he would survive. Unlike some they'd come across.

Shredded bodies. Missing limbs. Closing her eyes, she pushed images of the dead away.

Kei, Garen, and other Fey still searched for survivors, even though they hadn't found any more in a while, there were still a couple of Fey unaccounted for. Baelan remained by her side at the Fey camp by the river, helping her tend to those she worked on. He'd only left her side when they first arrived at camp, returning slightly more mussed and with lumps of bandages showing under his clothes. He didn't look to be in serious pain, so she let him be.

Rising on weary legs, she stretched her back and then moved toward the next wounded. Only a few more. She would have felt relieved about that, but she planned on heading to the Were's makeshift camp when she was done here to see if there was anything she could do to help.

Baelan handed her a cloth and she wiped at the blood on her hands as she walked. Not that it did much good. She would need a long soak to get it all off. She'd be lucky if she got to that before darkness fell.

"You'll be clean before you sleep," Baelan said firmly. "Even if I need to steal a bucket and scrub you down myself."

Raising her eyebrows, she looked over at him in surprise.

Jen Wylie

He frowned. "I actually didn't mean for that to sound inappropriate." His lips turned up into a saucy grin. "For once."

Shaking her head, she looked away. Guilt once again twisted her insides.

"You and I..." she started, her voice trailing off as she tried to put into words what she wanted to say.

"There is no 'you and I.' I know that, Aro."

A large breath huffed out of her and she nodded, looking away.

"It's done and over. I do not regret it," he added, "and neither should you. Sometimes, things just happen. But I..." Worry crossed his face as he looked at her intently. "I keep forgetting," he muttered. "Are you...?"

She looked back at him. He gave her a surprisingly soft smile. Understanding. "I'm fine."

He visibly relaxed. "Good. Good. That was quite the kiss though." He grinned.

She shook her head. It was. Her entire body tingled with the memory. She certainly wasn't going to admit that to him, though.

They walked silently for a moment before he glanced over at her again. "What's wrong?"

"Nothing." She shook her head and huffed out a breath. "I just...feel guilty. Like I betrayed him. I'm angry that I do. I walked away." She grimaced. "You were right. He wasn't who I thought he was."

"Love is rarely something that just stops, Aro. It turns into something else, or fades away on a memory."

She glanced over at him when he didn't continue. He looked off into the distance, a wistful look on his face. She wondered what he was thinking about. Perhaps someone who had broken his heart once. "There you go being all wise again," she said lightly.

His lips curved into a smile as he came back to her. "You so easily forget I am over a century old?"

"Of course not, with all that gray hair."

"Gray! It's not gray, it's silver!" The outrage on his face as he pulled at a lock made her smile.

"It's a bloody mess right now," she pointed out.

He sighed. "So it is."

"If Bay was out, you'd be rather terrifying."

"He is, isn't he?"

She shrugged.

Glancing at her, his brows rose. "You really aren't afraid of him."

"I know he won't hurt me, even without the spell."

"True."

Her head shot around quickly at the change in his voice. Stormy eyes regarded her for a moment, before turning lighter as she watched.

"Not your turn," Baelan muttered. He flashed her a grin that looked rather forced. "He was angry I pushed him aside and took over the kiss. Since he was considering ripping off Kei's head for interrupting, I thought it would be wise to intervene."

She wasn't quite sure what to say about that admission. "Ah...good idea."

"Plus, I got a kiss, too."

Without even thinking she reached over and smacked his arm.

He, of course, laughed delightedly.

Crazy Elf.

"Oh my. That doesn't look good."

Turning her attention to the Fey they approached, she grimaced. She swallowed and pushed down the emotions wanting to flood her, to take over and make her scream and cry. She didn't have time for such nonsense.

By the time she finished with all the Fey, more blood soaked her clothes and skin. The faces of the wounded kept flickering in her mind. Haunting her as much as her own lost family, even though she knew little more than their names. Arlen, who lost an eye. Hylr, with his gaping chest wound. Especially Gwist, who died under her hands.

At least now, there were only a few Fey with minor injuries who hadn't been tended to.

How do things fare by you?

With a sigh, she rubbed at her cheek before answering the Were. The drying blood was getting itchy. *Almost done tending our wounded,* she answered the alpha.

Good. He paused. *The prince has been harassing my Were. He wants to see you.*

Her heart fluttered for a moment before she shook her head and looked at the blood and death surrounding her. *I don't want to see him.*

He's insisting.

She snorted. *Ignore him.*

I wish I could, Aro-En.

Well, rot. *Tell him I said to go home.*

It wasn't long before the alpha relied. *Unsurprisingly, he's not agreeable to that.*

She huffed out a breath and stood. *Fine. I'm busy. I'll see him…when I'm not.* She winced at her poor choice of words.

The alpha chuckled. *He has been told. Now we can ignore him.*

It was her turn to smile. It faded quickly at the mournful howl of a wolf in the distance. Rhee-En didn't need to be dealing with this now. Selfish Elf.

I apologize for all the trouble he's causing because of me.

No need. She could almost hear his grin. *It is a…distraction. It's quite amusing seeing him in such a state.*

With those words she was quite certain the alpha didn't care for the Elven prince at all.

Do you need extra hands over there? I'd be happy to come and help when I'm done here.

Ah, you delightful woman. It would be greatly appreciated.

I will head over shortly then.

We will watch for you.

Kei lightly touched her arm, gaining her attention. "Do you want to get cleaned up?"

She shook her head. "When I'm done here I'm going to go over and see what I can do to help the Were. And then..." She closed her eyes and grimaced. "Then I need to go and talk to Prince again. He's been asking for me."

"You don't *need* to."

"I know."

He nodded, understanding. "I'll finish here. The sooner you're done, the sooner you can rest."

She stood, not having the energy to argue, and moved through the Fey camp. Baelan stayed close to her side, murmuring under his breath now and then.

She asked for any volunteers to share their power with her in case she needed it. Many stepped forward, without hesitation.

Pride welled within her, nearly bringing tears to her eyes. The Fey were such *good* people. They didn't deserve the fate that had befallen them.

Before leaving the camp, Kei rushed up to her. He glanced at Baelan for a moment, then back at her.

Her brows drew together in confusion at the sudden unease she felt. "What is it?"

"The Were aren't here. None have seen what you can do."

"What are you talking about?"

Kei shifted from foot to foot at Baelan's question, but his eyes met hers. "Giving power back to the Fey." *Does he know? You can give to others?*

I...don't think so.

Might be best to keep it that way. From everyone.

Her mouth opened and closed when she wanted to argue. But he was right. She didn't know how much she could trust Baelan, or the Were. If they found out she could give power to them, she might find herself a target. Or worse, they would ask more questions. They could *never* know all that she could do.

Nodding to Kei, she pulled him in for a quiet hug.

"I'll be over soon," he said.

Baelan cast her numerous glances as they walked across the battlefield before finally speaking. "Is he being overprotective, or are you hiding something?"

She grimaced. At least he kept his voice low. "I'm a freak enough, as it is. He always worries."

He gave her a long, thoughtful look before looking away. She wasn't sure if he believed her evasion or not.

It wasn't important right then. She worried more on if she'd be able to keep her power to herself if she came across a dying Were.

She needn't have worried. By the time she reached the Were camp, so much time had passed since the end of the battle any who were mortally wounded had either passed on or already been helped by their alpha. It had slipped her mind how the Were could share power with their pack bond, which was surprising as creating a pack to help Prince got her into a mess with the Were to start with.

Even so, many were weak enough they couldn't fully heal their wounds, and she was kept busy moving from one wounded Were to the next.

A hand clamped down on her shoulder and she looked up from where she knelt. Baelan took the roll of bandages from her and she stood, wiping bloody hands on her bloody pants. It didn't do any good.

"Thank you, Aro-En," the alpha said softly. His voice curled around her, making her breath catch. She really needed a nap. A faint smile curved his lips. Rotting Were knew he affected her.

"I don't think you needed us." She gestured to the many Were tending the wounded.

He shrugged. "It is appreciated all the same." He looked away. "We lost forty-seven. A handful more will not ever fight again. Two lost their wolves."

The sorrow in his voice made her chest ache. She stepped closer, resting a hand on his muscled arm. "It could have been worse."

He shook his head absently. "I failed as an alpha," he said so quietly she barely heard him. "I was not prepared for such an assault so soon."

"We can't prepare for everything, no matter how hard we try."

"What's done is done." He blew out a breath and forced a small smile. "What are your plans now?"

Kei stepped into view, his eyes shining. "We go to Furia." His gaze turned to her. "It is time."

Such simple words held a deeper meaning she didn't understand. Getting to Furia at a certain time was important, though she didn't know why. Kei had never said, and she wondered if he even knew. What was it like inside his head?

"Please let me know if there is anything you need," Rhee-En said.

"Thank you."

Baelan joined them. "Are you ready to head back to camp?"

She shook her head. "First I need to talk to an Elf."

Rhee-En grinned. "That should be interesting."

Interesting wasn't quite the word she'd been thinking of.

∞ ∞ ∞

Baelan and Kei walked on either side of her as they moved through the large Were camp. She checked in with Garen, who remained with the Fey in case they were needed.

They are still working on the pyre, he told her.

299

Her stomach twisted. The Fey burned their dead. Something she'd known but never been a part of. *I'll make sure we're back in time.*

It will be a while yet, Garen answered sadly. They too, had a large number of dead.

"Do you want to clean up first?" Baelan tugged at a bloody strand of hair.

"No," she said firmly. "Let him see."

The numbing sorrow for those they'd lost dimmed under her growing anger as they walked. If they'd been warned, or if the Elves had been here, not nearly so many would have fallen. As they drew closer to the wardwall, the fury within her raged higher. They passed a few dead Vor, maybe two dozen, their bodies full of arrows.

Baelan kicked a carcass. "Should we wait here?"

She turned her attention forward. Prince stood waiting, a number of Elves close behind him. "No. Come with me. Please," she added, trying to calm her growing anger.

As she approached she saw his gaze roam over her, flick to Kei, to Baelan, and then back. His lips pressed tightly together, distress clear on his face.

He was so stunningly perfect, so beautiful, tears clogged her throat. How could she have ever thought he'd love someone like her? Part of her still wanted to run to him. Wrap her arms around him and hope that this time he would tell her he loved her.

She should have known better. Such a foolish girl she was, thinking he ever would.

He made it easy to keep the anger, which she much preferred over maudlin thoughts. No blood stained his clothes or skin. The only thing out of place were a few strands of hair where it looked like he'd run his fingers through one too many times.

She stopped before the wall, close enough she could reach out and touch it if she wanted to. Close enough to be able to read his lips, the emotions on his face.

His eyes raked over her again, taking in every piece of rent clothing, every drop of blood. With a frown, his gaze moved beyond her. "You call this protecting her?"

Baelan huffed. "She's alive, isn't she?"

Her teeth clenched together as she tried to calm her emotions enough to speak. How dare he speak to Baelan like that. Maybe this was a mistake. She raised a hand to draw his attention. "What do you want?"

The Elves behind him stiffened and she looked to them quickly, ensuring they wouldn't be a threat. They all wore similar clothes, were all beautiful in the Elven way. Their eyes varied in color, their hair a range of blond, brunette, and black. One caught her attention for a moment, his eyes and hair the striking hue of a dark wine. He reminded her of the Elf Baelan had killed in the forest and she quickly looked away, not wanting to be reminded.

Prince's blue eyes caught hers, piercing and angry. "Why did you take so long to come?"

Arrogant bastard. Kei snorted behind her. "I am not your subject, *Prince*. I am not your anything."

"I was worried."

"And I was helping the wounded." She crossed her arms. "I'm sure the Were told you I was fine. I don't appreciate you harassing them."

"This is not..." He frowned and shook his head. His gaze dropped for a moment and he straightened as he looked at her again. "I am sorry, Arowyn. For everything I said."

The apology shocked her, stealing away more angry words so she could only blink at him stupidly.

He stepped closer, setting a palm against the wardwall. "We should be there. I should be there. With you." He bit his lower lip as his gaze searched her face for a reaction to his words. His shoulders sagged as she continued to stare at him angrily. "I am sorry," he said again. "Please forgive me."

She had no idea what to say. Her heart thumped away madly. He'd said what she wanted to hear, but was it enough? Her hesitation surprised her. Perhaps it was just too little too late.

She took a step back. "I need to see to the dead."

He quickly moved forward, placing his other hand on the wardwall. "Wait! Don't go. Please, don't go."

His stricken face stopped her. She wanted to scream. How could he do this? After everything he'd said, how could he act like this now? Like he wanted her. Like she meant something.

Kei, I don't know what to do!

Then listen to what he has to say until you do.

She let out a long slow breath and then nodded. Prince closed his eyes for a moment as his shoulders relaxed. When she met his eyes again, he smiled slightly. Sadly. "Come here."

After hesitating a moment, she moved closer. His fingers curved against the wardwall, as if he wanted to reach through it and touch her.

He stepped closer, dipping his head, resting his forehead against the wardwall. "I miss you. So very much. Every day. Every night."

Emotion plowed through her, tears burning her eyes. Unable to help herself, she raised a hand, pressing it against his. "I miss you, too," she admitted. "Always."

"I want to hold you, so badly. I want to hold you and never let go. I am so sorry."

Her lips trembled, and she fought harder not to cry.

Be careful, whispered through her mind, so softly she wasn't sure who said it.

"Arowyn, my Arowyn."

"My prince." A tear slipped down her cheek. Rot.

The soft smile on his face wavered. "I will come to you. As soon as I can, I will come."

Her brows rose as her lips parted in surprise. "You will?"

He nodded. "As soon as I can," he repeated. "I promise."

Letting out a shuddering breath, she blinked away more tears. He promised?

"Will you wait for me?"

She hesitated, her eyes searching his face. Did he mean everything he said? Could she trust him? He stared back at her, so earnest and hopeful, she finally nodded.

A huge, boyish smile lit his face and a small laugh escaped her at the sight of it. He leaned back slightly, still smiling, his gaze once again taking her in, memorizing her. "I should go then." His lips twisted into a grimace for a moment. "I have much to do to get free of her. Be safe, my Arowyn."

"I will, and you, too."

He grinned again, and then looked over her shoulder. "Take good care of her." His eyes returned to her as he stepped back. "I will see you soon."

She hoped so, but wasn't quite sure if she could trust him so just gave an awkward nod.

"You will wait for me?"

She hesitated but answered quickly as uncertainty suddenly crossed his face. "I will." He smiled again, relief relaxing his features, and began to turn. She stepped forward. "Shael!" He paused, tipping his head to the side. "I love you."

That huge smile returned, sending her heart fluttering. He pressed his hand to his chest. "My heart."

Not an I love you, but close enough. She pressed her fingers to her lips and then against the wardwall. He repeated the gesture, making her smile again.

With another grin, he finally turned and disappeared into the trees. The Elves followed, casting a variety of looks her way, mostly shocked or confused. Surprisingly none of them were hostile, which she didn't understand at all.

She turned around. Baelan stared into the forest where Prince had gone, looking completely baffled.

"Well, that was unexpected," she said as she began the walk back to the Fey camp.

Kei's lips curved up in a pleased smile as he walked beside her.

"Did you know?"

He shrugged a shoulder. "He is supposed to come." His lips turned down into a frown. "Not everything is happening as it should, like the Dragos said, so I wasn't sure."

She nodded absently. "So, he *will* come?"

"I hope so, Aro."

"Do you...do you know when?" She should have asked Prince that question.

"He will be in Furia in the spring. I'm not sure when he'll arrive. Spring is the only time that is mentioned."

Spring wasn't too bad. She could wait until then. He was coming. She almost couldn't believe it.

Baelan stepped forward to walk on her other side. "What happens in the spring?"

A brilliant smile lit Kei's face. "Our queen is chosen."

She couldn't help but smile back.

However, Baelan tipped his head to the side. "How will that be done?"

Kei's smile dimmed. "I'm not...I don't know." His brows drew together.

She threw an arm over his shoulders. "But we will. Perhaps the answer is in Furia."

He relaxed under her arm, his eyes lighting up. "Yes, it is time to go to Furia."

She glanced over her shoulder, knowing she wouldn't see her prince but unable to help herself. Emotions spun around inside of her. She should have listened to her heart, not what everyone else said. She and Shael often fought, but that didn't mean they didn't care about each other.

She loved him and he...she was his heart.

That was enough. More than enough.

I will see you soon, my prince.

Arowyn's tale continues in the next book!

Did you enjoy Broken Kei?
Please let the author know and leave a review!

Jen Wylie

If you enjoyed The Broken Ones don't miss Tales of Ever!

Available on Amazon

A few months ago, I was a normal girl. Life sucked, and just like everyone else, I took the simple things for granted. At least until I got this new power, a "gift" my mom called it. Apparently, I'm a firestarter. I didn't want to be. I didn't ask to be. It would be cool if it wasn't so dangerous and I knew how to control it. When an uncle I'd never heard of showed up to take care of me after my mom died, I should have been grateful. As it turned out, my whole family isn't normal and more than a little bit crazy. I thought things couldn't get any worse. I was wrong.

They banished me to Ever.

Other Works by Jen Wylie

The Broken Ones
   -Broken Aro
   -Broken Prince
   -Broken Promise
   -Broken Kei

Flashy Fiction and Other Insane Tales (anthology with Sean Hayden)
   -Volume 1
   -Volume 2
   -Bundle Volumes 1&2

Tales of Ever (YA Fantasy)

Ring Around the Rosie (FREE short story)

Jen Wylie resides in rural Ontario, Canada with her two boys, Australian shepherd, and a disagreeable amount of wildlife. In a cosmic twist of fate she dislikes the snow and cold.

Before settling down to raise a family, she attained a BA from Queens University and worked in retail and sales. Thanks to her mother she acquired a love of books at an early age and began writing in public school. She constantly has stories floating around in her head, and finds it amazing most people don't.

Jennifer writes various forms of fantasy, both novels and short stories. She loves to hear from her readers!